Tornado Ally

A Small Town Romantic Comedy
Lainey Ross

Foreword

For all who are too soft for this world.

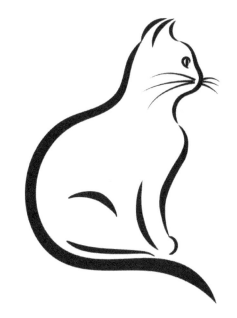

Chapter One

Ally

O livia meowed angrily at me, her fluffy face scrunched in disappointment. She hated me leaving her behind when I went into town. She knew that if she came with me, she was likely to get a treat from the small mom-and-pop creamery on Main Street. But I really did need to be quick today, and it was so hot I couldn't leave her in the truck while I went into the town hall.

"I'll be back later."

I ruffled her creamy, white fur before hopping into my truck. It was a little white Ford pickup, with mountains engraved in the back window. I'd inherited it from my grandpa. It had seen better days, but it still ran. And with the way vehicle prices were these days, I wanted to put off replacing it for as long as possible.

She stepped back reluctantly, going to sit on the wooden steps of the porch. Resigned to her fate, she curled her tail in around herself.

I waved goodbye, shut the door, and headed for town.

It was a ten-minute trip. But being ten minutes out of town here was like an eternity. The nearest neighbors were a mile away. I liked being a little secluded. It was quiet and peaceful, most of the time. The farmer I worked for lived three miles in the opposite direction, so I didn't have far to travel for my job. And it was nice that my tasks changed with the seasons, so I didn't get bored.

The radio was finicky out here, it worked better the closer you got to town. But there was only one rock station and one country station that worked even when you were in town. I didn't mind that either, but it would've been nice to have more variety. I wanted to get a boom box or CD player to have at home so I could have a few more options. Maybe someday when I went to visit a bigger city I could pick one up. I hardly ever left the small town of Blink, population 5684. Aptly named because if you blink, you'll miss it. That was life, living on a map dot.

My truck bounced and bopped on the bumpy road. I waved as I passed by a farmer I knew going the opposite direction. He'd probably already paid his electric bill for the morning at the town hall. Sheryl, the treasurer, did not like us being late. Heaven forbid you wait til later in the day, she'd considered anything after 2pm late. She was a funny, quirky old lady, but we all loved her for it.

I turned onto Main Street, red dirt turning into white gravel beneath my tires. The grain bin was up ahead, and there was a little office beneath it that held all the commerce the small town needed. That was where they weighed and tested the crops, held town meetings, and did all business.

There was even a little cafe nestled inside that served eggs, biscuits and gravy, and bacon every morning with coffee. If the farmers were bored, which they always were, or procrastinating, which they also always were, you could find them sitting in there shooting the crap over a cup of black coffee. That was all the office smelled like most of the time, black coffee mixed with grease and oil.

I parked my truck out back, making a mental note to get some gas before I headed back home. The gas pumps were right across the parking lot. It would be good to kick the can on that. I climbed up the stairs and pulled the door open, making the bell above my head jiggle. Everyone turned and gave a little wave, unsurprised to see me.

We all had a routine out here, and nothing exciting ever happened. Except maybe the cattle getting out. We'd all grumble about it, but as long as nobody got hurt, it really was pretty exciting. The neighborhood kids thought so too, mainly because they got to stay up watching cartoons and then hear about all the adventures when we came in muddy and exhausted after midnight, cattle in tow. Fixing the fence was the only part that wasn't so exciting in the aftermath of a late night like that. Especially in the Oklahoma heat.

"Hey, Mayabell! How are you doing?" I asked the woman who cooked and served breakfast every morning. "Breakfast smells amazing!"

She grinned at me, her face wrinkled and her hair perfectly permed the way so many older ladies liked to wear it. She was kind and genuine, but had an ornery streak a mile wide.

"Thank you, Miss Ally. I'm doing well..." Mayabell's voice trailed off.

I braced myself for what was coming next.

"You know, I could teach you to cook like this. Then you could wrangle yourself more than just cattle," she said, "you could wrangle a man!"

Her white eyebrows wriggled with excitement. Or what was left of them, anyway. She was so adorable, and... *so persistent.*

All the older ladies in town thought I needed to find myself a man. But it wasn't really a priority. Who was I going to date, someone I'd known my whole life? It was kinda hard to be attracted to someone you'd been in diapers with. Maybe not for every woman, but it was for me. We all already knew everything about each other, which was arguably too much. Where was the fun in that?

Mayabell always said she thought my standards were too high. Maybe she was right. I didn't know.

I smiled politely.

"I would love to learn to cook as good as you, Mayabell."

A chuckle came from beside me as the old farmers sitting in the bar stools got a kick out of my attempt to defuse the situation. Every single one of us knew that if I didn't get a move on, this would end up being a long lecture from Mayabell about how it wasn't good for a woman to live in a house alone like I did with my chickens and cat, and didn't I want a family?

I started inching my way toward the door as Mayabell beamed.

"I got the recipes from my Mama, and from her Mama before her, and her Mama before her. They are fool-proof in getting a man! The best way to any man's heart is through his stomach, ya know?"

"Can't wait, Mayabell. Let's set up a time for you to tutor me? I gotta run for now!"

I threw a little wave in her direction, making eye contact with a few of the local farm hands on my way down into the basement where Sheryl was. They smiled politely, and it occurred to me for the first time that maybe some of them were interested in me. The old men just thought it was funny, but the farmhands might secretly be hoping Mayabell would hook them up with me. She was quite the little matchmaker in this town.

I thought about it for a moment. Would I be willing to go on a date with one of the farmhands around here? I tried to picture myself eating a banana split with one of them at the Creamery. I shook my head. They were all so quiet, and I couldn't live like that. I already lived with deafening silence for years, I didn't want to live quietly with another person. If I was going to live with a man, I wanted him to be a yapper. Maybe even more of a yapper than me. That way, I'd never get bored.

I didn't feel like the men around here had much... finesse, either. Not that they couldn't, if they wanted to. They just chose not to. It was a point of pride for them. Different priorities, I supposed.

Their idea of wooing a woman was to take her on a tractor ride in the sunset. Which, there was nothing wrong with, but... I don't know. I just knew they didn't have what I wanted. I wasn't sure that what I wanted existed.

I knocked on Sheryl's office door, standing awkwardly in front of it. Sometimes she was on the phone and didn't like to be interrupted like that. But how else were we supposed to get her attention? And besides, if we didn't get the payment to her for our electricity during this small window of the day, she would be upset. We were all doing our best here with her very particular standards.

"Come in," she called, sounding bored.

I opened the door to find her typing away furiously at her keyboard with one hand. Beside it, her fingers flew over a calculator with a paper ribbon flying out the back of it. Back and forth, back and forth. She was a machine.

"I um," I fumbled, holding up my envelope with the cash for my electric bill in it, "was just bringing this by."

She stopped momentarily to smile at me.

"Thanks sweetie, put it right here."

She tapped a spot on her desk where several other envelopes sat, and I added mine neatly to the pile so as not to disturb it.

I looked at the calendar on the wall, the one with all of her grandbabies in the picture. Her daughter always had those printed for her for Christmas so that she could have a rotation of pictures of the kids. It was adorable.

"How's everybody doing?"

I tipped my head to the calendar. If I was going to go to the trouble of coming all the way into town, I was going to get some human interaction out of it, even if I had to go back upstairs and get hassled by Mayabell.

"They are doing so wonderful! The littlest just turned three on Tuesday. Can you believe that?" she crooned, looking over at the calendar.

"That's incredible," I grinned. "Time sure does fly, doesn't it?"

Her face fell just a little bit, almost imperceptibly.

"It does. Faster than you even know. It's lovely to have a husband to share it with..."

Oh my gosh.

These folks were laying it on awfully thick today.

"I bet so," I said, getting ready to bolt.

"You know," she said, a mischievous hint to her voice, "there is a dance coming up in a week..."

A dance? I didn't know how to dance. I had two left feet, at least that's what I'd always been told. Nooooo thank you. Besides, who would I dance with? Did any of the men in this town know how to dance? It seemed to me as though knowing how to dance and knowing how to rope cattle were mutually exclusive. The men here were either completely practical or completely impractical, with no in-between.

Maybe my standards *were* too high.

"I didn't know." I shrugged sheepishly.

She raised an eyebrow, typing furiously despite carrying on a conversation with me. She was truly scary sometimes.

"You should go..." she prodded.

"I suppose it could be fun to show off."

I awkwardly did a little chicken dance move.

"... with someone." She narrowed her eyes at me through her bulky black pencil eyeliner.

"I'll think about it," I said hastily, retreating out the door.

I waved at a farmhand coming out of the bathroom on my way out. I was pretty sure his name was Marcus. He tipped his hat to me and gave a polite smile.

I felt uneasy at the amount of matchmaking happening in this building. I could only imagine Mayabell and Sheryl giving subtle hints to every eligible bachelor they saw. In fact, what if they were in cahoots together? Oh goodness. What must the men think of this? Maybe they found it amusing. I shuddered to think any of them gave it serious thought. I would simply pass away of embarrassment.

I climbed the stairs to the other side of the parking lot, the bell ringing upon my exit, and crossed to retrieve my truck.

I stopped in my tracks, kicking gravel forward with my boots as I took in a man leaning up against my truck. His smile brightened when he saw me.

It was one of the guys that worked at a farm north of town. I knew him well enough to know that, but not well enough to know his name.

"Hi," I said, a little more aggressively than I had meant to.

He was leaning on my driver's side door. I couldn't get in without him moving. I didn't want to be rude but—

"Hey," he said. "I just noticed your tire pressure is low."

He kicked at my tire, which felt unnecessary.

"Oh!" I said, feigning appreciation. "Thank you so much, I was just about to go get gas. I'll air them all up while I'm over there."

I pointed to the pumps.

"I could do it for you." He extended his hand to the tire. "A lady shouldn't have to work so hard all the time. That's what men are for."

I was pretty sure men were actually for being a pain in the butt, but I bit my tongue before that escaped my brain and tripped out of my mouth.

After forcing a laugh, I insisted that I could handle it, and thanked him for the offer. He looked a little defeated, then something crossed his expression. A change settled over him. Was he angry? I couldn't tell.

But he moved away from my door, blessedly giving me the ability to get into my truck unimpeded.

"There's a dance next week," he said. "Do you want to go with me?"

He held his hat in his hands. Was this him trying a different tack? Was he flirting with me before, and I just missed it? I gulped. I didn't know it could hurt so much to swallow air.

His jaw worked nervously as he awaited my answer.

"Um..."

I shoved my hands into my jean pockets, rocking back and forth on my feet. What words could I possibly say? You're not my type? I'm not a good dancer?

I was beginning to contemplate faking my own death when he spoke again.

"Somebody already asked you, didn't he?"

His drawl came out more now. He looked dejected.

"No," I blurted out, then immediately regretted it.

I should've lied and said yes. That would've really gotten the town talking. I couldn't even imagine the clucking and carrying-on that would happen in the cafe had I said that to him. It could've easily been mistaken for a chicken coop. Missed opportunity.

Now the poor man just looked confused. I decided to punt this whole situation.

"Sorry, can I sleep on this?" I said, lacing my words with honey. "I just have a busy week this week and I want to make sure I'm not doing too much."

That wasn't a lie. Harvest was right around the corner and I had a lot to do to prepare. This would give me more time to let him down easy.

He seemed to perk up.

"Of course, miss," he said, a smile returning to his face.

He tipped his hat and moved further from my truck.

"I'll let you know in a few days, I've got some errands to run. Take care!" I blurted out quickly as I jumped in and shut the door.

He sprinted up the steps with vigor, dipping back into the cafe. I immediately felt the nervous butterflies take over in my stomach.

Had I made a mistake?

My mind and stomach whirled as I checked my tires at the pump. He had been right; they were low. I appreciated him pointing it out. While I was pretty good at keeping up with the farm vehicles I was paid to pay attention to, I wasn't necessarily good at keeping up with my own. Can't be good at everything, I supposed.

After I filled up on air and gas, and stress, I decided to stop in and get Olivia a little bit of whipped cream from the Creamery. The vet said as long as it was only occasional, she could have it as a treat. I owed her for going to town without her, anyway.

The little creamery was adorably decorated with a mint chocolate chip cone as the logo out front.

The building had been many things over the years. A coin shop, a pizza shop, a spaghetti shop, even a flea market. Businesses usually didn't stick around for more than two years after they set up here. We didn't have enough foot traffic for most people's liking, but the Creamery was about to celebrate its third anniversary. I suspected that they were doing so well because of the dairy they also ran. The whole town loved the little ice cream shop, and I tried to support them whenever I could.

Inside, a line of ice cream sat behind a frosty glass counter. One of the teenagers in town stood behind it, helping an elderly lady with a dish of vanilla ice cream, chocolate syrup oozing on top. He smiled at her as she rambled on about having to be careful about sticky stuff in her dentures. I couldn't help but smile to myself. He helped her to her seat, grabbing a spoon and napkins for her on his way to her booth. I stood patiently until he got back.

"What can I get for you today, Ally?" he said as he bounded back up to the counter.

"I think Olivia is due for a treat," I explained. "I left her at home today and she's quite upset about it. Gotta make it up to her, ya know?"

I winked, handing over the cash and a small tip as he rang in her usual cup of whipped cream.

"Anything for the princess." He pushed the tall tower of whipped cream over to me.

"Tell her hello for me," he hollered as I departed with the goods in tow.
"I will."

I waved back at him, thinking about the look she would have on her face. It might even make her forgive me. Maybe.

Chapter Two

Jack

U gh. Meetings were SO boring! I had to stop myself from jabbing a pen into my closed eyelid, as I often did at home during virtual meetings with my camera off.

I straightened my posture, catching myself slouching. I was not at home on my couch. I was ten hours North of home in a stuffy boardroom.

I hoped nobody would call on me. We had been in meetings, collectively, for six hours. We'd only stopped to eat lunch. Corporate's idea of lunch was a salad with a single piece of chicken on top.

I was starving, and that was putting it mildly. I couldn't believe everyone else sat so attentively, without a care in the world. How were they focusing on words after all the words we'd already had to focus on? There was so much jargon and repetitive, pedantic concepts that we'd already gone over. Was this helping anyone?

"Jack? Did you have anything to add?"

Oh no. I was being called on. Had my facial expressions given away how annoyed I was? Oops. I had no idea what we were talking about at this point.

"No, I don't think I do. Wonderful information being shared here. I don't think I could possibly contribute better than what's already been said."

That was corporate speak for sorry, I wasn't paying attention. It wasn't much more socially acceptable than straight-up admitting I hadn't been, but it softened the blow a little. I sat, stifling my inner screams. I would let them out later, in the car. This felt like a hostage situation at this point.

"Well then, let's dismiss. For those that would like to stay on grounds for the evening, dinner will be catered in the Jillian room down the hall. See you in thirty minutes!" Rob, our Chief Operations Officer, set us all free. My coworker nudged me in the ribs the second the man walked out of the room.

"Dude," he said, frowning.

"Sorry, I was hungry! And tired."

"How could you possibly be tired? You don't have jet lag like the rest of us!"

Yeah, yeah, so I didn't fly in from different times zones like most of them. So sue me.

"I still drove the whole way here," I reminded him. "That was tiring."

He rolled his eyes and stood, dusting his suit coat from the invisible fuzzies that seemed to plague it given how often he did this gesture.

I felt so out of place here. I was competent at my job, but not at navigating this part of working life. Why did it all have to be so complicated? Why was it not enough to just do a good job? I didn't like trying to navigate all these unwritten social rules and this inability to speak plain English. Why couldn't everyone say what they mean and mean what they say? I couldn't understand why people valued being obtuse in this industry.

I considered skipping out on the company dinner. Odds were I could probably find better at McDonald's. I'd bet money that the dinner would be a single radish, a carrot, a dollop of some fancy sauce (the name of which I wouldn't be able to pronounce), and the protein equivalent of a chicken nugget.

Besides, the dinner conversations were going to be as dry as the meeting had been. Like the Sahara desert on steroids.

I clicked the pen in my hand off and set it down on the table. There was a stack of papers for all of us to take home to review new policies and procedures, only some of which were covered in the meeting. I had no idea how I was going to get it all done. At least all of it would be paid time on the clock.

Stiff from sitting for so long, I pushed myself up and stretched. I stood to my full height, uncomfortably wiggling my toes in my dress shoes. Who designed these things anyway? If I was going to feel like a clown, couldn't they at least make it fluffy and cozy?

I ambled over to the door, glancing to see how I could dodge the pre-dinner business conversations. I was worn out of business conversations already after this week, and I needed to build back up some stamina if I was planning on going to dinner. I was still warring in my mind with deciding on that.

I didn't want to be perceived as anti-social. It could be bad for career advancement to skip out on the schmoozing. At least my coworkers could get through it with some booze. I didn't much care for the stuff, or maybe better said, it didn't care for me. So I'd be going in completely sober.

I saw an opening that parted in the swarm of people and took it, shooting out like a bullet from a gun. There was a nice fountain in the middle of the hotel that seemed like a great place to decompress. I'd come back in plenty of time to sit and eat this fancy, finger-food dinner with the rest of the corporate employees.

The only problem was, we were on the second floor. And the fountain was on the first. Which wouldn't be a problem except I hated elevators. They were just so... confined. Restricting. The thought of being trapped in one made me shiver.

I'd have to find a staircase outside of the eyeshot of my coworkers. They already thought I was silly for driving the whole way up here instead of flying. People just didn't realize how many things could kill you, or make you wish you were dead. Or they didn't care. I didn't know which.

The carpeted floor of the hotel was chaotically patterned, such that it made me dizzy. I stared at it as I passed people to try to avoid getting caught up into a conversation. I needed a break from listening, just for a little while.

I passed the elevators, their shiny metal glinting at me. Death traps, I thought. I wanted to die with my boots on, not screaming like a girl in a metal cage.

Had my anxiety been this bad before I took this job? I couldn't remember. But the thought startled me. I needed to make sure I was taking care of myself. I couldn't be cracking.

The pressure was only going to get worse from here and I needed to figure out how to handle it. My dad had made six figures for as long as I could remember. I'd always heard that's what women wanted. A wealthy, tall man. Someone who could provide for them. What if I couldn't do that? What if I never made it to his caliber?

The staircase sign up above a door frame caught my eye. I dipped through the door as my palms sweated. Maybe if I just jogged down the stairs. A little fight-or-flight therapy. Heavy on the flight.

I was winded by the time I reached the bottom. I needed to start working out, apparently. But I did feel a little better. The gray concrete walls of the stairwell were significantly less overstimulating than the bright LED lighting inside the hotel and all the colors and eclectic decor.

I wondered how my dad handled the pressure of this life. Maybe he didn't. Maybe that's why he had been cranky for much of my childhood. I wondered if things would've been different if he had had a different job. Would Mom have been happier? Or was he right, and money was the most important thing in a woman's life? She did seem to like her shopping sprees. Though she was running out of places to put the things she bought.

I rushed down the hallway, past a maintenance man and a nice lady with a cleaning cart. They seemed to be working together to locate something in the hall closet. A bottle of window cleaner fell off the cleaning cart as I passed. I bent to pick it up and hand it to her. She thanked me, her wrinkled hands wrapping around mine just slightly as she took it from me. Her face was just as wrinkled, but she looked happy. Maybe women could be happy in lots of different situations in life? I was overthinking. I needed to go sit.

So I did. I plopped down right in front of the fountain, teeming with life. It was at least fifteen feet high and surrounded by real greenery. Tropical plants of every variety.

The plants were so exotic looking, I wasn't sure if I'd ever seen some of them before. I decided to lie down on the cold concrete rim of the fountain and stare up at the climbing vines on the pillars and along the wall. They ran all the way up to the ceiling. If I closed my eyes, I could almost envision myself in a rainforest.

Far away from meetings, staples, papers, graphs, and oddly specific handshakes. I felt my blood pressure coming down to a normal, acceptable level. I didn't want to think about getting up. So I decided I wouldn't. I'd just lay and listen to the sound of the running water...

"Man, he must be tired." I heard a woman giggle.

Was I asleep? I shifted, feeling a cold sensation on my back.

"Guess so."

A man stood beside me with his arms crossed. He was the first thing I saw when my eyes popped open. I straightened up, my cheeks flushing with embarrassment.

"You missed dinner," the lady that sat in the cubicle next to mine said, extending out a to-go box of food in my direction.

I was pretty sure her name was Rachel. I felt bad that I couldn't confidently remember.

"Oh!" My eyebrows knit together. "Thank you so much."

That was kind of her to bring me food.

"You're welcome," she stifled another giggle.

She was a little younger than me and still had a happier disposition than the rest of us. It hadn't been beaten out of her yet. I'd thought about asking her out. She was a cutie. But office policy prevented it, which was smart. So I had tried not to learn any more about her. Easier that way.

Hey, had I drooled on myself? Is that why she was giggling? I not-so-discreetly ran my hand over my face, not feeling anything. Phew.

After today, I was sure she thought I was a doofus. Oh well. I didn't make enough yet to keep a woman anyway, if my dad was right. Devin, the dude standing over me, seemed less enthused and forgiving. His eyes were harsh, his body language rigid and imposing.

"We've got to get a move on," Devin said in a nagging sort of way. "We can't miss the flight."

"Oh!" I sat up with relief. "I've made alternative arrangements. Thank you for thinking of me."

He must not have known that I exclusively drive. Or maybe they thought I'd change my mind on the return trip? But then what would happen to my truck?

"Don't mention it. When you didn't show through all of dinner, the boss man asked folks to keep their eyes peeled. He tried to get a hold of you and couldn't. Started getting worried."

I frowned, searching my pockets now for my phone. George, my boss, was not going to be happy with me. This was exactly what I meant by not saying what they mean. Dinner was supposed to be optional, but obviously it hadn't been.

"We'll let him know you're OK," Rachel said chipperly.

"Thanks." I tried to smile, but it was more of a distracted grimace.

"We'll see ya later, bud," the man said, wandering off to the exit.

Chapter Three

Ally

O livia pounced on me the second I opened my white pickup door. It couldn't really be considered white, but that was the original color. I wasn't sure some of the red clay stains and splatters that lined the bottom of the truck would even come out at this point. But white had been the original color when my grandpa bought it.

"Hey you, hold on a second." I chided Olivia as she climbed up my leg with her claws.

I precariously balanced my purse over my shoulder, my car keys, my receipt from my electric bill, and her treat cup. She might as well have been a little spider monkey for the level of agility she had.

"Ok," I said, taking shuffling steps away from my truck and nudging the door shut. "Alright."

I eased her down to the ground, bending over so that her feet could touch it so she wouldn't fall. No doubt she would've landed on her feet if she had, but I just always worried about her hurting herself. Her eyes were absolutely feral as she tapped her paws against the cup holding her whipped cream treat, crinkling the plastic.

I took the lid off and jumped back as she attacked like a ravenous wolf. She didn't do this at the shop. She ate it out of the cup gently while I held it in my hand. Because she had a reputation there for being a dainty little lady, and she was quite partial to every single person who worked there. Here, however, she had no such reputation to upkeep.

She started purring loudly, like the motor of a souped-up car. Whipped cream clung to the top of her nose and in between her eyes. She used her paw to scoop it off and lick it up.

"Was that good?" I teased her. "You crazy girl."

She rubbed up against my leg as a thank you. The folks at the Creamery never believed me that she acted this way when I brought some to her at home. I made a mental note to take a video next time. I needed some photographic evidence of my little psycho.

I sighed. Enough break time. It was time to get to the chores. Days off were really just work days at home.

Chapter Four

Jack

F lyover country could never be more beautiful to me. I drove into the setting sun surrounded by plains and winding hills, with stunning citrus shades of orange and yellow shining on the whole earth.

And in my eyes. I dropped my sun visor down to get some relief. Wheat fields flanked me on either side, their bounty swaying like waves on the ocean.

Though this was the end of a work trip, I appreciated the opportunity to soak in the scenery, even if it was just out the window of a vehicle. I conveniently ignored the stack of papers nestled in my suitcase that I'd have to read when I got home. For now, they didn't exist.

Sitting at a desk every day was a soul-sucking experience. I was tired of living in beige and shades of grey. I could almost trick myself into thinking this small break of driving to and from a week-long training was actually a meandering, scenic vacation.

I turned up the radio dial in my trusty Ford pickup, searching for a channel that wasn't crackling static. In between searching for a station that worked, I took a swing from my soda nestled in the cup holder. Only a swig though, I didn't like having to stop to use the little boy's room often. There really didn't seem to be a signal I could pick up on, so I sat in silence. Miles passed with no distinction between one county to the next. I wouldn't even know when I was crossing state lines on this trip if the highway signs weren't posted!

A few miles before the Oklahoma border, the radio awakened from the dead. It was a Frankenstein-ian mix of voices and drums until I started turning the knob.

Guitar riffs from a country radio station poured through the speakers, so much so that I reached to turn the volume down a little. It was a nice little tune, once the decibels weren't threatening to blow out my eardrums. I settled in, ready to enjoy. My coworkers hated country and teased me about it regularly, so I had to make it a private indulgence.

This was the perfect backdrop to witness the moon rise over the landscape and take its place in the sky. It was a cloudless, still evening, with no other traffic on the road. I chuckled as I thought of the rest of the office flying home in an airplane, smashed together like sardines in a can. I much preferred this. Sometimes it paid to be a scaredy cat...

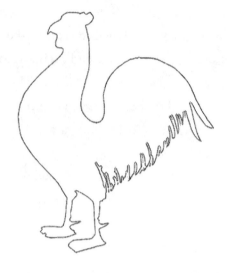

Chapter Five

Ally

"Ah!" I yelped as my rooster tailed my ankle with the dedication of a piranha in the Amazon.

Gerald had clearly never heard the expression, "Don't bite the hand that feeds you."

Did it count as a bite if the creature didn't have teeth? A beak could be just as scary... and painful.

I danced around in my overalls, deftly avoiding most of its lunges at me.

"Look here you... you..." Nugget of terror? Bane of the barnyard? Soon to be chicken dinner?

I shook a stick at the rooster, who only acted offended, not intimidated, by the gesture. Sighing, I ran toward the coop, hoping that he'd at least follow me. The sun was setting and I needed all the chickens in for the night. I'd already lost one to a coyote two weeks ago.

The squeak of the coop door opening was enough to get the attention of the rest of the chickens. While the rooster was interested in trying to assault my foot, he was more interested in getting away from the stick I was poking in his face. There were a few muted clucks and bocks as I shut the door and locked them in for the night.

I trudged to the door, Olivia rubbing up against me as I walked. She liked to disappear when the chickens were out. While you would think that they would be more scared of her than she was of them, that was simply not the case. She was the biggest scaredy cat in the history of scaredy cats. Which was why I had mouse traps under all of the furniture in my tiny house, because she was even scared of mice. She was a huge cuddle bug though, and that made up for this flaw in her work ethic as guardian of our little slice of paradise.

Olivia insisted on walking on my feet before I could fully open the door, even though we both could've waltzed right in had she let me. She was very particular about her routines and ways of doing things. Who was I to judge? I was pretty particular about my routines too, now that I was an old maid living in a tiny house out in the county. You get set in your ways, ya know? I always did the same thing every night.

Eat noodles, play exactly two rounds of solitaire, and read a few chapters of a book before falling asleep with it on my face. I'll never be able to loan them out to anyone because they all had drool stains.

So embarrassing!

My friends lived too far away to loan out books to, anyway. They all either left the state when they graduated high school, or moved all the way across it in their mid-twenties. If it weren't for cell phones, I'd never hear from them at all. My reception was bad out here, so occasionally I'd wait until it was my day to go run errands and talk to them while I was in town. Less dropped calls that way. But even then, it was rare that I heard from them.

The smell of the taco soup I'd made the night before wafted through the door when I opened it, and I decided maybe I would have leftovers of that instead of my usual noodles. I had to keep things interesting occasionally, right?

I snatched the pot from the fridge, ladling out a scoop into a clean bowl and sticking it in the microwave to warm up. Olivia trilled as she hopped up onto my bed. I didn't even bother scolding her. That was a battle I'd lost a long time ago. I walked over and plopped down beside her, snuggling into her fur. She gave me a side eye, but didn't protest.

A shed of annoyance only graced her expression when the microwave beeped and she popped one eye open. I jumped up, eager to shut off the noise. Then I opened my wooden kitchen drawer, or at least I tried. One of the spoons always made it stick.

After some shaking, rattling, and rolling, it finally popped loose. I procured a clean spoon, holding it like a trophy for a split second in victory. I plopped it into the bowl before walking over to the paisley-patterned, cobalt-blue curtains and drawing them closed for the night.

There was this irrational fear I had that I couldn't get over. A fear that someone might look in while I was sleeping. I remembered even as a little girl in my grandparents' house; I hated the curtains being open at night. It made the hair on the back of my neck stand on end.

My nearest neighbor being a mile away and not having a lot of reliable cell service didn't help the equation. I tended to be a light sleeper as a result, unless I was really, really tired. It was hard to live alone sometimes, but there were perks too. Like not having to share my food!

And not offending a roommate with my garish slurping. I savored the soup, thankful for the way it soothed my aching body. It was particularly humid outside tonight, and for some reason, this type of humidity always made my joints hurt.

Olivia nestled in beside me again, purring loudly. It helped ease the pain somehow, and I appreciated her for that. Even if she was a terrible mouser.

I was so thankful that tomorrow was Saturday. I mindlessly drank the rest of my broth in the bowl, dreaming about doing nothing. I didn't have any work to do except on my own property. The farmer that I worked for had me tinkering on a harvest truck all day today. It was in a mighty state of disrepair. We had a running joke that there always had to be one piece of non-working farm equipment at any given time. I was sore from laying over and under that thing all day trying to figure out what its problem was. Car repair classes from high school could only go so far.

I sighed, sitting the empty bowl on my bedside table. That was a problem for tomorrow morning, I told myself as I pulled out my pack of cards and book for the evening.

Chapter Six

Jack

Despite the fact that I really had to use the bathroom, had the radio volume up as high as I could tolerate, and had the A/C blasting, my eyelids were growing heavy. I tried to prop one open, but that proved to be unsafe. Who would've thought!

No amount of stimulation was adequate to keep me awake. At least I didn't have to be in the office again until Monday. I could find a hotel, but I didn't really want to pay for one. Would anyone really bother a man sleeping in his truck on the side of the road? Wait! Don't answer that... the world was crazy. There would surely be someone who would. And if not a concerned citizen, perhaps a cop or a sheriff. I didn't need that kind of a wake-up call.

I turned off the radio and turned down the A/C, resolving to brute force the situation. I looked over at the clock. 12:27am. Had I really been driving for that long? I probably needed to stop for the night somewhere. Stretch my legs so I didn't get blood clots. I slowed down, pulling over for a second to look up hotels on my phone. Maybe I could get an Airbnb somewhere in Oklahoma. I'd heard they had some interesting ones.

A frown tugged at the corners of my lips. No service. My GPS wasn't even entirely certain where I was. Maybe that's why I was on a dirt road and not a highway right now. Had it given me the wrong directions when it couldn't find the coordinates? I'd have to keep driving and see if I could get a signal.

I pulled the truck back onto the unoccupied road, hoping that it wasn't far. Maybe I would just see signs for a hotel and just cruise right into one. Surely the hotels wouldn't be full for the night. I'd sleep in a closet if they'd let me at this point. I missed my bed, small as it was in my tiny apartment in Texas. Though I had to say, being away from the light pollution was incredible. I could see all of the stars shining brightly through the top of my dash and—

A blur flashed in front of me as I turned the wheel to try to swerve away from it. My tires screeched, deafening me.

As the dust settled, a deer appeared next to my passenger window. It blinked stupidly at me as if it hadn't just tried to kill the both of us in one fell swoop. Why were they like this? Overgrown, suicidal rodents...

I was thankful I hadn't hit it. I wasn't sure a tow truck would've come this far out in the boonies. And I certainly wouldn't have wanted to see the bill for that.

My knuckles gripped the wheel, drained of all their blood as I took a few steadying breaths. That was a close call. In fact, I was surprised to find I hadn't peed my pants. That was perhaps the most miraculous part of this entire encounter.

I leaned over, cranking my passenger window down just a crack to yell at the deer. Yes, my truck was old enough to have to crank the window down. It was vintage, ok? Vintage was cool! The deer didn't even blink. I rolled my eyes and laid on the horn. That did scare it, thankfully, and I pulled the truck back into a legal position on the road. I took off, a little more shaky than I had been before. But at least I was awake!

Chapter Seven

Ally

The wind began to howl outside of my window. Between that, and Olivia anxiously meowing trying to tell me about it, I was awake. I rubbed my eyes with the back of my hands, sleepy sand roughly grating against my skin. What was all the fuss about?

I stood up, the chill in the floor seeping into my bare feet, and walked to the window. I pulled the curtains back, trying to see anything in the pitch black of the night. I saw a few rain droplets clinging to the window, but there wasn't much visibility beyond that. There were no street lights out here. I had been meaning to get a flood light out on the back porch, one that could go off with motion detection and deter predators from getting close to the property. But I hadn't been able to get by the hardware store to pick one up just yet, now that I had saved up the money. Farming wasn't always very lucrative.

I shushed Olivia, who was now anxiously stepping on both of my feet, giving me hugs fit to knock me right over.

"It's ok, sweetie," I crooned. "It's ok."

She did not believe me. I wasn't sure I believed me, either.

I padded to the front door, turning the lock and opening it gingerly. I didn't want it to fly off its hinges from the wind.

Hot, humid air flew into my face. It clung to me in stinky, gross waves. I held my breath instinctually. I hated breathing in muggy air. There was nothing discernible I could see as I looked out into the pitch black. I flipped on the porch light right as a lightning bolt struck in the distance. A chill ran up my spine. Had there been something there, on the horizon? There had been a black chunk taken out of the sky, hadn't there? Or was I seeing things? I had to have been seeing things.

I closed the door, locking it behind me, and fumbled in my bedside drawer for my weather radio. I turned it on, setting it on the counter. My hands were shaking so much that it was hard to mess with the knobs of the channels. I plucked my phone from its charger, clicking the button on the side to light it up. No bars. Perfect. No bars meant no weather alerts.

The weather radio crackled with static, and Olivia's meowing only got more intense. It was hard to focus when there was so much noise and adrenaline. I turned the knobs, hoping and praying to find a clear signal. Dread filled my stomach as the seconds ticked by without any sign of a station that I could tune in to.

I went to open the door again, Olivia hot on my heels. Her fur was ruffled in discomfort. I picked her up, comforting her with soothing words and pets as I waited for the next lightning bolt to illuminate the sky. I heard something pelt the ground. I flipped on the porch light to see hard, icy balls hitting the porch. Hail. I winced, thinking of my roof, and my truck, and the roof of the chicken coop. A crack of thunder sounded and I looked up just in time to see the same sight I had earlier. A sight that I desperately hoped I had hallucinated.

A large, black, twisting cyclone.

Chapter Eight

Jack

E ven though I loved taking backroads, I didn't love the potholes. My truck bounced up and down with every impact. Normally I would avoid each and every pothole, not wanting to damage the suspension, but on these roads? They were unavoidable. You just had to aim for the lesser of two evils.

The radio still wasn't working, and neither was my phone. I had taken up entertaining myself by singing, loudly, and off-key. Was it really off-key if you were the only one that could hear it? I didn't know.

I decided that I wasn't going to tell my coworkers about getting lost when I got to work. I didn't need them teasing me about my life choices. This was still better than a plane. I thought. Marginally, at least.

I did wonder when I would see civilization again. With my GPS out of commission, it was hard to know where I really was. Road signs were scarce out of here, and when they did appear, they were often bent up to the point of illegibility, or shot through with bullet holes.

Not a comforting sight, but I told myself it was some farm kids' idea of fun. Because it probably was. I had seen a few county road signs, and I was starting to be on my grandma's side about carrying around paper maps at this point. That would've helped a lot right about now.

Maybe I could ask for an up-to-date map of every state for Christmas. Didn't need to tell the family why. Everyone is allowed to collect at least one weird thing without questioning or judgment, right? My sister collected gnomes, for goodness' sake. It couldn't get much weirder than that.

My truck continued to rip, rattle, and roll down the country roads. The trees were starting to shake more than they had been, their leaves violently twisting in the wind. It made me nervous. Could it become strong enough to push my truck off the road? What did they say about Oklahoma, it was where the wind came sweeping down the plains? Based on what I was seeing, I could understand why that was a talking point in the state song.

I stopped singing, gripping the wheel intently. Another vehicle whizzed past me. I couldn't believe they were going that fast down a road like this.

I took a sip of soda to calm my nerves. Dark clouds were starting to blot out the stars, and before long, the moon was completely blocked, too.

My truck's A/C could only do so much to filter the humidity that was outside. I felt like the air was clinging to me, like a wet blanket. Something unsettling washed over me.

Another check of my phone told me I was on my own. I silently prayed I would find somewhere to stop and get some directions, a bathroom break, and lose this sense of isolation and unease. The trees lining the road became more and more sparse as I broke out of their envelopment and across a railroad track, into more open field terrain. A railroad track was a good sign, right? Trains stopped near towns. Hopefully there was a town coming up soon.

The rumble of thunder sounded, and I cursed myself for not changing the windshield wipers before my trip. They were falling apart. I had meant to get that done and it just... slipped my mind. I was planning on doing that after I got my clothes from the dry cleaner. What had happened? I tried to remember. Oh, I had gotten a call from my buddy on my walk home. He was pestering me about getting out there and dating. Then I was preoccupied, wondering if I really was the problem.

I didn't think I was. How was a person supposed to date these days? So many bad actors out there. I didn't want to be someone's wallet. And after that one date where I showed up to a man who had impersonated a woman on a dating app... well, that was enough of trying to date for a while for me. At least the waitress that day took some pity on me and comped the drink I was white-knuckled consuming after that jump scare.

I just wanted a nice, quiet life. With a girl, a dog, a white picket fence...

A crack of lightning went across the horizon. My hair stood on end. That was way too close for my comfort. I wondered how bad of a storm this was supposed to be. My GPS usually showed me weather advisories, but with it out of commission and the radio not working, I didn't really have any way to get information.

After a few more claps of thunder, and heavy, fat raindrops pelting my windshield faster than my wipers could keep up with, I made a snap decision. The next crossroads I came to, I was going to turn right. This road seemed to lead only through the backcountry of farms, fields, and forests. The only houses I'd seen were dilapidated, condemned, or flattened from time and neglect. There weren't even any barns that were in good shape.

I spied a green sign up ahead. Though I couldn't make out what it said, I could tell a turn was coming up. I honored the deal I had made with myself, slowing down and turning the wheel to the right. I immediately felt regret as my truck dropped down off of a small drop off. That couldn't be good for the shocks. I would have to profusely apologize to my mechanic when I got home. At this point, I was starting to wonder if I would make it home. Or at least, how long it would take me.

The road wound this way and that, making me wonder if I'd be able to remember how to get to the main road again if this ended up being a dead end. There were several unpaved roads that veered off this one, and the few that were paved didn't look like they'd been kept up.

A crack of lightning raced across the sky again and illuminated a 35-mile-an-hour sign. I looked down. I was going 50. Whoops... Maybe I should slow down. I didn't want to accidentally hit someone's goat or something.

But then another lightning bolt flung itself down from the clouds and put a spotlight on a large, black mass of swirling clouds. Terror swept through me. Whatever that was, I didn't want to stick around to find out. I couldn't tell what direction it had been going. Should I turn back around? Every second that slipped by made me more and more worried. When the next lightning bolt hit, I was ready and watching as I rattled down the road.

It didn't seem to be moving. I figured that was a good sign. Maybe it was just a really scary cloud? I sped up. Any animals should be cowering in fear, like I wanted to.

The road straightened out and in the distance, I saw a glowing yellow light in between drops of water on the windshield. My heartbeat quickened. Maybe that meant that there was a person there. The distance between us felt astronomical. The truck moved as though it was in a slow-motion time warp. The wind felt like it picked up even more, and I couldn't imagine that was possible. I grabbed my phone, stowing it in my pocket as I closed the gap between myself and the light.

The closer I got, the more confused I became. It wasn't a streetlight, but a porch light.

There was a little wooden home that looked like a small cabin. A woman ran frantically from an outbuilding, through the porch light, into an underground thing with a metal spinner on top. I slowed my truck down, pulling it off the side of the road and into her yard.

Then it occurred to me that I, a strange man, was approaching a young woman in the middle of the night in the middle of nowhere. This was perhaps not the best plan. As soon as I stepped out, I saw that she held a squalling blonde chicken. I approached loudly.

"My name is Jack, I am traveling and this storm seems pretty bad. I have no cell service and—"

The sound of a wailing train cut me off. Her wide eyes locked onto me.

She screamed something at me, but the wind broke her words up and carried them away.

She motioned with her hands and screamed, "GET IN!"

I heard her that time.

Another lightning bolt hit and I turned around to see the black, swirling mass was behind us, about to be on top of us. Was this a tornado? I hadn't seen the movie Twister, and I hadn't lived in this part of the country long enough to have been caught up to speed on them.

I ran to her and the shelter, where she shoved me in, rather aggressively I might add — did I like that? I wasn't sure... now was not the time — and scooped up a cat before closing the door and locking it behind us.

She breathed out an aggressive puff of air as she sank into the wall of the tiny shelter.

"That was close. Way too close."

Chapter Nine

Ally

Pitch black was all that lay before me.

The sound of frantic chickens clucking, the metal air vent spinning, and Olivia meowing anxiously filled the enclosed shelter. A cacophony of chaos and anxiety. Rain pelting the top didn't help matters, either. The train sound was coming up on deafening levels of decibels.

I felt around in the dark, searching for the lantern. My hands found purchase and I turned it on. Suddenly every creature crammed into the shelter was bathed in light.

And there, in the corner, on the floor, sat a stranger. A man.

He looked as though he'd been teleported from another world. He sat in the wet, red dirt-covered corner in business casual with a button-down shirt and slacks, his blue eyes wide with wonder and concern.

"Are you ok?" I asked.

He didn't seem to understand the gravity of the situation. I envied that. Except for the part where his ignorance could've gotten him killed. He was lucky to be in the right place at the right time.

He looked up from studying the chickens all around him.

"I think so." He swallowed, hard.

"Do you need something to drink?" I asked, pointing at the pack of water I kept down here.

I could slice it open and get one out. It might taste a little plastic-y, but it was the best hosting I could do at the moment. Unless he wanted to grab an onion hanging from the ceiling. That was the nice thing about tornado shelters, you could use them as a root cellar under the right circumstances.

"No, no," he said, almost too forcefully.

He winced, then explained, "I drank a lot on the road, and I haven't been able to find civilization or a gas station in a long, long time. And my phone didn't work at all for several hours now. I don't want to drink anymore. I've needed to use the bathroom for hours."

I laughed, which he thankfully didn't seem to be offended by.

"Sounds like you got caught on No Man's Highway. Were you taking a highway and then ended up on a bunch of run down roads?"

"Yes..." he said, his voice a mix of confusion and hesitancy.

"That always traps out-of-towners. Usually they don't get as far as you did before they turn back. They tend to freak out when the cell service doesn't work out here," I explained.

Before he could say anything back, the shelter was filled with the sound of the tornado right on top of us. I couldn't even hear myself think. I hugged Olivia as she shook, fighting back tears.

This wasn't the first time I had been close to one, but the sound was so, so scary. And the carnage after was even worse. I wondered if it would hit my house. Or his truck. I hoped it didn't hit his truck.

Welcome to Oklahoma, where the wind takes all your stuff and throws it. I did not want to have to call the insurance lady in the morning. It was so hard getting them out to the house when it just hailed, let alone with an event like this. That thing, what I saw of it, was huge.

I stroked Olivia's fur gently to calm her. The chickens had all gone quiet because of the noise. The man looked scared to death.

"We'll be ok in here," I hollered at him reassuringly. "This shelter rated for an F5."

"Is that good?" he asked, raising his voice to match mine.

He wiped his hands on his pants. It was so humid, it was hard to breathe. My hair was sticking to my neck in sweaty, sticky patches.

"Yes," I nodded, yelling back, "tornadoes only go up to F5."

"Is this an F5?" He gestured up, then shifted as my rooster jumped onto his leg and pecked at his knee.

"Gerald," I scolded, jumping up and shooing him down with my brow furrowed.

Then I looked back at his face, taking my seat again. I realized I hadn't answered his question.

"Sorry, they are menaces, every last one of them. Tornado ratings usually happen after the fact, so we won't know officially until it's over."

I found it exhausting to try to loudly pronounce every syllable over the noise.

He smiled at the chickens, not seeming to mind, but being a little wary. He nodded, acknowledging that he had heard and I didn't need to repeat.

A large cracked sound reverberated through the shelter. He jumped about a foot off the ground, and I did too. Olivia dug her claws into my skin. I winced, trying to coax her to let go of me.

The chickens were running into each other, frantically trying to get away from the noise.

"What was that?" he yelled, his face splotchy in this light.

"I'm sure it's just a downed power line nearby or a tree that got uprooted," I shouted.

But really, I wasn't sure. And I was worried.

Chapter Ten

Jack

B eing trapped in a shelter during a tornado with a stranger was not how I planned on spending my night. In fact, if someone had bet me that I would be doing this at any point in my life, I would've laughed, told them they were crazy, and lost all my money in one fell swoop.

The chickens were admittedly adorable, running around like little brainless dinosaurs trying to understand what was happening. I felt just like them at the moment.

It was a little embarrassing being completely clueless in front of this beautiful woman, but she didn't seem to hold it against me. She seemed more concerned about her unruly chickens. I was honestly really surprised her cat wasn't trying to eat any of them, but she seemed pretty well-behaved.

Despite the sweat dripping off of both of us, I found her so pretty. Her dark hair clung to her and her dark eyes swam with genuine concern and compassion. She seemed like a sweetheart. Her turquoise overalls were caked with red mud and blades of grass stuck to the bottom.

There was a new noise, some loud thumping on the metal door on the roof, but it seemed like the train sound had disappeared. I never wanted to hear that sound again.

"I'm so sorry," I said, now that I could talk at an acceptable volume in between the thumping sounds. "I hope I didn't scare you running into your yard like this at night. My name is Jack."

She laughed. Snorted actually. It was cute. A smirk tugged at my lips and I had to use all my willpower to keep it under control.

"Ally," she said, her eyes sparkling, "and I'm not scared. If I can deal with a coyote, I can deal with a strange city slicker in the middle of the night."

Ally. That was a cute name.

I sat back, trying to decide if I was genuinely offended by her calling me a city slicker or if I was going to run with it.

She tipped her head up, challenging me.

"What makes you think I'm a city slicker?" I said, hand over my chest like a church lady clutching her pearls.

She looked down at my dress shoes, slowly made her way up my outfit, and back down. My heart beat faster when she did that than it had when I was driving away from the tornado. But, I wouldn't mind if she did it again.

She said nothing, just giggled.

Point taken. But I wasn't going to let the banter go that easily.

"Maybe I was going to a funeral," I said, "you don't know."

Her face dropped. "Were you?"

Her eyes got wide, but before she started apologizing I put my hand up.

"I was just messing with you. Nobody died. Except me almost, apparently."

"I'm glad you didn't die," she smiled, petting her cat and then surveying all her animals. "I'm glad we all made it down here ok."

The cat was wide-eyed.

"It's ok, Olivia," she said soothingly to the cat. "You're ok."

Olivia. There was a name you didn't hear much anymore.

The noises outside seemed to be gradually disappearing more and more.

"How do we know when it's safe to get out?" I asked her.

Not that I was feeling claustrophobic. Ok, maybe I was. That had been the whole reason I hadn't taken the plane home. That and the fact that it was claustrophobic AND in the air.

While it was fun sitting with the chickens and all, we were down here in an enclosed amphitheater with a single air vent. I could use a smidge of fresh air.

She looked thoughtfully up at the door.

"We should probably wait a few minutes. My weather radio wasn't working, so I have no way to tell for sure, but as long as it doesn't sound too bad out there, I think we'll be good to go up in a few minutes."

I could handle a few more minutes, couldn't I?

Chapter Eleven

Ally

I was glad this stranger had a sense of humor. I'd never had to shelter with anyone but my family and elderly neighbors before. I would've never guessed I'd shelter with a strange man that I didn't know from Adam. But life was unpredictable that way.

I thought about my neighbors down the road. They were almost a mile away, and I hoped that they were ok. I didn't know how wide the tornado had ended up being, but I thought that based on what I had seen that it should've missed them. The storm could've always dropped a second one, or changed directions, I supposed.

"Can we get out soon?" the man in the corner asked, clutching a chicken as though it was an emotional support animal.

I had to stifle a laugh at the sight.

Surprisingly, the chicken didn't seem to mind. Maybe this man was a chicken whisperer. I could use one of those around here.

I stopped in my mental tracks. Where had that come from? That was such a silly idea. He couldn't stay. I shook myself.

"Yeah," I assured him.

It had been quiet for a few minutes, and I really doubted there was anything else. But I had heard of storms dropping down multiple tornadoes in a row, so I was always cautious. I really wished my weather radio would work. That would've helped us so much with this.

But truthfully, I was stalling. As weird as it was having a strange man in my cellar, it was an equally scary proposition to go upstairs. I hadn't been in or near a tornado since I was a child. And my grandparents took care of all of the damage then. We'd just gotten a glancing blow that time. I had a sinking feeling this blow hadn't been so glancing.

Would I have a house? Would I have a chicken coop? Would we have our trucks when we went upstairs? Would you find them slammed into the house? It was Pandora's box, and I wasn't ready to open it. As long as we stayed down here, I could stay blissfully unaware.

But the guy, Jack, looked anxious. Really, really anxious. Which made two of us.

"I'll crack it open and just take a look to make sure," I told him, rising from my spot on the floor and plopping Olivia down.

The floor was a little wet. She meowed at me in protest, shaking her paw. For a farm cat, she had a dainty streak a mile long.

"You're ok, Olivia," I told her.

I climbed the stairs carefully, hanging onto the railing as I went. Even with the lantern, it was quite dark in here.

I grabbed onto the handle, turning it to unlock it. The metal creaked. It was rusty, but that was to be expected with how old of a shelter this was. I tried pushing up on it. I had forgotten how heavy this door was. I couldn't get it to budge at all.

I climbed another stair, needing a bit more oomph. I pushed again. Nothing. My heart took off racing. I looked back at my new companion, his eyes wide.

"Don't worry, sometimes it just takes a good shove," I said reassuringly, though I was not reassured.

I inhaled a deep breath through my nose and braced myself as I slammed the door with my full weight.

Pain surged through my shoulder and down my spine.

That was not supposed to happen. A hiss escaped my lips.

All of a sudden, this perfect stranger was on his feet, his hands around my back.

"Are you ok?" his eyes swam with concern.

He was gentle but insistent as he drew me back down the stairs.

"Yeah," I blinked back tears. "I'm ok."

"I'll try it," he said quickly, guiding me to sit.

He almost refused to look away from me to actually go and test the door himself. I would be fine. I thought. Black spots swam in my vision from the pain, but I didn't think I was going to pass out. I just needed a second to absorb the pain.

He grabbed hold of the handle, pushing gently to test it. If he got that thing to budge without body-slamming it, I was going to be upset. That was like trying for forever to open a pickle jar and the next person being able to open it with no problems.

And knowing my luck, he'd be some chauvinist jerk that said something about women being weaker. Men's work. Yada yada yada. I heard that a lot around here, despite having gained the respect of many men, young and old, for keeping up mechanically and in the fields.

He was far more calculated and cautious than I had been about this. Probably because I'd already screwed up my shoulder. Maybe he would've been clawing his way out at all costs, given the chance, before he witnessed that. He definitely seemed like an animal trapped in a cage about to gnaw their leg off. Poor guy.

I watched as he wiped sweat away from his brow. It was super hot in here. Olivia sat, purring in my lap, overheating me even more than I otherwise would be. But the purring helped the pain, and I would feel bad pushing her off when she was just trying to help. The chickens all clucked, watching this new man stand on the stairs. I think this was one of the few times I'd seen them focus on a singular thing outside of food.

Impressive.

"I'm sorry," he said.

Before I could ask why, he started unbuttoning his fancy dress shirt. He shucked it off quickly and hung it on the railing of the stairs. My jaw hung open, undoubtedly, as he stood there in nothing but a wife beater undershirt. I'd seen a lot of those in these parts, but he fit it better than anyone I'd ever seen. Maybe familiarity did breed contempt. Maybe I needed to get out of town more.

His back flexed as he pushed against the door, displaying eerily lit lines of muscle. It wasn't overt or gaudy. He wasn't a bodybuilder.

But he was... gorgeous. Focus, Ally, focus. On what? I don't know. Hm. Was there anything better to focus on? At least his back was turned so he couldn't see me ogling him.

He stood steady on the stairs, completely oblivious, pushing up with both hands. The door didn't budge.

"You sure it's unlocked?" he queried.

And suddenly I was paying attention to the depth and texture of his voice.

It was a pleasant voice.

I glanced at the door handle.

"Yes." I frowned, sobering to the circumstances again.

"Ok."

He gave the door a huge shove, with more force than he had used on it yet. Probably more than what I had put into it body slamming it. And it still didn't budge.

I started to feel dizzy. That... that wasn't a good sign.

He pulled out his phone from his pocket, the screen illuminating his face. Now that his hair was wet from sweat, it curled just slightly. Adorable.

"I don't have signal." He looked at me. "Do you?"

His voice was surprisingly calm for the conclusion we were both coming to.

I pulled mine out with my left hand, which was harder but not impossible. Moving my right side at all hurt quite a bit.

"No." My voice betrayed me with a crack.

I blamed the mold down here. It had nothing to do with the fact that I was now terrified.

Chapter Twelve

Jack

We were trapped.

Underground.

In a tornado shelter.

I should've taken the plane.

But I couldn't bring myself to believe that. Despite my claustrophobia being fever pitch, I actually felt like I was managing OK. My new friend, however, was not looking good. The little lamp in the shelter was definitely not a normal indoor lighting color, but she was looking green even factoring that in.

"Are you ok?" I sat across from her.

I didn't want to invade her personal space. She already looked like she was seconds away from hyperventilating. I did not want her to pass out. Not only would she would be scared when she woke up, but I could be accused of something untoward by whoever ended up digging us out. If someone came to dig us out.

I just wanted her to feel safe.

"Yeah," she murmured, looking dazed.

I began to wonder if she had actually broken something by body slamming the door like that. I wasn't sure if that was possible. I suddenly regretted not paying closer attention in first aid class in college.

Unless I missed my guess, there was something on top of the door keeping us from getting out. And it was heavy enough that it wouldn't even bunch from either of us pushing. I didn't know what that would mean for us getting rescued. I hated to ask her questions that were stressful at a time like this, but I was sure she'd come to the same conclusion that we were trapped.

"Does anyone know you have this shelter?" I asked.

As long as someone knew a storm came through here and she had a shelter, we had a chance at being rescued, even if debris was completely covering us up. I didn't know where the nearest emergency crews would be coming from and how many other people could be trapped, but hopefully I could get a basic estimate.

"Yeah," she said, seeming to perk up a little, "everyone in town and the farms nearby."

Good. That sounded like it was a lot of people who it would cross their minds to check on her.

"When are you scheduled to go into town or work next?"

That would give us an indication of when people would start looking.

"I was supposed to go to work on Monday. I didn't have any solid plans for this weekend."

Well crap.

It was 3:30 am early Saturday. That meant nobody would be expecting her for a two days.

"Is this road a high-traffic area?" I asked, hopeful.

She laughed. She didn't even answer.

The hope that I had that we wouldn't be trapped down here for a while was starting to fade. But I was sure we'd make it out alive, just a little bit worse for the wear mentally. I was thankful she'd put water down here. At some point I'd break down and drink some.

I really didn't want to have to pee in front of her, and I was sure she felt the same in reverse. I was suddenly extremely grateful for the takeout meal Rachel had given me for the road. Though small, it was better than nothing under the circumstances. I wondered about the animals though, would they be ok?

An idea struck me. I'd heard of people being able to call 911 even without a signal. I'd never tried it, never needed to, but it was worth a shot. There was nothing to lose, really. My phone was mostly charged, and I imagined hers was too, since she'd probably been in bed for the night when this thing hit.

I whipped it out, dialing those three little numbers. All my hopes and dreams hung on a thread as I watched and waited. Waited for the call to start connecting. Waited to hear it ring. Nothing.

I got an idea. She eyed me as I climbed the stairs and dialed again, putting my phone just under the little wind spinner. It seemed like that would be the best chance of getting the call to go through. But the phone screen blinked red and disconnected.

I sighed, sitting down on the stairs. What was already going to be a long night had turned into a very, very long night. Even if we got rescued, what had happened to my truck? Had we been directly hit? Would it be intact?

Would it be drivable? Would it be fixable? What about her house? Would she be homeless?

So many logistical considerations ran through my head. But the one thing I knew for sure was that there was no use worrying about much right now. The storm was probably still raging through a local neighborhood. It seemed unlikely that anyone would discover us until morning.

So tonight, we ought to rest. In the morning, we could take shifts banging on the door and yelling to try to get someone's attention passing by.

She sat with her head slumped against the wall. She looked exhausted. I got up and moved back to my corner.

"Goodnight," I said quietly.

I don't know why I said goodnight to the random stranger whose tornado shelter I was trapped in, but it seemed the polite thing to do.

I was pleasantly surprised when I heard a weakly whispered, "Goodnight."

Chapter Thirteen

Ally

T he air was so oppressively hot and humid. I felt like I was dying when I woke up. Rather abruptly and rudely, I might add. My rooster took it upon himself to crow, in this enclosed space, like the maniac he was. Right at 6:30am, per usual. Which meant we'd gotten what, three hours of sleep?

I woke up just in time to catch the man I'd spent the night with in this insane asylum startled awake, his arms flying backward. I couldn't contain my laughter at his unassuming, shocked face.

He rubbed his eyes in confusion. His face morphed into hurt, and finally orneriness as he interpreted my laughter as playful and not hostile.

"Does he do that every morning?" the man asked.

"Yeah... he's got a great internal timer."

I rubbed the back of my neck, peeling off some of the stuck-on hair.

My neck felt stiff from sleeping against a concrete wall all night. The few times that I had woken up, I had chosen to go back to sleep immediately. If the storm had hit town, they had a lot more going on than we did.

The chickens pecked at some spiders crawling across the floor, for which I was grateful. They were giving me the heebie jeebies. I would've never thought to put them down here for pest control, but I was thankful at least that they had something to eat. I had no doubt that Olivia would start eating me if we didn't get her food soon. I needed to get them all some water because the damp spots in the corners of this thing were not sufficient.

"Do you have a knife on you?" I asked my new friend.

He gave me a concerned look in response. The wheels in my head turned slowly until I realized I'd just accidentally accused him of being a serial killer or something.

"Oh my gosh, no. Sorry. I left my pocketknife in the house. I need to water the chickens, and Olivia, and I figured we could drink out of some water bottles and then slice the top off to give them something flat to drink out of," I explained, to the point of almost rambling.

OK, no, I was rambling.

"Oh," he said, "that makes sense. Um..."

He picked up his button-up shirt and patted the pockets. I didn't blame him for not putting it back on, it was way too hot for that. And so was he. *Not that it was any of my business.*

I was going to be shocked if he actually had a knife. He didn't seem like the type. Did they even allow weapons in the fancy offices he frequented? But he did pull something out of his pocket. It was a square-looking piece with a pointy hook.

"It's a letter opener," he explained as he saw me squinting at it. "It's got a sharp piece. We could break it off and saw into the bottles that way or we can puncture the bottle and cut around it, I think."

That was smart. Maybe his big city brain was going to be worth something in this situation after all.

I opened a bottle, handing it to him, and then opened another one for myself and chugged until it was half gone. I wished it didn't taste like plastic so much, but it was hot down here and we couldn't afford to overheat. The quicker it went down, the better. He handed me the letter opener and I pierced the bottle with it like he had suggested, carefully carving through the plastic. I got almost all the way around and then tore the top off.

I sat it down, offering it to Olivia. She wandered up to it, lapping at the water. I felt bad that the edges were a little sharp and ragged, but I knew she would be careful. The chickens, however... I wished I had a file to blunt the edges for them. They weren't exactly the sharpest tools in the shed. Don't tell them I said that, though. They would get their feelings hurt.

He handed me his half-drunk bottle and I butchered it too, offering it to the chickens. They pushed and shoved each other trying to get a sip. I would have to open another to refill these, and then we could have another dish for them to share. Hopefully it wouldn't be too long until help came.

"Do you think it's daylight out?" he asked.

I wondered the same. I supposed, since the rooster had crowed. But usually, I could see light through the air vent, even when it was cloudy out, and I couldn't right now.

"Who knows?" I offered. "It could just be cloudy out."

He frowned, burying his head in his hands.

"Are you ok?" I asked, now worried.

"Yeah," he said. "I just can't imagine how many missed emails I have from my boss now."

I recoiled. "You get emails from your boss on the weekends?"

"Usually," he knit his brows together, "that's pretty standard for corporate jobs, I think."

"Ohhh fancy," I mocked, "no free time."

I meant it good-naturedly, but I was actually appalled. That seemed inhumane. Nobody could be on 24/7. I mean, farming was sometimes a job with long days and nights, but there were off seasons and lighter loads days, and at least working for a farmer and not having my own farm, I definitely got days off. Every week. And I only got called out if there was an emergency with a cow giving birth, cattle getting out, or some other genuine problem that could put the life and limb of an animal or person in danger. What could possibly be so pressing with an office job that they would need to email you on the weekend?

"It is kind of annoying," he conceded, "but that's just the way it is."

"Is it?" I narrowed my eyes suspiciously. "Or is that just what they tell you so that you think it's normal?"

I knew city life was different, faster, more brutal to the spirit. But this seemed not worth it at all. No amount of money would be enough for me to not have uninterrupted weekends.

He laughed. A genuine laugh that lit up his face in a gorgeous way. I wanted him to do it again. That revelation surprised me, but I decided to let it go. It was nice to have some company that was enjoyable. And for now, a complete secret. The ladies in town couldn't tease me about someone they didn't know about.

Maybe the people that pulled us out would be from a bigger town nearby and the only thing Blink ever found out would be rumors. They'd never know about this man, and about what really happened to us. I could write it into urban legend myself, embellishing and omitting as I wished.

It was rare to have control of the narrative in a small town. I quite liked the idea.

"Corporate is full of all sorts of silly rules. They don't say what they mean, they don't mean what they say. You have to guess at things, and if you guess wrong, you get to sit through a lecture about professionalism and how things are done, and it's... exhausting," he finished.

"Sounds like."

My mouth turned up into a smile, curiosity getting the better of me.

"What do you do for fun, when you're not navigating life in a foreign language?"

This time he laughed really hard. I could get drunk on that laugh. It made my spine tingle. I realized that even through all the sweat and anxiety, he smelled good. Really good.

"That's a great way of putting it." He gave me a wink that made my heart skip a beat.

"What do I do for fun, let me see..." He tapped his chin. "I like to go on walks when nobody else is awake yet and it's quiet, no hustle and bustle yet. I like to play this little farming video game."

He paused, blushing. Probably because it sounded ridiculous to him to tell a woman who lived in the country that he liked to play a game that simulated her life. And it was pretty funny, but I'd tease him about that later. I was still listening.

"I secretly like to listen to country music."

Ok, I had to interrupt to ask a question.

"Secretly? Why?"

"My coworkers hate country music. They say it's like nails on a chalkboard. But I like the storytelling, you know? It's always got a narrative. I like other music too, but I don't get to listen to country very often. My roommates in college didn't like country music either, so it's been a guilty pleasure for a long time," he recounted.

I laughed.

"So let me get this straight. You like country music, you like farming games, and quiet? Seems like you're a fish out of water... either that or a rhinestone cowboy... "

I gave him a scrutinizing glance, meant to make him nervous. When he shifted uncomfortably, I knew my work here was done.

"I don't see that being the case, though. Rhinestone cowboys usually have bejeweled cowboy crap like boots, hats, and belt buckles. Unless I miss my guess, you probably don't own any of those."

"No," he said nervously, but with a touch of relief, "I don't."

"So what's your plan?" I asked, just being nosy now. "Live the rest of your life wishing that you had a different one? Answering emails in between feeding your pixel cows on the weekend? Sneaking country music like it's an illegal drug? That does sound like quite the interesting way to live, if you ask me."

"Well," he chuckled, "when you put it that way..."

"What way would you put it?"

I decided I was going to turn this man every way but loose. He was fun to tease. Whether it was the heat or embarrassment, there was a cute creep of red flush that ran up his neck and across his cheeks.

"I think everyone hates the life they are living, don't they? Everyone wants to escape from what they are doing, at least for a little while, so things can be a little more bearable? Are you telling me you never want to escape from... whatever it is that you do?" he asked earnestly.

That was a good question. I would have to think about it. Was there anything I wanted to escape from? Usually I didn't mind the monotony of small-town farm life. I loved almost all of it. And the rest I could tolerate really easily. Except for the loneliness. That was killer.

Chapter Fourteen

Jack

That question seemed to send her into some deep contemplation. I hadn't meant to ask something profound, I was just trying to see if it really wasn't normal to hate most of your waking hours and dream of a life outside of the one you were already living. I thought it was a universal experience, and I supposed the jury was still out on that based on the look on her face. She'd gotten so quiet that I began regretting my question.

I nervously picked at my fingernails as I tried to look anywhere but at her. I wondered if I had dug up some kind of personal hurt. I sure hoped someone dug us up soon, speaking of. It was unbearably hot in here and I didn't want to fully strip in front of this poor woman. She was sweating buckets too, and it wasn't fair for me to be able to shed clothes and not her. The cat was velcroed to her legs, which probably didn't help matters.

"I suppose there are downsides to my life," she admitted, "but they are a price I'm more willing to pay compared to some alternatives. What happens if you don't answer your boss's emails on the weekend?"

I thought about how to answer that. I didn't want to misrepresent the severity to someone who didn't know anything about corporate America.

"It depends on the email. It could be something silly, like someone needs to order more paper for the copier on Monday, or it could be something urgent like a client wanting to move their investments immediately even though we can't on the weekends. Those aren't fun emails."

She frowned. "That sounds like a lot of stress."

"It can be," I admitted, "but the pay is good, at least in the long run."

"I can't think of a pay high enough for me to be willing to deal with that on the weekends." She scratched her head.

Suddenly we heard a noise. I couldn't be sure what it was. Was it a vehicle passing by? A helicopter? My eyes went wide. Whatever it was, now was our chance to bang on the door and try to get the attention of a passerby. We both jumped up. She started yelling, and oh my gosh, she had good lungs. She was LOUD. LOUD and energetic. I had to cover my ears.

She let out a few good screams for help before she stopped and let me have a turn banging on the door. My fist stung from the impact, but we had to press our advantage. There was no telling how much the sound could be deafened by whatever was on top of us. We both stopped our efforts, waiting for any sign of a reply or acknowledgment. But the noise seemed to be getting more and more distant.

"What do you think that was?" I asked her, leaning against the wall for a break.

She thought for a moment, checking her phone again for a signal.

"Sometimes they send out helicopters to assess the damage a tornado has done. I remember seeing it on TV as a kid. Depending on the damage, they assign certain ratings to a tornado to tell how bad it was. Remember how I told you this shelter is rated for an F5, and that's the worst one? So it's possible the person might not have heard us at all. But if they ran a helicopter over the area surely they'd see... " Ally's voice trailed off.

Would they see the tornado shelter if it was covered by debris? Would they at least see the damage and send someone to check, as there was clearly a house inhabited out here? I chose to believe yes. For my sanity, and for hers. We had to keep a good attitude in here. I strained my ears trying to hear, but the noise was well and truly gone.

"Anyway," I changed the subject, "you didn't tell me. What do you do for fun?"

I sat down again on the floor, awaiting her answer with bated breath. She looked surprised for a second, then she got a wicked grin on her face.

"What?" I demanded to know what put that beautiful smile on her lips. Whatever her hobby was, it must be positively scandalous.

"Nothing." She grinned like a banshee.

"I don't believe you," I countered, arms folded.

"I like to read," she said carelessly.

"Oh really? Reading makes you smile like that? Must be *some* book."

I had to dodge as she tossed a water bottle right at my head. Her aim was impressive, I had to give her that. She giggled as I wiped the shock from my face and set the bottle down at my side.

"It's only fair," I teased her. "I told you my hobbies, even the embarrassing ones..."

"Oh yes, country music is *so* embarrassing."

She flipped her hair over her shoulder in a mocking gesture.

"To me, it is."

I pretended to pout.

Right when I thought that our little game was about to be over and she really wasn't going to tell me, she leaned forward and whispered, "If I tell you, I'm gonna have to kill you."

"What if I'm ok with that?" I whispered back.

Her mischievous grin shook off her face.

She composed herself, jutted her chin up, and said very matter-of-factly, "Skinny dipping."

I thought my ears weren't working. Maybe it was a heat stroke. They seemed to be ringing like crazy. What had this wild woman just said to me? This adorable, country bumpkin of the highest degree? This innocent little farmhand with an army of chickens and a pampered cat?

She skinny dips?

Jack, don't do it. Don't picture it, I told myself.

Be. A. Gentlemen.

Wow.

I liked her. She was crazy. Did I like crazy? I guess I did. I could live with that. There were worse things.

"Oh really?" I asked, my face not at all composed.

I wasn't sure I could get my face under control for the rest of my stay in this shelter. But one thing was for certain, I was not telling my coworkers about her. She was going to be my secret.

I'd tell them about getting stuck in a tornado, I'd tell them about the crazy roads. But she was sacred. She was a wildflower in my concrete jungle. I couldn't get enough of her. Her wild swamp eyes effervesced as she laughed, the sound bouncing off of every piece of concrete in this place.

Chapter Fifteen

Jack

Were there any countries that used enclosed spaces as torture to get information out of people? I was beginning to see why, if so. Though I doubted that it was particularly legal anywhere.

I felt like spilling my guts to this woman, as though that would somehow keep me from dying in this concrete cell. I bit my tongue, figuratively, until it nearly bled. Usually I would nervously drink water, but I still really, really had to pee. I couldn't risk making that worse.

I couldn't tell if she felt the same level of antsiness that I did, but it didn't seem to make her as talkative as me. She did seem to be starting to fray at the edges too, though. Just in her own way. The cracks were starting to show. I worried about what would happen if she started hyperventilating. I wasn't exactly a medic. I had no first aid really, though I could put on a bandage. I wondered if we'd both need counseling by the time this was said and done.

I wondered how much longer it would be until someone came to find us. Or if we would be found. I tried to push that thought out of my mind, but it came more and more frequently as the hours passed by. We were lucky to not be suffering any signs of a heat stroke at this point.

The chickens seemed to be feeling it though; they were practically wilting. Ally kept pouring water on them, and the cat, which the cat didn't appreciate one bit. She angrily groomed herself every time.

I periodically checked my phone. It was finicky about turning off from being too hot or too cold. I wasn't sure that the time on it was right anymore, either. The fact that it hadn't shut off in this heat was a good sign. But it was draining the battery very quickly despite me not using it. I didn't ask about hers. I supposed it wasn't relevant considering neither of them worked down here.

Chapter Sixteen

Ally

The heat was finally getting to me. And the exhaustion. I was finding it harder and harder to doze off under the circumstances. I wasn't worried about Jack. But I was worried about not opening my eyes up again. About never seeing the sun again. I felt like a pirate with scurvy out sailing the seven seas, not having seen land or another human in weeks. At least Jack was here.

That would be a whole other can of worms if we did get rescued, though. How would I explain this strange man? Earlier, I had been excited about all of the possibilities of urban legends I could make up about him. But in reality, I had to live here. And I had to live with whatever the actual rumor mill spun up about this situation. Would I be the talk of the town for the next nine months while they waited to see if I was gonna give birth to this man's baby?

I almost laughed at the absurdity, but I stopped myself. And Jack noticed. He probably thought I was cracking, which would be true, but it wasn't necessary to point out.

"You know what sounds good right now?" I said in a haze, not looking directly at him.

"What?" he asked with trepidation.

I was sure this poor man had no idea what was about to come out of my mouth.

"Ice cream," I said with a beaming smile, "with fresh strawberries."

He visibly relaxed. Then he chuckled.

"You're gonna make me hungry."

How long had it been since we'd eaten? Was the time on our phones even accurate? We'd been down here for almost eighteen hours. In one way, that was a good thing. The temperature would start to dip and we would start cooling off again. But on the other hand, nobody had come for us yet. Would we have to wait until I was supposed to go into my job on Monday?

"Did your coworkers or boss know what route you were taking to go home?" I asked, wondering if maybe a search party would be sent out for him. "Do you location share with someone or anything like that?"

He frowned. "No, I was kind of winging it based on what my GPS was saying was the fastest route. I don't have anyone that I location share with."

Ok. I tried to make my brain move in a positive direction. If debris really was on top of the shelter, anyone who was driving by, whether for an errand or a trip to town, would see it. And they'd think at least to check the house in that instance, wouldn't they? What if there were other people trapped too? What if the storm was so bad that all of the resources and manpower were already doing as much as they could?

I remembered a time when the whole area had been struck by a blizzard, which was highly unusual. We barely ever got snow. It was so dire that nobody had electricity. A generator had to be hooked up to the town hall.

I remembered sleeping under a table with the secretary's son while people chattered away. And when I woke up, the Red Cross was there. I thought it was the coolest thing. Probably because I wasn't the one dealing with the insurance companies or food supply. To me, it was an exciting change in my small world. This was not exciting. This was scary, and the responsibility of picking up the mess fell on me.

What was I going to do if my house was gone? Would insurance put up a fight? Didn't they usually put people in hotels when their houses got hit by tornadoes? There wasn't a hotel within thirty miles of here. And what about my truck? Would it be functioning?

I put my head in my hands, Olivia purring constantly at my side.

"It's going to be ok," Jack assured me, and he sounded so confident about it.

"How about we play a game?" he offered.

"A game?" I asked.

I couldn't tell if he was serious or joking. I didn't know finance guys played games. Seemed too stuffy of an industry for that. Except maybe golf.

"Yeah, you like games, right? I assume someone who likes skinny dipping would like games..." He gave a coy smile.

I wanted to be offended. But my curiosity was stronger.

I leaned forward. "What kind of game?"

His face took on a boyish quality. Like one of those boys in school who pulled pigtails, or blew spit wads into your hair. I struggled to picture this guy in a professional role...

"How about twenty questions?" he pitched.

"Nah, that one is boring and SO long," I said, shooting him down.

He frowned, and I almost felt bad. But I really didn't care for it. Might put me right to sleep though, which wouldn't necessarily be a bad thing.

"Well, we could play truth or dare," he offered, and though his face was innocent, his voice was not.

I hadn't played truth or dare since I was in high school. It was notoriously... scandalous. Was he flirting with me? Or just trying to pass the time?

"Isn't that a kid's game?" I folded my arms, eyeing him suspiciously.

"Maybe, but we don't exactly have a card deck to play poker down here," he pointed out.

I tried to picture him playing poker, and I couldn't see it. But he was full of surprises, so maybe.

"True... I'd kick your butt at poker, anyway," I said with a smile.

He laughed. "You think so?"

"I know so." I tipped my chin up.

"I might take you up on that challenge when we're out of here. But for now, you can go first." He leaned forward.

How devious did I want to be? I thought about it.

I could always make him kiss a chicken. And if I wanted to be really mean, I could take a picture of it on his phone and make him send it to one of his coworkers when we finally got out of here and had cell service. That would certainly be something he'd have some explaining to do about later. I tried to think of a question I could ask him. I supposed I could come up with something on the spot, so I decided to just jump in.

"Truth or dare?" I sat forward, elbows on my knees, watching him intently.

I could tell he was calculating the risk, and I honestly didn't know him well enough to know how he was going to play the game. We'd known each other for less than a day, even though it felt like we'd been down here for at least three. Not seeing the sun could do that to a person.

"Truth." He smiled earnestly.

He seemed eager to know what sort of things I would like to know about him.

"Tell me something embarrassing that you don't think I would ever guess about you."

He tilted his head, thinking.

While he thought, I wondered what I should choose when he asked me. I supposed his answer would inform me of how dirty he played.

"I slept with a stuffed animal until I was 19."

My jaw hung open.

"No way! What kind of stuffed animal?"

My shouting upset the chickens, who all ruffled their feathers in protest.

His cheeks turned pink.

"It was a cow," he admitted.

I was laughing now, probably harder than I should have. This was way more wholesome than any game of truth or dare I'd ever played before. I could just picture his little self, his cute blue eyes and blonde hair snuggling with a cow stuffy.

"What was its name?" I asked, taking a drink of water as I realized my turn was coming up. My mouth was turning dry at the prospect.

"Betsy."

"AWWWW!" I exclaimed loud enough to wake poor Olivia up.

She trilled at me, one eye open and then shut again as she went back to sleep. I gave her some consolation pets in recompense.

"Your turn," he said, eager to have the ball in my court.

My hands suddenly felt more clammy than even the humidity had had them feeling.

"Dare!" I said quickly. I wasn't sure where that came from.

"I didn't even ask yet," he said, a quizzical but amused look painted on his face.

Chapter Seventeen

Ally

As I drifted in and out of sleep, I wondered about the fields. Had they been hit by the tornado? By the hail? Those fields were everyone's livelihood around here. If the farmers didn't get paid, I didn't get paid. Neither did any of the other farmhands. The town would suffer. Oil money could only go so far. It wasn't stable, and it wasn't enough in the long run to support the local economy.

I longed to reach out and touch the blades of wheat, feel the texture. Reassure myself that this was all a dream. That nothing was going to change. That there wasn't a bunch of work to be done, potentially right above our heads. And let's be real, I'd be doing it alone.

We shouldn't have played games like that. I got a little attached and started picturing what my life would be like with someone like him, twenty-four-seven.

Joking and laughing, standing in the kitchen swatting at each other with tea towels while we made supper together. I shouldn't have let my guard down like that. This was temporary insanity. A cruel trick of the mind. Trauma bonding.

Hadn't I read about that in a book once? Two people caught in the middle of something crazy, like being stranded or shipwrecked? Who was to say any two people in that situation were ever really in love? Maybe they were just bonded together by crazy survival chemicals forever, and they just thought it was love? Whoa, how had love even entered my mind? I nearly growled, out loud, at my own brain. Things would be better in the morning, I told myself, when we'd hopefully have been rescued already.

This stranger, who slept so beautifully and peacefully in the corner of my humid, damp storm shelter, was just passing through. I reminded myself of that.

I would continue to do life alone, just as I had been. He would be on the road sooner or later, and this little reprieve would be over. I'd have to swat away farmhands and little old ladies wanting to play matchmaker.

Everything would go back to the way it was. Except, it probably wouldn't, depending on what the tornado had done. Not to mention any hail that came with it. I wished so much that I could just have some certainty about what was going to happen. Where would I stay if my house was gone? Would I still have my job? Would the whole harvest be gone? My senses felt more and more deprived with each passing moment down here. And overloaded at the same time. There was only so much humidity and moisture sticking to skin that a person could take.

Chapter Eighteen

Jack

A loud noise jolted us all awake. The rooster and chickens started angrily squawking and the cat gave a surprised, prolonged hiss. That was perhaps the most intimidating she had ever been.

Ally held back a curse and rubbed the back of her head. She must have hit it on the concrete wall being jolted awake. She'd need all sorts of bandaids by the end of this.

An unearthly creaking sound filled the shelter from above. Were we being rescued?

My heart pounded in my chest. I had to admit, my hope was starting to wane. Not enough to become paranoid yet, but inching ever closer. This was not how I wanted to die.

I had definitively decided that I was now scared of both airplanes and tornado shelters, thus scared of anywhere a tornado could be. Were there tornadoes in Texas? I was sure there was. I might have to relocate. If I worked hard enough to prove myself, maybe I could convince my boss to let me work remotely. But the very prospect sounded daunting, honestly. One thing at a time. We needed to get out of here.

I heard voices. Ally did too. We both jumped up instinctively. She started screaming while I banged on the metal above us. Maybe people were just checking the property, but they surely could hear us now.

"Hello?" came a warbled voice from beyond the confines of our dungeon.

"Help!" Ally screamed. "We're trapped!"

Silence stretched on for a few seconds, then we heard that voice talking with another voice. I could only hear bits and pieces. Ally's name came up a few times. Then a man's voice yelled back down to us.

"Don't panic!" he said.

It was a little late for that. While we weren't acutely, actively panicking, we had been gradually panicking for over a day.

"We're calling for help, just got to find a signal on the property," he called down again.

Ally frowned, then yelled back up, "Go toward the chicken coop! That's where the best signal is!"

I wondered how she functioned regularly with such bad cell service out here. I was sure it wasn't storming right now, which meant this was just an everyday thing for her.

"I don't see no chicken coop," the man yelled back down.

I watched as Ally's face turned white as a ghost.

"It's back to the West of the house, you can't miss it," she argued.

Silence again.

"Miss, there's no chicken coop."

She sank down, despondent. I supposed that chicken coops were probably expensive, or at least not quick to be replaced. I wondered if you could get insurance on a chicken coop.

"Just head to the West of the house and see if you can get a signal," I hollered up at him, moving toward Ally.

I gauged her comfort level. I didn't want to invade her space if she didn't want some nearness to calm her down. Not that her cat cared, the cat did what it wanted. She was currently curled up beside Ally, either pretending to sleep or trying to sleep with her ears firmly pinned back from all the noise.

"Don't worry," I told her, sitting about a foot away, "it's going to be ok."

I didn't know exactly how it was going to be ok. But I knew it would be.

She was stoic, but I could see the quivering in her lip. Oh goodness. Tears. I couldn't handle tears. I had to think of something. Fast.

"At least the animals are all ok, in here with us. It could be worse. The coop can be replaced."

At that, she burst into tears.

That had apparently been the wrong thing to say. I was hopeless at this. How had my dad done this? Or had he? I couldn't really think of a time when he had comforted Mom. He wasn't really the nurturing type, I supposed, even with us kids.

"Grandpa helped me build that coop," she sobbed, hands covering her face.

Oh. Sentimental. Yeah, that couldn't exactly be replaced. Functionality wise, yes, but not emotionally.

"Maybe he could help you build another one?" I offered.

"He passed away," she said softly.

Foot, meet mouth. I was terrible at this. Maybe this was why Dad just focused on money. But I didn't see money fixing a situation like this. And we didn't even know what the house looked like. I hoped that if it was bad, the guy would at least spare telling us until we were out. It was crazy that I was so invested in this woman's life now.

"What if..." A crazy, hair-brained idea popped into my head. "What if I helped you build a coop? It wouldn't be the same, but you could always look at it and remember that time when a random stranger blew into town and spent two nights in your tornado shelter. I'm sure it'd be a great story to tell at parties. You'll always have something to remember me by."

She stared ahead, then smiled.

"You're crazy."

"I don't deny it." I shrugged, smiling back.

"Do you even know how to use a hammer?" she challenged.

"Of course I do."

I did not. I hadn't hung any pictures in my apartment or anything. I'd never seen my dad use a hammer. But it couldn't be that hard, could it? Just whack at an object, right?

"Hmmm," she said, suspicious. "Deal. You help me rebuild the chicken coop, and I'll feed you."

Honestly, that seemed like a fantastic deal. I was starving. I never wanted to see a tiny, fancy restaurant dinner again. I was willing to bet she was a good cook, too. Just something in her affect told me it was so.

"Deal," I said.

I was going to have to google how to make a chicken coop now. But it was worth it to get her to stop crying and smile again.

The man came back, calling back down, "Help is on the way!"

Chapter Nineteen

Ally

I groaned. I didn't know what help meant to Wilbur, the old farmer from a few miles over. It could mean that he had called 911, or it could mean that someone was about to drive a tractor onto my lawn to pull things off of us. I wasn't sure which would be faster or safer. But with the lawn presumably being muddy, it would be all torn up no matter what I supposed.

I couldn't help but grin again at the idea of my new friend helping me build a chicken coop. It would be chaos. And what was I going to fix him for supper after that? Maybe some fresh bread. He'd probably never had homemade bread before. If I still had anything left of my tiny little garden, I could make some vegetable soup, too.

My stomach growled loudly.

He laughed and said, "Me too."

I put my hand on my abdomen, embarrassed.

"Maybe we'll be out of here by breakfast," he said.

Breakfast? What time was it? I pulled out my phone. It was still overheating. It had 5% battery left because it got drained so quickly from extreme weather. The clock read 4:53 am. If that was correct, then we very well might be out before breakfast. I wondered if I had lost electricity all night in the house. I would have to call town hall and see how long it had been out, so I could decide if anything in my fridge was still good and....

I realized I was going to have to put the chickens in the house if they didn't have their coop overnight. I wracked my brain, trying to think if any of my neighbors had a chicken tractor. That would be a good temporary fix. I really, really didn't want the chickens in the house. I would never feel like it was really clean again. Olivia was a prim and proper house guest. The chickens, however... not so much.

I sighed. The logistics of the next couple of days were going to be wild.

Jack tried to check his phone, but it had died from the heat. His face was ashen.

"You ok?" I asked.

"Yeah, I will just have a lot of explaining to do to my boss when I get out."

I recoiled. "I'm sure he'll understand. You can't anticipate a natural disaster, and honestly, I have never ever heard of someone getting trapped in their tornado shelter. New fear unlocked."

I gave him a sympathetic smile as I attempted to joke.

"I hope so," he said, stuffing the phone back in his pocket.

The lamp was just about spent, I could tell. It was starting to flicker. I was glad that someone had found us in time before we spent hours down here in the dark with the chickens and cat. At least this way we could avoid where they had pooped. I made a mental note to put a litter box down here next time. Could a person litter box train chickens? Maybe I could put diapers on them. I'd heard of people doing that.

Of course, at the same time I was planning all of these alterations, I also never wanted to do this again. And I wouldn't have Jack next time. If there was a next time. I absolutely would've driven myself crazy and lost my voice screaming in the first two hours had he not been here with me. And probably hurt myself even worse than I already had. But I was convinced a good, hot shower would take out most of the sting in my shoulder.

The anxiety of possibly not being rescued seemed to be bleeding out of him, too. I could see him mentally taking stock. Being trapped down here may prove to have been the easiest part of this week, depending on what the upstairs world held. But at least, for a few days, while he fulfilled his promise of making the chicken coop with me, I wouldn't be alone. I wondered if he knew that it was going to take a few days.

Maybe he wouldn't have a choice anyway, depending on the state of his vehicle. I could probably help him fix that. Maybe I'd even teach this city boy how to change his own oil. Give him the ol razzle dazzle and send him on his way. He probably thought I was feral compared to all the other girls he knew. And he probably wouldn't be wrong in that assessment.

About thirty minutes went by with us stewing in our own thoughts, eagerly anticipating seeing the sky again, in all its beautiful blue glory. I heard the distinct sounds of a tractor puttering down the road. I was sure it was washed out as all get out from the rain, hitting every pothole as it went. Tractors weren't fast, so there was no telling how far they'd driven to get it here. I guessed that whatever was on top of us was bigger and more complicated than what a truck could pull. Or maybe they just wanted to have some more traction with the ground wet.

We heard a chain scrape across the top of the shelter door. They must be wrapping whatever debris with the chain so they could pull it off. I hoped that it would be a quick process. It was almost more agonizing knowing someone was going to get us out, but not quite being there yet.

"Y'all hang on tight down there. We're gonna get ya out," Wilbur called down.

I reached out, bracing myself for the noises about to come. I anticipated a slow, horrible scraping sound to drag across the top of the door, like nails on a chalkboard. My left hand landed on something hot, and I looked down to see what it was. I didn't feel Olivia's fluff. My stomach fell as I saw I had landed on the top of Jack's hand.

If he minded, it didn't show. And while I was sure he had noticed, he was acting as though he hadn't. What a gentleman. He stared up at the door, bracing for himself as well.

"Sorry."

I moved to take away my hand, but he looked directly into my eyes with his own swimming with blue.

"Don't be," the light flickered beside us in the middle of the room. "It's ok, really."

It went out at that moment, the same moment that the awful scraping sound started. We both jumped, like something out of Scooby Doo.

I wondered if there was anything we would be able to salvage out of the chicken coop or if it was just a pile of scrap metal and wood now, scraping across the top of us.

This was all so crazy. What were the chances of some random stranger taking that highway and landing in my yard right before a tornado hit? I'd say I should go buy a lottery ticket, but I still hadn't decided if this was good luck or bad. It was something, that was for sure.

I heard Wilbur hollering at someone above us, and the tractor shut off. Was that it? Was the door about to open? I couldn't see if it was unlocked. I got up, trying to blindly feel my way in the dark. That would be so crazy if they tried to open it and it was locked. That would cause some hardcore unnecessary panic for us all.

One of the chickens squawked at me, letting me know that I had, in fact, almost stepped on her.

"Sorry ol girl," I apologized, hoping that she would forgive me.

I needed to get them some serious treats after all of this. Were there chicken therapists? If so, they needed one. I was sure that Olivia at least would forget about it by next week. She might never get back in the shelter to explore it after this though.

I got smacked in the face by one of the onions.

"Ugh," I huffed, and I heard Jack get up and start making his way toward me.

"Are you ok?" he asked, concern lacing his voice.

"I'm fine," I said, shuffling forward and connecting with one of the steps. Finally.

I groped in the dark for the handrail and grabbed hold. I took careful, tentative steps up and blindly reached for the door so I could turn the lever that locked it. It was stuck. Stupid rust.

I yanked at it and lost my footing.

"Whoa!" I exclaimed as I tried to right myself.

I didn't want to get hurt worse than what the town doctor could fix. That would require spending time in a hospital in a local city and I was not in a place to pay for that. Farming money wasn't lucrative enough to carry insurance on.

My heart started pounding as I fell in slow motion, unable to orient myself at all. I reached out for something to hang onto and came up empty.

"Oooph!" Jack's lungs emptied as I fell right into him.

Anger boiled up in me. Why was he right behind me? He should've just stayed seated where he was and let me handle this.

Then concern rushed through me. Was he hurt? We couldn't both be hurt. That wasn't allowed.

Then... an emotion I wasn't sure about bubbled up as I realized his arms were wrapped around me. They were... lovely.

No they weren't. What was I thinking?

Warm.

No! I tried to shut myself down. Was this touch starvation? I'd read about that somewhere, where if you were isolated enough, you could get touch starved and basically be ravenous for physical contact.

Pathetic.

But I lingered in his arms for a second longer, or maybe two, than was really necessary. It was shock. That's what I told myself. That's what he could believe. Feeling his breath on my neck sent a shock down my spine.

I straightened up, uselessly brushing myself off in the murky darkness.

"Are you ok?" I asked, trying to keep my voice from cracking.

"I'm fine!" he said incredulously. "Are you?"

"Of course, but you shouldn't have done that. You could've gotten hurt."

"I could say the same to you," he said, a little bit of irritation creeping into his voice.

We both needed food. We were hangry. And sleep-deprived. And overloaded on stress. I remembered my grandma saying once that you should see someone in every season, but I felt like being trapped in a shelter for a day was the equivalent. I felt like I had seen every facet of this man in some ways. And not enough of him in others.

Oh hush, Ally!

"Sorry," I huffed, annoyed and exhausted, "I just want out of here."

I didn't want to be done with him, just done with being stuck. And I couldn't decide which I was more frustrated with.

"I know," he said softly, "me too."

I stared at the sounds being made above the door of the shelter. Reality awaited us.

Chapter Twenty

Jack

I t wouldn't be long before we were busted out of here. I didn't know what things would be like in the world above. Every second that passed was a second closer to freedom, and a second away from freedom. Being unreachable, while in a traumatizing way, had at least been a break from the twenty-four-seven on that I had to be with work. Maybe I could just shoot my boss a short text when I got up there, in the West corner of the property by the house, of course, and let him know that there was a tornado and I'd been trapped.

Would he actually believe me?

I'd never called out of work before, even for illness, so I hoped so. But maybe they'd think I'd cracked, especially after I'd just missed that dinner and fallen asleep on the fountain. I supposed I could take a picture for proof. I wondered if I would even be able to charge my phone. Would we be able to find my truck? I doubted the town that Ally spoke of up the road had a place that sold phone chargers. Would there even be a gas station with snacks inside?

A few creaks and the sound of metal scraping metal came from upstairs. I was anxious to see what all had been on top of us. At the same time, I was debating not looking at all. I was sure it was the stuff of nightmares.

I squinted in Ally's direction, or what I hoped was her direction. She better not bolt up the stairs again. I tried to see any sudden movement in the dark. She had scared me earlier, trying to climb the stairs with no light like that. I could still feel the warmth of her in my arms. It was electrifying. I had to remind myself to breathe like a normal person. Even through the sweat, she had a pleasant smell to her. One that made my nerves tingle with anticipation.

I kicked myself. Of course I'd fall for a woman miles away in a no-name town. Why couldn't I get anything right? I didn't even want to think about what my dad would say about a woman like her. It wouldn't be good, I knew that. But the sort of women he would approve of, I wasn't sure I would ever be happy with. They lacked substance, hopes, and dreams of anything other than mani-pedis and vacations to the Bahamas. No drive. Meanwhile, Ally was out here all on her own, running a little homestead with an army of chickens and a cat.

I felt my whole body jolt when someone tugged on the door and it actually budged.

I couldn't believe it.

Voices came in clearer. Air wafted in cleaner. I hadn't realized how much the chickens smelled. No offense to them, of course, they couldn't help it.

The door swung all the way open and stopped on the hinge. Soft, early morning light filled the shelter, and a hand extended downward. Ally stood close to the stairs, reaching out to take it.

I saw the relief on her face, mixed with some other emotions I couldn't quite place.

"Hi Wilbur," she said, her voice trembling. She'd spent all of her bravery inside this concrete box and the last bits of it bled out onto the stairs as she climbed them.

My heart broke. I had to do something. I picked up a chicken, who surprisingly didn't try to murder me for it. It was a blonde hen.

I handed her up to Ally, who looked impressed and distant in the same breath. The hen placidly transferred hands, probably as equally relieved to be above ground as we were. I realized as I picked up chickens and handed them over that I had a headache. Probably from the heat. Now that the adrenaline was wearing off, I was starting to feel the physical effects of all the stress.

I wondered if she was too. Maybe we ought to go get checked out once things were settled. Olivia bounded up the stairs into her waiting arms. Ally pulled her close. She turned away for a moment, then turned back at me with desperate eyes. My stomach dropped.

I gripped the siding on the stairs with chilly hands despite the heat. My legs ached with each step. Wilbur was there with a few other men and, for a moment, my view was blocked by them. But as soon as I stood on solid ground, I understood the reason for the sobriety.

More than just the chicken coop was gone.

My truck was too.

A mess of twisted metal and wood sat in the yard behind the tractor, some of it still in the confines of the ties that were wrapped around it to pull it. The original shapes were almost unrecognizable.

Oh no.

The house.

I looked over at Ally's house. It was surprisingly still standing, but the roof was damaged. I couldn't tell how much, but I suspected it was enough that it might need to have a tarp or something on it until it was fixed. Her white truck was not parked where it had been. It sat in front of a tree that it had crashed into, the hood crumpled like a piece of paper in a wastebasket.

I wasn't sure if that was fixable, but at least it was still recognizable. I didn't know if my car insurance company would cover a natural disaster like this. But I supposed I was going to find out on Monday. For now, looking out at the carnage, I was glad to be alive.

Ally and the men were talking, but I could barely focus on the words. It was hard to believe I could've been on the road when this thing hit, completely oblivious. If it weren't for Ally and her shelter, I'd be dead right now. And now I wasn't sure I wanted to go back to the life I was so worried about before all this started. Near-death experiences sure offered some perspective.

The breeze on my skin was such a welcome change. It washed away all of the unnecessary concerns I had, forcing me to take stock of what was right in front of me.

Ally.

She walked to me, and I felt like I was in a dream when she crashed into my chest with sobs wracking her body. I instantly wrapped my arms around her, pulling her in tight. My cheeks flamed red as all the men looked at me, a complete stranger to them and to her. I was sure they wondered what exactly happened down there. I decided to simply nod at them in acknowledgment and thanks for saving us both. The time for explanations could come later.

Chapter Twenty-One

Ally

Tornadoes were so finicky.

They could go through a singular area and leave some things completely untouched, while absolutely destroying other things just a few feet away.

I'd seen it all my life. One field would be spared, another had wheat that had been beaten down. One neighbor's house stood while another's was gone. Barns, greenhouses, and even cattle went missing sometimes. But thankfully, for this tornado, there were no casualties.

Seeing my property in the morning light made the nightmare come to life. My ears rang as I looked around. I could barely hear Jack asking to go inside to use the bathroom. I couldn't even remember what I had said to him, but it must've been understandable because he went in.

I watched numbly as the town mechanic hooked my truck up to be towed.

The ride into town in the wrecker was eerily quiet. I sat in the middle seat, which was hardly legal considering the seatbelt had broken a long time ago. The radio was hanging from the console by a thread. This thing was halfway to the trash heap already, but it ran well enough. Jack sat to my right, and the mechanic to my left. I tried not to touch either of them, holding my breath with each bump in the road that we hit.

The mechanic had taken one look at Jack's truck and apologized, looking him straight in the eye. There was no saving what was left of that thing. Everyone knew the value of a good truck around here. It was a tragedy to lose one, especially when it was tied to your livelihood like it was here.

Laying eyes on the carnage that we passed was chilling. It was more of that same story. Barns, outbuildings, trampolines, play places, pieces of roofs, and random planks of wood were scattered across the countryside.

It was hard to believe what was right in front of my own eyes. It looked like something out of a movie. Like a monster had risen up from the earth, ripped trees out of the ground, and thrown them during a temper tantrum. But in reality, all it boiled down to was the fury of the untethered wind.

At the house, the mechanic had said he just thought my hood needed replaced. I was anxious to see if that was actually the case. I didn't want to have to ask to be picked up for work because inevitably, one of the farmhands would volunteer. And I didn't want to be alone in a truck with any of them. I would sooner walk to and from work every day.

We backed into the shop.

"Hope sweet home," the mechanic, Adam, said sardonically.

He set to work immediately, getting my truck down off the tow truck. Jack sat, looking bleary-eyed past the windshield. He didn't move until I did.

We stood around in the mechanic shop, the smell of oil and grease permeating the air. Adam rubbed his forehead, tracking grease right across it.

Jack looked around curiously, like we were in a museum. Tools were splayed out everywhere, as well as tires and various car parts. Adam never got rid of anything, ever. He liked to go on rants about how cheaply made cars and trucks were now, and how it was nearly impossible to replace parts on some of the older ones. He basically had a mini junkyard in here of the parts he anticipated being most in demand and important.

"I'm glad you're alright," Adam said to me, eyeing Jack standing in the corner of the shop reading an antique sign.

"Me too," I said, remembering that I could take a full breath without it being sweltering hot and humid.

He worked his jaw.

"Who's he?"

He was to the point, and I could respect that. I knew he wouldn't go gossip about it like everyone else in town. He was just looking out for me.

"He blew into town with the storm. He was taking No Man's Highway and realized it wasn't going anywhere, so he took a few turns and landed in my yard right before it hit," I explained.

Adam gave a low whistle. "That was fateful."

Fateful? Adam was always surprising me. He spoke so infrequently, and often it was simple, but occasionally he made me feel like I needed a thesaurus.

Was it fateful? I supposed it was. At least for Jack to make it out alive. But did it go beyond that? I could admit, at least to myself, that I wondered if fate meant for it to be more than that.

"Yeah," I affirmed. "I'm thankful that there were no casualties at all."

He grunted, getting back to his work on removing the hood of my truck.

My stomach rumbled. Jack and I were still covered in sweat and grime from the shelter, and I hated to show up at the Co-op or the Creamery like this, but I was hungry. And both were within walking distance.

"I think I'm going to go try to find some breakfast," I told Adam, who tipped his head up, chewing tobacco in his mouth.

I walked over to Jack, breaking the spell the history of this place had on him.

"Hungry?" I asked, studying his face in the light. It was so different fully illuminated. He looked much younger, but also more exhausted.

"Yes," he admitted sheepishly. "I thought you'd never ask. Are there any good places to eat around here? I'll buy. It's the least I could do after you allowed me to stay in your shelter like that."

I waved the sentiment away. I didn't need accolades for human decency. But I was very grateful that he wasn't a serial killer that I'd had to spend two nights with. Looking back, without the adrenaline pumping, I could fully see how the situation would've ended badly in the vast majority of circumstances.

"There is a Co-op where they serve breakfast."

And snoopy old ladies, I thought to myself.

"And there is a Creamery. They mostly have ice cream and some sandwiches."

He followed me out of the garage doors, keeping stride at my side. The quaint neighborhood just outside greeted us, with birds chirping and kids playing. The road was rough, just like it was near my house, but they did a better job of patching potholes here in town. Even so, you had to watch your step walking down it, or you could easily roll your ankle.

I stepped into the role of tour guide, pointing out the Co-op at the end of the road, and the Creamery off to the side.

"The gas station is off that way, just beyond those trees."

Jack took it all in, the sights and sounds of a small town buzzing with excitement. Any big event, good or bad, made it all come to life. People who never spoke to each other would call a temporary truce for the sake of something exciting happening. It was kind of funny, honestly.

"Do you have a preference of where to eat?" I asked.

I personally wanted the food at the Co-op, but I wasn't sure about feeding him to the proverbial wolves just yet.

"I think I'd like to go to the Co-op," he said. "I'd definitely like some coffee."

Ripping the bandaid off, it was.

I wracked my brain for the correct words to tell this man that he was about to get the interrogation of a lifetime. The Spanish Inquisition, Blink style. Nothing could be adequate, but I had to try.

"Everyone meets at the Co-op most mornings for breakfast, it's kind of the town watering hole," I started, to which he nodded excitedly.

He seemed to be looking forward to meeting everyone.

"But I should warn you... "

Was warn too strong of a word? I didn't think so, but I didn't want him to dismiss me for being hyperbolic.

"Some of the elderly ladies are snoopy, and they like to be busybodies."

His eyebrows shot up, and he let out a resounding laugh. "Oh really?"

At least he thought it was funny. We'd see if he still thought it was funny after it was all said and done.

We passed by a few kids swinging in the yard, and he waved at them like he'd been here his whole life. They waved back, beaming. I blushed. There was no reason to, but it felt like I was introducing a new boyfriend to my parents or something. Except there were a lot of people in this town, and they all seemed to feel like they had a say in who I ended up with. Sometimes I wondered if it was for the entertainment value or if they were genuinely just wanting to see me end up happy with someone.

"They've tried to set me up with everything with a pulse in this town," I said, and then I immediately wished I could take it back.

"Interesting..." he said, looking me over after that truth bomb.

"They aren't the best matchmakers," I babbled, and I realized I was making it worse.

"Are you telling me you don't like the men they so lovingly pick out for you?" he said teasingly. "They sound like a bunch of grandmas."

"That's because they are," I said. "And no, they aren't my type."

"What's your type?" he said, turning around so he could walk backward to see my expression as he asked.

I almost tripped, but tried my best to pretend it hadn't happened.

"That's none of your business," I said matter-of-factly.

He was just as bad as they were. I started to worry that them meeting him might be even worse than I originally thought. But there was no going back. We were at the bottom of the steps of the Co-op, and already being spotted by at least a few of the men they'd tried to set me up with in the past.

Awkwardness filled my body. I forgot how to walk, talk, and breathe. I climbed the steps, Jack right behind me. At the top, we were met with one of the men in question holding the door open for me. I said an uncomfortable thank you, then slipped inside. At which point he closed the door before Jack could enter too. I glared at him, diving for the door myself.

But Jack had already caught it, effortlessly holding it up as though it wasn't heavy when I knew good and well that it was. Guess they could only bother to be chivalrous when there was competition. Figured.

"Friendly people," he murmured.

I looked around, trying to see if anyone else had seen that. My face felt hot. This was a disaster. Take me back to the shelter!

Mayabell spied us, her face lighting up with absolute glee.

"Hey handsome!" she declared loudly, for the whole Co-op to hear. "What can I get for you?"

It was in that moment I learned that this man could charm the skin off of a snake if he wanted to. His smile only added fuel to the fire as he ordered a black coffee, scrambled eggs, and grits.

"Have you ever had grits?" I asked, surprised.

I didn't care much for them. I thought they were an acquired taste.

"Nope."

He pulled out a stool for me to sit at and held his hand out for me to hold as I climbed up. I almost refused the help, but I recognized that I was unsteady in more ways than one.

"I figured I'd get out of my comfort zone."

"Like living through a tornado and being trapped in the shelter wasn't enough of that?" I teased, keeping my voice low so the whole town couldn't hear.

"Maybe I've decided to be a daredevil now." His mouth twisted into a devilish smirk. "I got a taste and now I want more."

I could tell he wasn't serious. I mean, maybe he was excited to try new things, but this man was far from a daredevil. But I didn't mind the flirting. I just wished it wasn't happening in front of Mayabell. But that seemed to be part of the fun for him. Didn't he know I'd still have to live in this town after he left??

My heart gave a little pang. I was such a softie, somewhere in there. He was so fun, so full of orneriness tempered with actual gentlemanly affection. It was a combination that I didn't know existed, and now I didn't know how I was going to live without it.

"What'll you be having today, Ally?" Mayabell asked me, spryly bouncing over as though her joints weren't older than the dinosaurs.

I was starving. But I didn't want to eat like a ravenous wolf in front of this man. Didn't men hate that? But we had spent a whole day in the storm shelter. He seemed to sense me warring with myself.

"You need to replenish your strength," he prodded. I appreciated that.

"Can I have some eggs, bacon, sausage, a few pieces of Texas toast, and milk?"

"Sure thing, sweetheart. I'll have those both right out for you two."

Whatever I didn't eat, I'd put in a to-go box. From what I had gathered, the electricity had been out long enough that everything in the fridge and freezer at home was definitely ruined. It was good that I had been working on collecting more canned goods recently. I'd been eating a lot of that for the foreseeable future. That and eggs.

"I love that you're not stuffy about food," Jack said.

I looked at him, bewildered. That was so out of the blue.

"What?" I asked, baffled.

"Sorry," he backtracked, "I'm just used to so many of the girls I've been out with being on fad diets. Sometimes it can be a little high maintenance. I understand allergies and health problems, but it's a bit much when they're just doing it to be trendy, you know?"

All I got from that was he had been out with a lot of girls, and I suddenly felt very, very inadequate. He'd seen so much of the world and other people and I... hadn't.

"I didn't realize you were a regular Casanova," I said, trying not to sound bitter or jealous.

One of the farmhands definitely picked up on it though, and side-eyed me from his seat across the other side of the counter.

I stuck my tongue out at him before Jack had a chance to see. He was reading the signs on the wall again. We had a few vintage ones of oil and gas companies. The thing about living in a small town like this was that you basically lived in a functional museum. It gave me a new appreciation for it, watching him look at everything in such wonderment.

"Casanova?" he asked, unfamiliar with the terms.

"Never mind," I said quickly, wanting to forget I'd ever said it.

I didn't want to explain the intricacies of how I'd just negged him.

"She's calling you a cad," a cowboy sitting behind us at a table said, chuckling to himself.

"A cad?" he asked again, looking more concerned now.

"Oh my gosh!" I shot a death glare at the cowboy, jabbing my finger in his direction. "Thanks for that. You stay out of this."

He looked smug, his job causing chaos completed.

"I meant," I said, my words punctuated, "I didn't take you to be such a ladies' man."

That seemed to be a term he was far more familiar with. This was why I couldn't date in this town. Dating was a group project, and one in which I had the least input, no matter how much I tried.

"Oh, I'm not, my dad just—"

Mayabell blessedly interrupted his protestations that I had already decided I wouldn't believe by popping down two steaming plates of food and sliding a coffee mug off her thumb.

"Eat up kiddos, I hear the cleanup is going to be brutal."

So someone had already told Mayabell about my property. I wasn't surprised. The whole town probably knew I was trapped in the storm shelter before I got out.

At the very least, the house was livable. I couldn't wait to go home and take a shower and...

What was I going to do with Jack? He'd probably have to come home with me. Logistical nightmares and embarrassing scenarios floated through my head like sugar plum fairies.

We were both adults, I told myself. I could sleep on the floor, he could sleep in the bed. It would just be one night. We'd already survived TWO nights together. That was crazy to think about.

I watched as Jack dug into his grits like he was a starving calf with their first bottle. I didn't think I'd ever seen anyone enjoy grits that much, and I was certain I'd never seen anyone do it again. I was relieved to know that the habits I'd picked up eating alone at home could not rival his desperate, twenty-four-hours without a meal eating habits. I stuck my fork in the pile of eggs on my plate, humming happily as I chewed them. Food had never tasted so good.

Chapter Twenty-Two

Jack

I could admit, I loved a challenge.

I could not even originally want something, but be presented with a challenge on it, and it would turn into the thing I most needed in life.

But in all honesty, I wanted Ally before I saw the way every man in that small Co-op cafe looked at her. I doubted it took Mayabell much to convince them to go on a date with her.

It seemed like any of them would be happy to have her, but the feeling was clearly not mutual. I wondered why that was. They were all tanned, muscular men. Hard workers. I wondered if maybe it just didn't pay well, though Ally didn't seem to care overly much about money. I didn't peg her as materialistic, even though my dad said all women were. There had to be some other reason she was so fervently turning them down. She treated them more like annoying brothers than marriage prospects.

There was one in particular I noticed shooting me daggers with his eyes. But the reality was, I was just a stranger that got trapped with her in a storm shelter for a couple nights.

I would have to watch my back around these dudes. Some of them seemed fine enough, but others definitely seemed to be resentfully scoping out my intentions with Ally. I'd have to find a good way to ask her more about them without her deflecting or shutting down.

Her truck hood wasn't ready by the time we were done with breakfast. I threw down a very generous tip for Mayabell, both because I was highly entertained by her and because her grits were actually the best thing I'd tasted in a while. Way better than the food I'd had on the work trip by some of the alleged best chefs in the city.

I couldn't wait to try the ice cream shop Ally had mentioned so much later. Right now, she was intent on taking me on a trip through town. I was quite certain she might intend to show me the whole place by the time her truck was ready to drive home, and with as small as it seemed to be, that was infinitely possible.

I listened to her chatter on about the people, places, and things in this area she called home. She seemed to grasp earlier in the day that I loved historical things. We came upon a railroad track, and I was shocked to find that she had an encyclopedic knowledge of it. Why it was built, when it was built, what it was used for during each stage, why it was shut down. She even walked me up to a railroad car that had found its final resting place on the track. Then she fixed me with a wicked grin.

"Do you want to go inside?"

I blinked. "We can do that?"

Ally reached out for me, begging me to follow her. She was so beautiful. I watched her when her back was turned, mesmerized by the way her hips swayed as she walked. I took a swig of water from the bottle Mayabell had given me as we made our way to the railroad car.

She grabbed hold of the aging metal railing and took each step in stride. I followed her, eager to see this treasure hidden in plain sight. There were a lot of gauges, bells, and whistles. I didn't have the faintest idea what they were for or how to read them.

"In here," she beckoned, opening the door. It seemed heavy, but it didn't slow her down at all.

The inside of the car smelled like hot metal and a little bit of wood. There was a sink to our right. I wondered how the water had been hooked up to it. I felt like I was getting a tour of the Wild West, frozen in time. I supposed in a way, I was. There were a lot of chairs, or maybe booths, hooked on the walls of this part of the train. The flooring was cracked, but still sturdy.

"It's so hot in here." She pursed her lips, fanning herself.

Ally grabbed a bookend off a shelf next to one of the booths and stuck it in the door so it was forced to stay open. It did take the edge off. It was quite sweltering in here.

She led me down the hallway, which was quite narrow. I couldn't imagine anything being built like this these days. It would be considered a health hazard and inaccessible. It was crazy to think how times had changed, and how many other time capsules like this existed. I was surprised this had just been abandoned. Couldn't they have repurposed parts or sold the metal for scraps?

We passed a lot of cubbies along the narrow hallway. I tried the doors on them, curious as to what was inside. One held a first aid kit that was surely no good anymore. I didn't know what medicines had been in it, but I was sure the heat had rendered them unusable or unsafe now.

Still, it was a metal box with metal hinges, nothing like the plastic one we had in my office. We came upon an opening in the narrow hallway. Both sides had what amounted to a second floor. If people had been in it, it would have been quite crowded. Unless maybe it was for children. The stairs, if they could be called that, were very small horizontal bars built into the indents on the side. Ally reached out for them, determined to crawl up there.

She shot a look back at me, beaming. I was beginning to think she might secretly be an adrenaline junkie. I looked up to where she was climbing, seeing crude, metal, rectangular cutouts that served as seating. The other side looked much the same. Both sides were flanked by long, horizontal windows where the occupants could watch the scenery flying by.

"There was a time when you could take the train to all sorts of festivals and events, and it wasn't very expensive," Ally explained. "I used to sit up here as a kid, and there were people who would walk the isles and bring pop or snacks. We didn't always get it, but when times were good, Mom and Dad would buy us some. It was one of the highlights of the year!"

I admired her as she sat, lost in her reminiscing. I tried to picture myself riding on this train. I wondered if it would've made me motion-sick. Probably, knowing my luck. But it was fun to imagine anyway.

"This is so cool," I said, turning to the other side to look up for a second.

I wondered if I should climb it, but decided against it. I wasn't sure it could support my weight. Ally was petite and significantly shorter than me. I didn't want to break anything.

I heard her moving behind me and turned around just in time to see her lose her footing and start falling. I lunged forward, catching her awkwardly in my arms.

"Are you ok?" I asked, eyes wide. She hadn't even seemed to realize she had fallen yet, her eyes were clamped shut.

She popped one open, then the other, and took a deep breath.

"Yeah," she said sheepishly, "sorry."

"It's ok," I said, relieved.

I didn't need her to have a concussion. She still hadn't gotten checked out for her shoulder yet.

She tried to squirm out of my arms. "I'm heavy, I'm sorry."

I bit back a laugh. She felt perfect in my arms. I didn't even notice whether she was heavy or not, and my heart ached at the idea of putting her down.

"Nah," I teased, "you're a lightweight."

I guided her to the floor with ease. "See, I didn't even break a sweat."

Never mind that my heart was pounding. It wasn't from exertion. It was because of the feel of her skin, the smell of her hair, the cute expression on her face.

I was in deep, standing there in a dusty railway car in the middle of nowhere Oklahoma. What was I going to do?

Chapter
Twenty-Three

Ally

U gh, that was so embarrassing! I had to believe the sleep deprivation was making me clumsy. First I fell in the shelter, which was totally because it was dark, in my defense, but then this! He must think I was such a klutz. Apparently I was around him.

My whole body burned from being in his arms. I couldn't get out of them fast enough, but it also physically hurt to be put back down, which had nothing at all to do with the slipping and falling. It had felt so perfect.

Now I was acutely aware of Jack behind me as we walked the rest of the train car. I wondered if he felt his stomach flipping too. Was it just from falling, or was there some kind of chemistry brewing between us? What if it was just because we'd spent every second together of the last two days in a crazy situation? If I took away the circumstance, would I feel the same? But nothing was ever clinical like that.

I tried to think of a time I'd felt like this before and couldn't. When all of my friends in high school were talking about the boys they liked, I was focused on my schoolwork. There was never anyone who rose to the level that they described. I thought they were pulling my leg when they talked about butterflies and topsy-turvy feelings in their stomachs. I'd noticed one or two boys that were cute, but I didn't feel like this about them. What was happening to me?

"What's this?" Jack asked, in a voice that didn't betray any of the tension that had existed in the last minute or two.

I whirled around to see him opening the little closet space for the latrine.

I giggled as his nose wrinkled and he coughed, closing it back up.

"The bathroom." I felt a little bit bad. "It's not exactly first class, but it did the job."

We walked into the part of the car where meals were served during longer travel. It still had some of the fancy containers that kept food warm while it was being served out, though there was no actual food left. It occurred to me that if this had been abandoned in the city, it would probably be covered in spray paint. I appreciated that this part of history hadn't been defaced. It wasn't interesting enough for anyone to break into and break things around here. The kids liked to pull other kinds of pranks, like making fake crop circles to freak out the conspiracy theorists in the town.

I watched as Jack gently traced the cover of a book that had been left on one of the tables. The cover had faded with the time and sunlight. A thick layer of dust coated it, except where his finger had traced. I wondered who had been the last to read it, and if it had been any good. I loved the care he showed to the object. It reached into my heart and squeezed it, and I couldn't explain why. I was almost jealous of that stupid little book.

Move on, I told myself. That's such an insane thing to think.

I looked out the window at the town. It was interesting to see from this angle. I could almost see it the way he must, someone just passing through town. It was quaint, a little community that wasn't necessarily frozen in time, but certainly moving at a slower pace than what he must be used to. Stable, consistent, not exciting. I wondered if he considered these things positives or negatives.

Ringing filled the railcar, startling me. I jumped, spinning around to look at Jack. He was fishing his phone out of his pocket, scowling.

"Hello?" His voice was suddenly professional, albeit tired.

The transformation was jarring.

I could hear some fast-paced speech on the other end of the line, far faster than what I could keep up with. I felt my heart beating faster from the franticness of it, and I wasn't even the one having the conversation.

I stepped out of the back door to give him some privacy, surprised that there was a signal in there. It was good to know there was a private place that I could go to have a conversation while in town.

I paced outside on the raised platform, looking toward the edge of town and the grain bin in the distance behind the Co-op. I snuck a peek in every once in a while to see him with the phone glued to his head, his expression not at all matching his voice.

He looked irritated, frustrated, and exhausted, but his tone was business as usual. I wondered if he often felt this way, like he was leading a double life in some ways. Having to pretend for his work, while secretly dying a little inside. Or maybe a lot.

I counted the holes in the grated floor beneath me, then looked at the chipped paint on the train car. I wished that this thing still ran, it would be so fun to take Jack on it to a carnival or something. I wondered what he would think of the snake festival that still happened every year, though everyone had to drive to it now. Would he be freaked out? Or would it fuel his alleged adrenaline junkie streak?

I lingered at the door, shifting nervously back and forth as his voice started getting louder.

"Yes sir," he said, moving the phone away from his ear as though the person on the other end was yelling. "I'm sorry sir, the reception out here is terrible."

More yelling, to the point I could hear it all the way outside the door. More grimacing. I watched the life drain from his eyes. Anger boiled in my stomach. This man had just survived a tornado, and it was the weekend. Were these big shots in suits heartless? Did they not recognize that maybe there were more important things than pushing papers from day to day? I was exhausted just watching and listening to all this.

"I'll make arrangements to be back to work as soon as I can on Monday." I overheard him promise.

Disappointment settled into me. That wasn't much time at all. Did he really have to go so soon? And why was I hanging on to something this transient so tightly? I was letting my heart make all these plans, my head think all these wistful things, and here he was about to leave.

He looked in my direction, and I ducked down, ashamed of myself for eavesdropping. I heard his footsteps coming toward the door before he pushed it open. Acting nonchalant was not necessarily my strong suit, but I tried.

"I don't suppose this town has people that Uber?" he asked.

I blinked at him. Was that a root vegetable?

"Or a taxi?" he said more desperately.

"No," I said cautiously. "No taxis or Uber. I can give you a ride to a bigger city where you can probably find something like that, or I can just take you home, once my truck is up and running anyway."

I wasn't sure that the hood was actually all that was wrong with it, but we would know soon enough.

He ran his hand down his face. "It's six to eight hours from here to home depending on traffic. I can't let you do that."

I frowned. "I'm really happy to. It's not a big deal. I don't think my boss is going to be too upset with me for missing a day or being late, considering everything else that's going on right now. I have a roof to repair."

And a chicken coop to rebuild, I thought to myself.

"I appreciate the Southern hospitality, Ally." Jack's face softened with sincerity. "Would that everyone was as thoughtful."

"Did he at least ask you if you were ok?" I said, stewing over the tone I had overheard on the phone.

He laughed. "No, he just took the opportunity to say I told you so about me not taking the flight."

I rolled my eyes. Productivity over people was not a lifestyle I would be able to handle.

Chapter Twenty-Four

Jack

My head was pounding. It could've been the heat, it could've been the sleep deprivation, it could've been stress. But I was pretty certain it was that phone call. I wasn't expecting a warm conversation, but I certainly wasn't expecting a complete lack of concern for my life and limb. I'd heard people say that jobs don't care about you, but it was something else to get it flung in your face like that.

Ally looked livid. I wasn't sure if there was an emotion that wouldn't look adorable on her, but it was in that moment I realized that I never wanted to be on the receiving end of that look. It was scary!

We stepped out of the railcar.

"Thanks for the tour," I said.

And I meant it. That had been so cool, even if my boss had put a damper on it.

"You're welcome," she said cheerily as she hopped down. I followed her as she walked over to the other side to close the door.

"Don't want any animals getting trapped in here. They'd be crispy critters."

She was like a rough around the edges version of a Disney princess.

Ally told me quite a bit of the town tea as we walked, and I had to say, this place was far from dull. And I was going to keep my mouth shut around all of the inhabitants. There were no secrets in this place. And based on what she was telling me, it wasn't hard to deduce that I was likely going to be the talk of the town. I reassured myself that maybe the tornado would overshadow my infamy. Though maybe not to the men who were vying for her hand.

"So you've always lived here?" I asked casually, kicking a rock and sending it skidding down the gravel road near the park. It looked nice apart from a broken swing and a few signs of aging, but otherwise hospitable.

"Yeah," she said, sounding contemplative, "all my life."

I nodded, turning into the park. I wanted her to show me this area. It seemed that every landmark jogged a story in her mind, and I wanted to hear them all. My time here was short. I wanted to know as much as possible.

I could already tell that this, whatever this was with her, was going to haunt me more than any girlfriend ever could. It was like I had been transported to another world, another planet. Beamed up and dropped into somewhere I never would've believed existed had I not been seeing it with my own two eyes. I wanted to savor every last drop of it, collect every sensory detail so I could visit again, if only in my mind. It would pale in comparison to having her here with me, but it was something to hang on to. Something to remind me that maybe life really was more than work and money. Prestige and corporate labels.

"Have you ever wanted to go see the world? Aren't you bored?" I asked, opening the gate to the park for her so she could step in.

She looked a little offended at the question, but seemed to actually be entertaining it, maybe for the first time in her whole life. Had she really never considered it at all? I supposed that if it didn't even seem like an option, it probably hadn't crossed her mind. Like something like this hadn't ever crossed mine. I wondered if she would think about it after I left, now that I had asked her.

"It never really occurred to me," she said. "My family has lived here for generations. They always taught me to stay where family is. The land that I live on now is family land. I don't think any of my family has even had the option to move because it would be so expensive to live anywhere else and everything here is paid off. Inheritances are kind of a big deal around here."

I chewed on what she said, hooked on every word. It was such a different world and way of thinking than what I was used to. My dad didn't plan on passing down his company to me, I didn't think. He expected me to strike it rich on my own like he had, to pull myself up by my bootstraps. There weren't a lot of inherited advantages that had happened in my family. I couldn't blame Ally for staying in her house on paid-off land with her animals. She wouldn't be able to find that kind of deal anywhere else, even if she sold it all to start over. Things just didn't work like that.

"That makes sense," I said, sitting down on a swing and pushing off lightly with my feet. I was sure I looked crazy in my suit, sitting in a child's swing in a dusty old town. I stuck out like a sore thumb. But, who cared?

Ally smiled, stepping back to watch me. She whipped out her phone before I could jump out, snapping a picture at the speed of light.

"Hey," I protested.

"Blackmail," she said simply, sticking out her tongue, "in case I ever need it."

Blackmail? What was she going to do, post it on the internet? She didn't even have good cell service out here, how much was she really connected to the online world? I supposed she could sell the picture to the local paper, I'd seen a few lying around at the Co-op, but that would only add to my lore as a legend around these parts. I wasn't worried.

But I was going to seize the opportunity.

I jumped up, grinning ear to ear as I grabbed for her phone. She shrieked and took off running, grass kicking up beneath her cowboy boots. I had to hand it to her, she was fast.

I had thought, since she was so much shorter than me, it would be easy to catch her. But it turned out she was pretty slick. She could change directions on a dime. Ally looked back at me, her untamed hair twisting in the wind. Her laughter was intoxicating, spiked with joy. It almost felt like we were little kids playing chase. I wondered what she had looked like as a little kid? I was willing to bet she'd always had a healthy dose of freckles across her nose and cheeks.

She zigged past a pole, and I zagged to the other side of it. She ducked under some monkey bars, which slowed me down a little. I could feel my lungs burning. Ally was in way better shape than I was, probably because of her farming work. It was putting me to shame!

I took the opportunity to dip behind the slide, completely out of her sight. I knelt with my dress pants on the dirty playground. It wasn't like they weren't already in bad shape after the two nights in the shelter and the sweat. I wasn't even sure that the dry cleaner could fix it at this point. It could be replaced.

"Jack?" I heard her call accusingly. Then suspiciously. Then anxiously.

I heard her footsteps getting closer and closer until she was about to pass me. I lunged out, trying to catch her by surprise.

She screamed, wrestling to try to get out of my arms. I grinned, snatching her phone from her hands. She lost her footing and in my attempt to catch her, I lost mine too. We both plummeted to the ground. I braced myself for impact, mostly mentally, because there wasn't much I could do physically. Upon opening my eyes, I saw her bewildered face, eyes wide, mouth agape. The clouds rolled on in the distance against the blue sky.

Thankfully, I had landed first, and she had landed with a thud on top of me. For someone who had hurt her shoulder less than a day before, she sure didn't have a tough time throwing it into me.

"Sorry," I said sheepishly, looking up at her a little bit proud of myself.

She made a grab for the phone and even pinned underneath her. I was able to jerk it away in time for her to miss it.

She looked shocked that I had reacted so quickly.

"You're something else, you know that?" She pushed up against my chest to sit up, and I had to say, I didn't mind it.

At least until I saw the blue and red lights flashing in the corner of my eye.

Chapter Twenty-Five

Ally

"Oh no."

All of the air left my lungs, and it wasn't from the fall.

The Barney Fife of our little town had found us, which was embarrassing enough on its own. But with his lights flashing, I didn't know if he was playing a nasty prank on me or if he thought something was wrong. I considered how it looked that this strange man who the sheriff had never seen before was chasing me around the park, hiding, then knocking me to the ground.

I was on my feet within a second. Jack propped himself up.

The sheriff's footsteps were heavy on the gravel as he lumbered toward us.

"Everything alright there, Ally?" His voice was reserved. His dark glasses concealed his eyes, which I hated. It was hard to get a read on someone when you couldn't see their eyes.

"I'm fine," I reassured him hastily, putting my hands out in protest.

This man had known me for half my life, and not once had he even so much as pulled me over. I didn't know how to act. I'd never been in trouble a day in my life. At least not with the law.

"Ya looked more than fine, little miss." He raised an eyebrow. "Ya looked like you were canoodling in broad daylight in a children's park with this..."

The sheriff searched for a word, but apparently couldn't find one.

Shame flooded through my system. I didn't. I'd never. I couldn't even find words. I couldn't force my mouth to open.

"We weren't," Jack defended... himself? Me? Us? "It wasn't what it looked like."

The sheriff looked curiously between the two of us now, and I couldn't imagine that he really believed us. I supposed it was better that he thought we were up to hijinks than if he thought Jack was hurting me, but it was an awkward situation all the way around.

The sheriff stood, one hand looped on his belt and the other extended to Jack, who took it and shook himself off.

The red and blue lights going off in the background splashed across his skin. It was silly to see a man in a suit getting washed out by the lights of a cop car.

The sheriff shook his head, laughing. He patted Jack on the back, tipped his hat to me, and mumbled, "Crazy kids," before walking back to his car.

"Stay out of trouble," he called just before he shut the door of the cruiser and took off.

Jack let out a breath. I stared straight ahead as the sheriff drove away. Then I looked at Jack.

This would definitely be the talk of the town.

"Hell of a way to make an impression," I said smugly, though I was still shaken up.

"Look, I'd say you're the one who made the impression. You were on top of me." He folded his arms.

UGH. I put my hands on his chest and lightly shoved with my fingertips. He was a lot sturdier than I was anticipating, both when I fell on him and now.

His lip twitched as he tried not to smile.

Hey.

Where was my phone?

I looked behind him. It wasn't on the ground.

He stood as still as a statue, watching my every move.

"Did you put it in your pocket?" I asked, my voice dripping with disgust and trepidation.

"Wouldn't you like to know?" He stared down at me.

I narrowed my eyes at him. If I really must pat him down like an airport TSA, I would. I didn't know exactly how they did it, and I expected with his aversion to flying, he might not know either. Which was great, that meant he wouldn't know if I was doing it wrong.

I moved closer toward him, which he responded to by taking a step back.

"Wow Miss Ally, personal space," he chided.

I felt my cheeks flushing. This man was insufferable.

"Yeah well..." My words were stilted as I made little grabs toward his pockets, always too late because he jerked away. "You. Have. My. Personal. *Property.*"

His voice echoed richly in the wind as he laughed, sending shivers up my spine. Something in my stomach tugged, and I realized it was pulling me under.

I was falling for this man.

Did he feel it too?

I studied his face, so carefree and happy.

My face must've fallen because his softened into a more sober expression.

"Ok, ok," he relented, "here."

He held the phone above my head. I glared at him. I had to jump, but I managed to snag it.

"*Thank you,*" I said dramatically.

I checked, but of course, I had no texts or calls. The mechanic would probably be working on my truck until the sun went down, or until it was finished, whichever came first.

I supposed we should be thinking about dinner soon and making arrangements to get home if my truck wasn't going to be done by the end of the day. But I wasn't ready yet. I was having fun. I couldn't remember the last time I'd been this genuinely happy.

"I've got more stuff to show you," I said. "Come with me."

He looked intrigued. "I feel like this town is a bottomless bag. It looks small, but you keep pulling out things to look at."

"We can go rest at the shop if you're bored," I said with a frown. I stopped in my tracks. I didn't want to wear him out.

"Oh, that's not what I meant," he said. "I was just saying I'm surprised how much there is to look at. It's deceptively small."

I looked toward one edge of town, then the other. He was right. It packed a punch. There was always something happening around here, good or bad, and we all knew about it.

Honestly, I felt like living in a small town was living more connected and accessible than Jack was with his cell phone.

Everyone knew everything about you, or at least they thought they did. And unlike with a cell phone, you couldn't exactly turn it off here.

Well, you could turn off the reliable source of information by just not saying anything, but these people were masters at filling in the blanks, no matter how convoluted their stories may seem.

Chapter
Twenty-Six

Jack

A lly didn't seem to tire easily. I was already sore from spending two
nights in the shelter. Then adding insult to injury by hitting the
ground at the park. But here she was, still going, going, going, with no signs
of stopping. That was ok, though. I could listen to her talk... and watch her
walk... for forever.

She decided that I absolutely must see the town grain bin that was next
to the Co-op. I wasn't sure how exciting a grain bin could be, but I was
willing to keep an open mind.

"Usually when it's time for harvest, we all make sure the grain trucks are
up to snuff. That's what I have been doing for work lately. Everyone will
harvest their wheat, as long as it hasn't been hail damaged or rained on that
day..."

My brain started to drift. This was SO much information! I didn't realize how complicated agriculture was. There were so many details of what was good and bad for wheat, how much people got paid for it, and all of the ins and outs of the machinery involved in it.

"So," I said as I tried to think of a reasonable question that I could ask to show her I had been paying attention, "how do they decide how good the wheat is?"

That seemed complicated? Were people actually looking at all the little grains and putting them under a microscope or something? That seemed very labor intensive.

"Oh," she said, positively glowing.

It was so cute that she was so immersed in sharing her world with me.

"A probe goes into the back of the truck where the grain is and sucks some of it up to test it. It'll be given a grade, the truck will be weighed, and then it'll be dumped. That gets dusty pretty quick. You either have to wear a mask, make sure your windows are rolled all the way up, or hold your breath. Some people do all three."

I would never look at my breakfast toast the same way again. This was a newfound respect and appreciation I'd grown for it.

"Are there crops that get harvested where you're from?" she asked, her eyes round and soft.

"Uh," I said, feeling stupid. If there were, I wasn't aware of them.

"Does grass count?"

She laughed. "Maybe if you're feeding it to your animals or something."

"Yeah, I don't think we did that with it. I think my dad just threw it away in bags," I said, trying to remember for sure.

"Oh," she said.

I looked up at the grain bin and whistled. "That thing is tall!"

"It has to be to store everything," she said with a smile.

If this town ever decided to be a tourist trap, she would be their number one tour guide.

She showed me some slated metal holes in the floor where she said the grain went in.

"The trucks have levers and stuff where they dump all of the grain down there."

I could believe it was a dusty operation like she had said. Positively everything was covered in a thick layer of what looked like sawdust.

"I remember riding in the truck as a kid, coming with my grandpa to drop off a load of wheat. The ladies in the Co-op would give us grape pops and peanut M&M's. And sometimes there were even cute teenage boys working. A lot of the girls I knew would ride with their families just to see them. I came for the grape sodas mostly," she said, suddenly seeming to realize that she might be admitting to more than she had wanted to.

"Mostly?" I lowered my voice.

She made a nervous noise, then tried to walk it off.

"Anyway..." she said.

"No no," I insisted, "do tell me about the cute teenage boys! What were they like?"

Her ears turned red. "I don't know. They were tan, I guess, and they'd been working hard, so they had lots of muscles."

She was creeping towards annoyed by the end of that sentence.

"So your type is tan, muscular farm boys?" I ventured, trying to bait her into sharing what her type actually was. If that was the case, I was sunk. But it hadn't seemed to be from what I'd observed so far.

She stuck her tongue out at me. "Wouldn't you like to know?"

Her taunting sent me back to high school, like our game of truth or dare had.

"Maybe," I said pointedly.

"Maybe," she said, getting close. Too close. My heart hammered in my chest. She put one finger on my peck and shoved it in. "You should mind your own beeswax."

She smiled again, retreating to safer territory on the other side of the grain bin.

"So when does the season start?" I asked, curious if I'd get to see any of it.

I knew it was almost an impossibility. My boss would come to haul me to the office himself if he had to. But I wanted to know. I could already picture myself riding in one of these grain bin trucks. One that Ally herself had fixed up, sitting in here dumping wheat kernels into the floor while all of the workers stared at me, jealous that I was in the cab with Ally and they weren't.

Man, these fantasies were out of control. I was acting like a teenage boy, if only in my mind. What was this woman doing to me? This was crazy.

She spun around, the dust swirling around her as the light hit golden hour. She looked like an angel, spinning in a spotlight with cowboy boots and crazy hair. What had I ever done to get to lay eyes on such a beautiful woman?

Suddenly, all the money in the world didn't seem adequate to be deserving of the love and affection of someone like her. I desperately needed to figure out what would be.

I walked to the side of the holes in the floor so I could meet her on the other side, not wanting to twist an ankle.

She looked back at me, patiently waiting. The mechanic shop was only a block or two away, and I was sure we'd be heading there next. Then probably to her house, and soon enough, back to real life.

Reality was a pain in the butt.

Chapter Twenty-Seven

Ally

"How's it going?" I asked, bounding into the mechanic shop. I was hopeful about my truck.

Adam turned his head almost imperceptibly, a little annoyed by my enthusiasm.

"It's not just the hood," he said, deflating all of my hopes.

I turned to Jack, who looked about as concerned as I felt.

"How bad is it?" I asked him. He was elbow-deep in the engine, which made me nervous.

"It might be a few days, and I might have to order some parts."

Order parts? That was blasphemy in his world. That meant that it was actually not good. This man hoarded every part for every old car and truck on the planet.

"I can fix it," he assured me, popping out from under the hood to look me in the eye, "just give me some time."

"Ok," I said, biting my lip. "Would it be possible for you to drive me — er, us — home at the end of the day?"

I hated asking, but I really wanted a good shower and sleep after the events of the last two days. It was hard to believe we'd been trapped underground less than twenty-four hours ago.

"Sure hon. Come back around nine."

Jack's stomach growled. I turned to him, smiling sympathetically. I had been growing hungry too. My plans for a nice, low-key dinner at home were foiled. But this was no big deal. I'd just take him to the Creamery. It wasn't like the whole town hadn't already seen us together all day, anyway.

Music poured out of the radio in the corner of the shop, tailing us on our way out. There was something magical about music out in the open evening air. It made me crave someone's arms around me, slow dancing under the moon. Someone being Jack. I sighed.

The dance! I'd almost forgotten about that. It was this coming Friday! And... Jack would be gone. My heart sank. I took a deep breath to hold back what could easily turn into real tears. The thought of going with the farmhand from down the road was painful now that I knew I had other options. I hadn't been thrilled about it before, but now... A thought hit me that I should've felt bad for, but I couldn't bring myself to.

What if my truck didn't get fixed in time? Maybe I could slip Adam some cash to hide a part or something, just until Saturday morning. How long would they let Jack stay here before they came to get him themselves? Surely he had some vacation time or something? I didn't know if he'd actually want to spend that on me, though. I was nobody. I was getting ahead of myself. Slow down, Ally. Hold your horses.

"Where are we going?" Jack asked, hands in his pockets as he walked beside me.

"I figured the Creamery," I offered, "but we could also see what Mayabell is cooking up this evening. I'm sure she'd love to see you again."

He smirked. "I'm sure she would."

I rolled my eyes and gave him a little shove with my hip.

He just laughed. Butterflies danced in my stomach. This wasn't fair.

"Let's go to the Creamery," he said. "I want to try everything while I'm here."

I was completely fine with this. I wanted ice cream. Needed it, in fact, after the last day or two.

"Sounds good," I said nonchalantly.

There was a little bitty bar down by the Baptist church on the corner, the sign buzzing to life as the farmers threw their towels in for the day. No matter how small the towns around here, they could all support two things: churches and bars. It might seem antithetical, but that's just how things were.

Somebody swung their pickup into the parking lot awfully fast as we were walking through. Jack's arm snaked around mine, dragging me off of the road and onto the grass. He stuck me on his other side, walking closest to the road and parking lot.

How chivalrous. Where had he learned that? I felt a little embarrassed. But I also was touched by the gesture.

I tried to think of something to say, but my brain wouldn't budge.

I was *so* good at this conversation thing. Maybe it was just because I was so tired.

"Look at that," he said, pointing to something near a patch of trees on the property ahead of us.

I squinted, not sure what he was looking at. A little flash of light. Was that... a firefly?

"That's so cool," he said in awe.

It wasn't dark enough for them to be super noticeable yet. In fact, I was surprised he saw it at all.

"Just wait until later, when we head back. It'll be even better," I told him.

"Really?" His voice was breathy.

"Mhmm."

I could show this man anything around here and he'd think it was amazing. I felt like such an exciting, interesting person for the first time in my life.

I was thankful when we made it to the wooden ramp and steps of the Creamery. My stomach growled. Once I had food in my system, I was sure I'd be a much better conversationalist.

Daisy, the lady who owned the shop, was working tonight. Her hair was teased up into a high updo, and her eyeshadow looked like she'd been teleported from the 80s.

It was easy to get stuck in the time period you grew up in around here. There weren't a lot of modern trends we were exposed to. Most of the exposure we got was through mail catalogs. The teenagers seemed to find out about popular trends somehow though. It was kind of fun to watch them try out all the new-fangled clothes and makeup styles.

The owner grinned at me when we stepped through the front door, before toning it down in time for Jack to miss it. Oh, man. This whole town was full of nosy people.

She probably already knew all about him. If these people had consistent internet connection, I was sure they'd already have done a background check on him. While it was a smart idea, I hardly felt it necessary. He hadn't hurt me in the shelter when he'd had every opportunity to. He wouldn't hurt a fly.

My palms started to sweat. What was she going to say when we got up to the counter? I suddenly had the urge to shove Jack back out the door. He, in contrast, looked with interest up at the hand-drawn chalk menu of meals and ice cream options. It would be fine. This would all be fine.

"Hey Ally," Daisy said enthusiastically, holding eye contact for a second too much. It was a look that said, "Let's talk about this later."

And by talk, she meant an interrogation was coming. Ugh.

"Hi Daisy," I said, barreling through my sentences. "We're starving. Can I get the usual, plus a banana split with extra fudge?"

Extra fudge, I had learned, fixed most of life's ills. If it couldn't be fixed by fudge, duct tape, or WD-40, it might as well not be fixed at all.

"And your friend," Daisy said, looking at me, then at Jack, "What's your name?"

"Jack," he said, awkwardly extending his hand and then turning it into a little wave.

"Nice to meet you, Jack!"

She looked at me with eyes that said, "He's cute."

Like I didn't already know that.

"What would you like?" she asked him.

He leaned forward, charisma oozing from him. It was like a switch had flipped and suddenly, Daisy was like putty in his hands. Even in a dirty suit.

"What do you recommend? You're the expert."

If I rolled my eyes in that moment, they'd have gotten stuck in the back of my head and never come out. I was still tempted to do it all the same. Maybe I should do a background check on him, make sure he wasn't a conman with a wife and kids in another state.

She glowed as she recommended the deluxe burger with steak-cut fries and a chocolate malt to him. The only modification he made was to make it strawberry because he said chocolate wasn't his favorite.

I gasped out loud. Daisy gave me a knowing look. I'd sell my soul for chocolate, it was no secret.

This was sacrilegious. Maybe he and I wouldn't work out, after all.

She turned to start working on our orders, and his facade with her dropped instantly. I scrutinized him. His confused expression as I squinted my eyes at him was nothing short of hilarious. I decided that he was just having too much fun messing with the old ladies in this town. His poker face was not that good.

"What do you have against chocolate?" I grilled him.

This *WAS* an interrogation. What kind of psychopath was he?

He threw up his hands in premature surrender.

"Nothing," he said, wide eyed, "I swear."

I glared at him through my eyelashes, as though I was about to pounce.

"I just really like strawberries," he whispered a confession, "and she said the ones she uses here are fresh from her garden. I couldn't pass that up. Seemed part and parcel of the tourist experience for me to try food grown right here, ya know?"

"So..." I said, trying to suss the situation out fully, "you do like chocolate?"

"Um, it's ok," he said, "I just don't like it as much as strawberry."

My face crinkled as I considered this.

"I suppose this is acceptable," I conceded. "I don't have to run you out of town now."

"Oh," he said, half with relief and half sarcasm, "I'm glad for that. Is the town mascot a chocolate bar?"

I shoved him with my hip, just in time for Daisy to turn around and catch a glimpse of it. Whoops.

"You're a violent woman, you know that?" he teased, putting his hand on my hair and ruffling it.

"And?" I said, straightening it all back.

Combing it later was going to be a nightmare, and that was before he had done that. I might braid it after just so I could get a break from it tangling. Oklahoma wind always had its own plans when it came to hair, unless you used military-grade hair spray.

"Now, now," Daisy said, turning around with a tray on her hip, "no domestic violence in the Creamery. I don't want to have to make a sign..."

Jack laughed, his hand on his belly as it shook.

I was being ganged up on, and I didn't like it. I folded my arms and glared at Daisy, who poised her face to look like a perfect angel.

"Shall we find a place to sit?" Jack offered, ushering me to the booths and high top tables.

I hated the high tops. I always felt like I was going to fall. I'd once had a horse as a child that liked to buck, and after one too many falls off of her, I was a little more concerned about gravity. But I wasn't going to stop Jack if he wanted to sit at the high tops. I wasn't going to make myself look like a wuss.

He looked back to make sure I was following him, like a mother goose with her goslings. It was kind of adorable. We passed high-resolution pictures on the wall of the Creamery's wares. From sandwiches, to salads, to ice creams. Daisy would call out to us when our food was ready to let us know to go get it. Most fancy restaurants would give you a ticket with a number on it, but Daisy was on a first-name basis with everyone around here. And if she didn't know you, she made sure she did shortly after you came in.

Jack picked the booth in the corner by the door. The Creamery wasn't bustling at this time of the evening. There were a few older couples who were sitting eating their dinners, and a few teens who filed through the door on dates. Besides that, it was pretty dead. Which was nice. Low chance for eavesdropping. The elderly people couldn't hear each other well, let alone us, and the teenagers were too absorbed in their summer romances to pay us any mind.

I wasn't sure how we were going to end up sitting. I could get claustrophobic jammed into the inside of a booth.

Jack inspected the table to make sure it was clean, then ushering me into one side of the booth. Once I sat down, he took a seat across from me. I could see the whole Creamery behind him, while he could see outside. This would be good. I would be able to see if Daisy was doing a drive-by eavesdropping under the guise of cleaning tables.

"So," he said, resting his jaw in between his fists, "got any big weekend plans?"

"Besides cleanup and repair?" I asked, tapping my fingers on the table.

He nodded in acknowledgement.

"Will you just not have weekends until everything is repaired?"

"You mean like your breakneck schedule, all the time?" I said sarcastically. "No, I'll take breaks."

He sat his chin on his hand.

"That's fair."

"Yeah," I said.

I looked down, like a teenager about to ask for a DTR of their crush.

"There's a dance this weekend."

"Oh," he looked intrigued.

But we both quickly got distracted as Daisy walked our way.

"Ally! Jack! Everything's ready!" she called.

I moved to get up and collect our food, but Jack stuck out a hand.

"I've got it, just wait here."

I wanted to protest, but waiting sounded nice. My legs were exhausted from giving the tour of the town, and my body ached more than it had in a while. It was nice to be doted on like this, I had to admit. I was so used to having to hold my own in every situation to prove that I could. I felt like I had to, so I wouldn't get unwanted attention or help with strings attached. It felt weird to let my guard down like this.

Jack came back with two trays balanced carefully on his arms. In another life, he would've made a cute waiter. He set mine down in front of me gently so as not to jostle the food. I was impressed. He set his down and took his seat again.

"Thank you," I said earnestly. He smiled with such genuineness that it felt like I was lying in the sunshine outside.

"You're welcome."

I took out my sandwich, my stomach rumbling. Jack shook his fries out onto his tray, picking out a few to snag. He practically swallowed them whole. He edged the tray toward me, eyebrows wiggling as he offered me some as well.

"These are good," he said.

My heart melted that he was sharing his food when we both knew that each other was starving.

I was a little embarrassed to take a bite of my burger. My "usual" was a hamburger loaded with mustard and a literal ton of pickles.

For as much as I was a chocolate person, I was also a sodium person. I hoped that Jack was at least amenable to pickles, otherwise this was going to be quite a shock when they started falling out at the first bite.

I suddenly became self-conscious. What did a ladylike bite look like? I didn't know. I ate with men that burped and farted during meals. We were all basically cavemen at this point. Unsocialized.

I tried to take a dainty bite, but that made the pickles shift even more. I abandoned my reservations and went for it, covering my mouth with my hand as I chewed. My eyes rolled back into my head as the fluffy texture of the bread, the savoriness of the meat, and the salt hit me. This was exactly what I needed. It felt like life was pouring back into me.

Jack was wrapped up in his food, practically inhaling it as well. He seemed to be enjoying it, for which I was grateful. It was nice to be able to offer such great hospitality to outsiders, even if they weren't exactly here of their own free will.

"So, who are you going with?" Jack asked before popping another fry into his mouth.

"Huh?" I said instinctively, still chewing my food. I swallowed, my face red at the social faux pas. "Sorry, who am I going with where?"

"To the dance," Jack smiled, taking a bite of his sandwich. I wished I had just taken a bite of mine. It would buy me some more time.

"Oh," I said, searching for something to save me, "I mean, I have an offer, but I don't..."

How could I nicely word that I was not interested in going with the man who asked me? I didn't want to sound like I was stuck up and too good to go with him. I just... would rather he not touch me. The thought of his hand on my waist suddenly made me nauseous.

"You could always go by yourself and just dance by yourself or with whoever suits your fancy at the time," he suggested, sensing my unease.

"That's true." I gave a tight smile.

"Unless..." he added in a tone that made me nervous, "you can't dance."

I gasped, almost choking on my burger. The pickle juice burned my throat as I coughed. His eyes got wide, and I felt bad that he felt bad. I was ok; I recovered quickly.

"I absolutely can dance!" I protested.

"Sorry," He said, rubbing the back of his neck with his hand, "I didn't mean to offend you. I'm sure you dance beautifully."

How did that suddenly make it worse? Ah!

Daisy came to my rescue. I gave him a look that said, we've got company. He immediately switched modes to telling me about the stock market, which made even her eyes glaze over. That would show her. Maybe she would think twice about coming to eavesdrop on people. I had to admit, while it was a little hard to follow the lecture he was giving, it was pretty interesting stuff. I had no idea what hedge funds and day trading were before this moment in time. It seemed convoluted. Maybe it was. But it worked like a charm.

"She's gone," I whispered as she disappeared with the empty tray she'd picked up from a vacant table.

"Good." He grinned, pleased with his handiwork.

I laughed.

"That was pretty great. Good job."

He did a mini bow.

"Do you really do that for work? I'd be stabbing my eyes out with a rusty nail after a day."

He blanched, then tilted his head to the side. "It is pretty boring sometimes."

"So this dance," he said, bringing it up again, "is it themed? Like, do you wear masks, or is it centered around a crop? I heard this one country song on the radio where there was a dance celebrating watermelons and..."

I laughed out loud. I knew exactly what he was talking about.

"No," I said, "it's more of just a harvest celebration. Sometimes it's before harvest really gets going, and sometimes it's after or during. It can be a busy, stressful season. It's nice to have something to focus on and look forward to in the midst of broken combines or low wheat prices."

"That makes sense," he said, sneaking in bites as he listened. "That's a good idea. All they give us in corporate America is pizza parties."

"Seriously?" I asked in disbelief.

He rolled his eyes and nodded. "Lame in comparison. I want a dance like that. Maybe I could find me a pretty cowgirl there."

Did he just wink? I think he did. I almost melted into the booth beneath me, liquidating onto the floor. Time to pick out a gravestone, because I was dead.

He wasn't serious. He was teasing. He had to be.

"Well," I tried to call his bluff, "you could always stay until Friday night. We could give your phone to Mayabell and she could handle your boss. Maybe she could even negotiate some ransom benefits for you, like no working weekends if she gives you back."

I crunched on a pickle that had fallen out. These things were so good. Daisy canned them all herself. She was a woman of many talents. Cooking, canning, gardening, meddling...

"As fun as that sounds," he said, "I won't be here Friday."

Disappointment settled back in. I knew that. Why had I let myself believe otherwise?

He eyed his strawberry malt, taking the wrapping off the top of the straw. I watched with interest as he tried to take a sip. Usually Daisy made them pretty thick. He struggled for a few seconds, his eyebrows going up up up as he tried to get it to go through the straw. He eventually took out a spoon and unhooked the lid, procuring a scoop of it that way. His eyes lit up as he savored it.

"Wow!"

"It's good, huh?"

"Oh man," he said. "No other malt will ever top this."

I wholeheartedly believed that.

I finished the last few bites of my burger and snatched up the fallen pickles. No pickle left behind.

I slipped the banana split out of its paper bag, eager to devour it. I stopped in my tracks when I saw two spoons sealed in clear plastic. I narrowed my eyes in the direction of the counter around the corner. Conniving crazy woman! Ugh. He probably would think sharing a banana split was gross. Cooties and all that!

"What?" Jack said, amused at the war happening on my face.

"Nothing," I said, a little too high-pitched for believability.

He stared me down skeptically, not even glancing at his malt as he continued to take spoonfuls of it and slurp it down.

"Daisy must just be going senile," I said as I pulled the whole thing out, "or she thinks I'm going to break a spoon."

He laughed so loud, all of the occupants in the Creamery turned around to see what the ruckus was.

My face burned. I covered it with my hands, running them down dramatically.

"I like the old ladies here," he said, "they've got gumption."

"They're bored," I rasped, embarrassed.

"But we're not." He dipped a fry into his malt and then ate it.

I did a double-take.

"Did you just?..." I motioned.

"Yeah," he said, "it's good. Really good."

I had never considered doing that.

"Here."

He dipped another fry into the malt and handed it to me. I cupped a hand under it to keep it from dripping on the table. I figured with all the close quarters we'd shared, if he was sick I was already on my way to catching it myself.

He eyed me intently as I tried it. I tried to keep my face neutral in case I didn't like it but it was surprisingly good.

"Told you," he said with pride.

Chapter Twenty-Eight

Jack

A lly was adorable as she kept a constant vigil for Daisy while we talked. Watching her try the fries with the malt was fun. Her face was so expressive when she ate. She was incapable of holding her thoughts back.

She opened the banana split she had ordered, tearing the plastic casing off of one of the spoons with her teeth.

She slid the other spoon to me, and I wasn't sure if this was an invitation to eat with her, to put on a show for Daisy, or just a polite gesture that she hoped I wouldn't take her up on. I was fine sharing my food with her. It didn't bother me a bit, but I knew not everyone felt the same and I didn't want to intrude.

"You can try it," she prompted, "but I will warn you, it is pretty chocolatey."

I could see that, from the syrup that drizzled across it and what I thought might be chunks of brownies or pieces of fudge. It looked positively decadent. I was surprised at how many plates Miss Daisy kept spinning around here. She was a force to be reckoned with.

I took the spoon, following her lead. She picked up a piece of fudge, ice cream, and a sliver of banana, so I did the same on the opposite end. She eyed me through her long lashes, watching me take a bite.

She was right; it was really rich. But enjoyable. I inadvertently hummed my approval, which made her face light up. I wondered if it was always this easy to be around someone, or if it was this effortless because I really did like her? None of my other dates had felt like this. And I knew this wasn't a date, but my mind kept trying to tell me it was. This was just... what exactly was this? I supposed I didn't know. And it didn't matter. I'd be gone soon, anyway. I tried to shut down my free-flowing emotions in light of that.

As I looked up, a man opened the door. The bell above him jiggled. Ally whipped around to see who it was. His face was dark, both from the stubble he was sporting and his expression. He didn't look particularly friendly. I wasn't sure if I had seen him around here, but I thought he maybe looked familiar.

Ally's face turned ashen.

I leaned forward as he passed by, keeping my voice down. "You ok?"

She nodded wordlessly, waiting for him to be at the counter talking to Daisy before she spoke.

"That's the guy that asked me to the dance," she explained.

"Oh," I said, understanding dawning, "I wouldn't want to dance with him either."

She laughed, and it sounded like twinkling lights. I savored every second of it.

By the end of dinner, we had instinctively leaned in closer and closer to each other as we chatted and finished off the banana split. That was the best meal I thought I'd ever had.

We got up to leave. I paid the tab and left Daisy a generous tip while Ally ran to use the bathroom. I took the time to try to clean up so Daisy didn't have to. Ally said she wasn't sure if there would be electricity at her house because sometimes they'd have to turn it on and off while repairing things after a storm, so I ran to the bathroom as well. I didn't want to spend another night holding it like I had before.

Once we were reunited, Ally walked up to the counter to pay Daisy. I hung back at the door knowingly. Daisy waved her away.

"It's already been paid for, enjoy your evening."

Ally turned to me, astonished.

"You didn't have to do that," she said as we walked out into the night air.

"I wanted to," I said. "Every woman deserves to be spoiled once in a while."

She looked like she was confused, or maybe on the edge of tears.

"Thank you," she said. "Really, this has been the most fun I've had in a long time."

"You're welcome."

I moved around her, taking my spot closer to the road as we walked toward the garage. We might have been a little late in getting back to the truck. I hoped the mechanic wouldn't be too displeased with us. I'd apologize to him myself. We probably could've been done with dinner way sooner had I not dragged it out by talking so much. I just wanted to make the most of it with Ally while I was still here.

Ally had been right about the fireflies. They danced in the darkness all the way back to the garage. The mechanic sat in a chair outside with his truck, smoking a cigarette. I tried not to inhale too deeply so I wouldn't start coughing. He put it out when he saw us emerge.

"Ready to head home?" he asked Ally.

"Yeah, thank you so much. Any more news on the truck?"

"Nah," he said, "still trying to figure out what's wrong."

I studied Ally closely, trying to see any signs of disappointment or emotion, but I came up empty. I couldn't decide if I was relieved or anxious about the news. But it was just one more day, ostensibly. As long as I didn't overstay with her or overstay my boss' nerves, everything would be ok.

The mechanic opened the door to his truck and hopped inside. I went to the passenger side, opened the door for Ally, and ushered her in. It was crazy how her jeans might as well have been a ballgown. She was so stunning.

We were fairly quiet on the ride home. Everything looked different in the dark. The broken limbs of trees and damaged outbuildings looked far scarier. My heart ached again for this community. I felt bad that I would be leaving Ally and all of them behind while life went on for me without this kind of chaos.

"Thank you," I told the mechanic as I stepped out, holding out my hand for Ally to take. Olivia interjected herself under us, meowing incessantly.

"Hey baby," Ally said, scooping her up in her arms like a real baby.

The mechanic tipped his hand as I shut the door. His tires kicked up a little dirt on the way out. I nervously balled up my hands as I realized that Ally and I were alone. Not that we hadn't been alone during the two nights in the tornado shelter. But that was different.

It felt like we'd lived a whole lifetime in the last two days. How was that possible? I looked at the shelter and shivered. Don't think about it too much, just keep moving, I told myself. I deftly avoided the muddy tire tracks that the tractor had cut into the yard as I walked over to join Ally on the front porch.

She fumbled with her keys and Olivia did a little tap dance on both of our feet. I pulled my phone out and used it for a flashlight; that was about all it was good for, anyway.

As soon as the lock clicked, she opened the screen door, unlocked the wooden door, and flipped on the porch light. It took a moment to adjust, but when I could see clearly, I saw the wide grin Ally was sporting.

"We have electricity!"

We? I liked the sound of that. A smile forced its way onto my face, despite my internal protestations. She ran into the front yard, looking up at the roof.

"Looks like they've covered it for now. And they already got the chicken tractor out here!"

"You have good neighbors," I noted.

"I really do," she said. She already knew that, of course, but I think it was sinking in on another level after this.

"Come on in," she said, opening the front door for me.

"Thank you," I obliged, following right behind Olivia. My heartbeat threatened to come out of my chest. I had only briefly been in the house this morning to use the bathroom in the dark. This scenario was something else entirely.

I looked around, taking in Ally's humble abode. It was so cutesy. Despite her ability to keep up with the guys in every aspect, her home had a very feminine touch. She had ruffly curtains and a tattered bedspread with what had to be a hand-me-down floral print. Her kitchen was well kept, not a crumb in sight. She had small pots and pans hanging from nails on the wall. There was a frying pan that looked like it was well-loved beside the stove. I imagined that she was an amazing cook.

"Make yourself at home," she said, dipping into the bathroom.

"Thank you," I said, continuing to admire her house as Olivia hugged my legs.

She came out of the bathroom with a hairbrush, angrily yanking at the tangles in her hair from the last two days.

"Whoa," I said, "let me help."

I didn't know what came over me. I really didn't. One second I was watching her rip her hair out, the next I was snagging the brush from her and holding it and her hair in my hands.

Her shoulders were a little tense, and I wasn't sure if I had overstepped or if she was just bracing for the pain from the tangles. I just couldn't let her yank all of her beautiful, luscious hair out. I took painstaking care to brush through the bottom edges, working my way up to the top of her scalp. I had her sit down on a kitchen chair so she would be more comfortable. She held her eyes closed.

"Let me know if I'm hurting you," I said, doing my best to be gentle.

"You're fine," she said, her voice barely audible. Something about the way she said it made little butterflies dance in my stomach.

I continued on until all of her hair was tangle-free. Very little was stuck in the brush. I was honestly pretty proud of myself. With how she was handling it, she would've needed a wig. I could understand being impatient though, it was quite the process.

"Thank you," she said bashfully.

She took the hairbrush back, feeling through her wavy locks.

"You're welcome." I cleared my throat, stepping back.

"Where'd you learn to do hair, hmm?" she teased as she got up. "Is that how you woo all the ladies?"

"Oh, did the wooing work?" My eyebrows shot up. I chuckled as she got flustered trying to come back from that.

I had not been trying to woo her, but if that had been the outcome, I was more than happy with it.

"Sorry," I apologized as her whole face had turned red, "no, I do not normally brush strange women's hair."

"Oh," she snorted, "I'm strange now?"

I tilted my head. "Maybe a little."

She threw the hairbrush in my direction. I ducked, laughing as Olivia skidded away from the commotion. She struggled to get traction on the wooden floor.

"Truce," I said, holding my hands up. Her eyes were twinkling.

I loved how being with her felt like being a kid again. She was so playful and flirtatious.

"Well," she said, "we should probably take a shower. We both stink."

Her eyes got big just a second later. "Separately, we should shower separately."

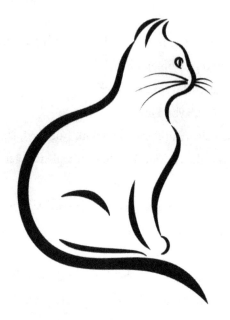

Chapter Twenty-Nine

Ally

"I knew what you meant," he said.

But his eyes said he was laughing his butt off at me on the inside. I was so stupid. How could I have said that?? Jack probably thought I was such a floozy. *We should probably take a shower.* Why couldn't I just be clear from the get-go? I didn't want to lead him on. I was already trying to figure out how to make a cot on the floor for me to sleep on. I couldn't have my guest sleeping on the floor. I considered sleeping in the bathtub, but it would be pretty damp in there after we both showered.

Whatever. That would be a problem for later. We both really did need a shower. I dipped into the bathroom to get a fresh bar of soap for him and a new toothbrush. I wished that I had been more prepared to host but it wasn't like I ever really had people come to visit.

I reemerged.

"Here you go." I set the soap and toothbrush in his hands. "You go first."

His smile reached his eyes.

"That bad huh?" He winked.

Before I could put my foot in my mouth even more, he added, "Kidding, I'll be quick. Thank you!"

He disappeared into my bathroom. I stood there, awkward and unsure of what to do with my hands. Or my heart. Or my head. This was a mess.

After a few moments, I went to check my pantry for things I could cook in the morning. Hearing the shower faucet turn on made me realize that there was a naked man in my house. I tried to put it out of my mind, with minimal success.

My face turned red all over again. Olivia meowed at me, and I bent down to scratch her behind the ear. She could tell I was a basket case.

I nervously made the bed, swept the floor up, checked the windows for hail damage, straightened the curtains, and generally fidgeted with everything in the house. This was crazy. This would definitely be the talk of the town until my dying day. But what were we supposed to do? There were no hotels within 30 miles, and it wasn't like we had a functional vehicle, anyway. And it was one night.

I decided to sit down with my book for a bit. Distraction was the best medicine in some cases. I got a few pages into the book, right before it got really good, when I heard the water turn off. My brain scrambled itself. I hadn't even considered what he was going to wear when he got out. He couldn't likely put on the same clothes, they were filthy. I could wash his clothes, but they wouldn't be completely done tonight. I did the only thing I could think to do. I went to my small cedar closet and pulled out my floor-length, pink, fluffy robe.

I knocked on the door, closed my eyes, and shoved it into his hands.

"Here," I squeaked, before slamming it back in the poor man's face.

I was not going to survive this. This made the tornado look like child's play.

Chapter Thirty

Jack

The hot water felt absolutely heavenly on my skin. Every muscle in my back relaxed as the heat glided over it. I had never been more relieved to be taking a shower than I was right now.

I felt like a giant in this small bathroom. Everything was built for someone much shorter than me. I had to reach down to use the sink. And I could see straight into all of the cabinet shelving when I opened it, looking for a towel before I got in. I'd found a faded one that had clearly been her favorite at one point. Ally was such a petite, secretly girly woman. I was definitely out of place.

Her soap was mild, which was nice. I did not want to go home smelling like a woman. I'd never ever hear the end of it. All of my coworkers knew I was not a player. They'd be shocked that I even had spent the night with a woman, though I hoped they wouldn't find out to begin with.

Suds stripped away the grime from my arms and legs. I scrubbed every inch of my skin, remembering how I'd slept in the tornado shelter with the bugs and chickens. When the last of the bubbles had finished running down through the drain, I turned off the water. I wanted to save as much hot water as I could for Ally.

I stepped out, careful not to slip. The last thing I needed was to die naked in this poor woman's bathroom. I decided to dry my hair first so it wouldn't drip all over the floor and cause a mess.

My pulse shot up when she knocked on the door. I awkwardly yanked the towel down to cover everything important.

Inching down the wall, behind where the door opened, I prepared myself for whatever it was that she wanted.

Suddenly Ally said something that I didn't quite catch and a pink, fluffy garment was thrust into my hands. Then the door slammed shut. I blinked in confusion and shock.

I finished drying quickly, scared of that door opening again. Then I inspected what she'd given me.

It was a woman's bathrobe. Very soft, actually. I held it to my cheek.

Then realization dawned on me.

I had nothing to wear. I didn't have a change of clothes. Everything I packed had been in the suitcase in my truck.

Ally meant for me to wear this.

My whole body felt like it was on fire.

"Oh my gosh..." I mumbled to myself.

"Are you ok?" she yelled, apparently hearing me.

"Yeah, I'm fine, thank you!" I yelled back.

But I was not fine. I was very not fine. I slipped the robe over my shoulders, thankful that it was longer than I anticipated. I reminded myself that lots of men had worn skirts over the centuries. Like kilts. That was basically a skirt. It would be fine. I could survive one night in a woman's

bathrobe. I'd already survived a tornado. Though the tornado was far less...
humiliating.

A belt hung in the loops of it. Relief flooded through me as I tied it
together. At least it offered that much protection. I scooped up my dirty
clothes, not keen on Ally seeing them, and made sure the floor was dry so
she wouldn't slip.

Opening the door felt like a monumental task. She was going to laugh at
me. I knew she was. I had to psych myself up to turn the knob. I clutched
my pile of dirty, emotional support clothes and took a deep breath.

Ally lay on top of the bedspread. She looked up from her book, then
her eyes roamed me up and down. She put it down, giving me her full
attention.

"Awww, you look beautiful," she said, sickly satisfied with herself.
"Maybe you should keep it. It drags the ground on me."

I stifled the urge to melt into the floor. "I don't think it's my color."

"Aww, come on Jack!"

She hopped up from the bed and walked up to me, picking a piece of lint
off my shoulder.

"Women love a man secure enough to wear pink."

Ally laughed maniacally as she walked over to her dresser and pulled out
a few things.

She pointed out the stacking washer and dryer set in the corner.

"You can pop those clothes in there and start it. That way they'll be ready
in the morning. I'll be out shortly."

"Thanks," I said, my voice cracking.

I checked the pockets of my dress slacks as I made my way over there.
There was a shelf with a basket of laundry detergent and other accou-
terments. Her house was so compact, but it was nice in a way. Only the
essentials. My mom would hate it. At this point, I was convinced that

maybe my dad didn't know everything about women. I wasn't ready to say I knew anything, except that they were all different.

The door opened easily, and I shoved my bundle of clothes in just as the shower water came on. My brain detoured and I had to shut it down. Do not think about Ally in the shower. My nerves were insane. I had been so calm and collected when we'd literally slept in the shelter together. Granted, it was on opposite ends of the shelter, but still. Somehow I felt like things were different now. There was some kind of electricity in the air that ran through our every interaction. I didn't know what to make of it.

I pulled out the tray for laundry liquids and poured a little bit of detergent in it, trying to bring myself into the present moment. It would be so nice to have clean clothes. I pushed it back in, then pressed the button to start a small load. The machine made a few beeping noises, then started right up.

I stepped away, wondering what I should do now. Olivia purred at my feet, and I bent down to pet her. She was such a love bug. Her purring was overshadowed by another sound...

Ally was humming a song from the shower. And boy, she could carry a tune. I was transfixed. I wondered if she was going to start singing, but I doubted it. Maybe she usually did, but was just humming tonight on account of me.

Olivia padded to the bed, and I followed her. I saw Ally's book that she'd put down. It had a pretty pink, fairly girly cover, which surprised me. Ally sure did a lot of work to seem the exact opposite of the way she was at home. What was this tough tomboy reading? I picked it up, turning it over to read the back. As soon as I did, I felt a little guilty. It was clearly a romance book. I felt like I was reading a private diary or something. I immediately put it down, and Olivia jumped into my lap, wanting more attention.

A few minutes passed by with me staring at the decor in Ally's house and listening to her hum. Olivia had completely fallen asleep. I was nap-trapped by a feline. Curiosity got the best of me, and I picked the book back up again.

I noticed a bookmark in the pages, and I turned to see where Ally had left off. I was an awful person; I knew. This was not nice. But I wanted to know more about her. What was it she liked about this book? I wanted to be inside her brain for a minute. And I really needed to be distracted from her being a door away from me, completely naked.

My eyebrows shot up as I read. I wasn't sure what I had expected, but it hadn't been this. It was a very sweet, romantic scene where the main character was getting kissed on the neck out on a balcony in Paris. I had to stop myself from saying "Awww" out loud.

Ally was a sweetheart. This was so precious. Is this what she wanted? She wanted to be wooed, genuinely, and someone to be gentle to her? No wonder she didn't care too much for the men at the Co-op. This definitely did not seem like their speed. I filed away this forbidden information.

The shower water turned off, and I immediately put the book down like it had suddenly caught fire. My heart pounded as I tried to make sure I put it back exactly how I'd found it.

Olivia trilled and jumped off of me, padding over to the door. She waited expectantly for Ally to open it. I tried to act natural, but there was no natural way for a tall man in a frilly pink robe to sit on the bed of a woman he'd basically just met.

Ally stepped out, her hair wrapped in a towel. She was adorned in an adorable pajama set with a baby blue satin shirt and shorts. She looked insanely cuddly in that.

I awkwardly splayed my hands behind me.

"Have a good shower?" I squeaked.

What was I saying? What was I doing? Making a fool of myself, that's what.

She looked at me suspiciously, bending down to pet Olivia. "Yeah... I no longer feel gross."

Ally walked to the kitchen and filled two glasses with water, then walked one over to me.

"Oh," I said, touched by the gesture, "thank you."

"You're welcome," she said. "Um, I was thinking..."

"Oh?" I took a sip. "Thinking what?"

"Well, I think you should take the bed tonight."

Chapter Thirty-One

Ally

Whatkind of host would I be if I made him sleep on the floor? I couldn't justify it. I would sleep on the floor, and he would take the bed. That was the end of it.

"What?" he said, bewildered. So much so he almost spit out his water. He looked like he may not have even contemplated the bedding situation.

"No, you can't do that! Your shoulder is hurt."

Admittedly, my shoulder did still hurt. But it was much less now that the warm water had eased out some of the kinks in the muscles.

"I'll be fine." I waved my hand in the air. "I'll make a cot on the floor."

"No," he said adamantly.

"You can't stop me," I said before I could stop myself. He'd hit my argumentative button now. I crossed my arms and stared him down.

"Wanna bet?" He grinned. He looked absolutely goofy in that robe. I couldn't take him seriously.

"Yeah, I do," I said.

"Fine," he said, "I'll just wait until you're asleep and then pick you up and trade you places."

My jaw hung open, aghast. Even Olivia gave out a concerned meow as she looked between us.

"You wouldn't dare!" My hand flew to my chest.

He laughed. "Oh, I would."

His face was completely open and honest. He was insufferable! Oh my gosh!

"Well," I sputtered, my eyes narrowing, "you couldn't even pick me up if you wanted to."

I was sure of that. There was no way a man with an office job could scoop me up and put me in that bed. Catching me when I fell was one thing, but carrying me was another. I wasn't a lightweight.

He cleared his throat, took a step closer, squatted, never breaking eye contact with me, and hauled me up into his arms in a fireman's carry.

"You were saying?" he said, his voice low.

He stepped closer to the bed with me cradled against his chest.

He was so pleased with himself. Meanwhile, my brain was scrambled. What was this I was feeling? I was overcome with a warm, calming sensation. His hands were touching my bare skin and being this close to his chest, I could feel his heartbeat. I could fall right to sleep like this.

WAIT A MINUTE. WE WERE FIGHTING! WHAT THE HECK?

I started squirming and he put me down. Smart man. I could... I don't know, I could do something crazy! He couldn't just pick me up like that.

"See," he said, "told you. You should get in the bed."

"No." I stamped my foot. "And if you move me when I fall asleep, I'll just... move back!"

"You are so stubborn," he laughed, absolutely bewildered as he rubbed his temples.

"You're the one who refuses to just take the bed!" I said, my fists balled up at my sides.

"How about I make you a deal?" He smiled softly, his eyes trailing the wet curls of hair that had escaped from my towel.

"How about I promise not to move you after you fall asleep and I take the bed?" I glared at him sideways. Was he giving up?

"Ok," I said, a little confused.

"And..." he said, brushing back some of my wet hair behind my ear. My breath caught at the gesture. "We both take the bed."

Chapter Thirty-Two

Jack

I t was a bold move, and I wasn't sure if it was going to pay off. But she wasn't backing down, and neither was I.

She seemed to melt down. I wasn't sure if it was because I'd moved her hair or because of what I had said. Maybe both. She sputtered, eyes wild, looking between me and Olivia as though Olivia could be a tiebreaker and talk some sense into the situation.

"People," she finally got out, "would talk!"

"Ally," I chuckled, "they're already talking. You saw the way Daisy was at dinner."

She looked thoughtful. "That's true."

"I swear to you," I assured her, "there will be no funny business what-soever. You stay on your side, I'll stay on my side, and Olivia can be our chaperone in the middle."

Olivia seemed to understand that I was including her. She gave my leg a happy head bunt, leaving a healthy dose of fur on the fluffy robe. I never thought I'd have a cat as a wingman in getting a woman to go to sleep in an actual bed.

Ally's eyes were full of racing thoughts. She was frozen in place.

"Or you can let me sleep on the floor?" I offered again, hoping maybe she would find that to be a palatable option now. It truthfully wasn't the one I wanted, but what was most important to me was her sleeping in the bed.

"No," she said, "it's ok. We can just stay on opposite sides."

"Great," I said, lifting up the covers and going to sit all the way in the corner against the wall.

"Just be aware," her face was stoic and serious, "I steal covers."

I burst out laughing, and she looked offended.

"I'm not worried," I said, "I think my luxurious robe will keep me warm no matter what."

Olivia settled in between us on the top of the covers. I hoped that Ally couldn't hear my heart racing in my chest.

Tiredness was starting to sink in for me, and I was sure it was for Ally, too. She yawned. I didn't know what tomorrow had in store for us, but I was sure we probably should go to bed soon.

"Goodnight Jack," she said, reaching to turn off the lamp.

"Goodnight Ally," I replied into the darkness.

Olivia sat beside my leg, purring up a storm as I drifted to sleep, replaying the feeling of Ally in my arms.

Chapter
Thirty-Three

Jack

M orning came extraordinarily early out here. I was surprised when
light started streaming through Ally's curtains, especially since
I hadn't heard Gerald yet. I had slept a little lightly under the circumstances... especially with her talking in her sleep.

It was a gentle orange glow that didn't feel forced or stressful. I wished
I could bottle it and take it back to the city with me to use instead of the
million alarms I had to set all the time.

I pushed those thoughts aside. I had to live in the moment while I had
the chance. I may never experience something like this again.

Olivia sat on the same pillow Ally's head rested on. Drool puddled on
it where Ally slept with her mouth open. She looked like the cutest little
gremlin I had ever seen in my whole life. I wished I could snap a picture of

this, but I knew she'd kill me. And I'd feel the same if she snapped one of me in this robe. Some things were just too sacred to be preserved forever.

Memory would have to be enough. I didn't dare move. I didn't want to wake her or Olivia. She needed all the rest she could get. I could tell she regularly worked too hard. I wondered if she did that because she had to, because she wanted to, or because she had nothing to pour her energy into. Just because she wasn't working over the weekend like I was, didn't mean she wasn't overdoing it. And I wondered if she was doing that to prove herself to the men around here.

I wished I could see more of the softness I knew she possessed. She seemed to dance around it. Every time she got close, she'd pull back, and the walls of forced toughness and edginess would come back. I loved all of her. I wished she felt comfortable with fully being herself.

My heart threatened to stop as she took a big breath and started moving. I immediately closed my eyes and laid back down on the pillow. I did not want the first thing she saw when she woke up to be me staring at her.

Chapter Thirty-Four

Ally

How could I sleep with this man in my bed? Even though he used my soap, he still had his own distinct, delicious smell. He was going to do me in.

I laid completely still, wondering if he was going to snore. I had to confess; I hadn't been paying attention to things like that in the tornado shelter. But now, I was curious.

Normally you only get to see a new person, or any person, during the day. Maybe a day or two a week. Maybe a little after sunset. But this? I had been with him nonstop for days. I took deep breaths, looking at the small sliver of moonlight that snuck behind the curtain and onto the floor. I wished my heart wouldn't beat so loudly.

My mind raced, and at some point, I must have just passed out. I didn't know how it happened. One minute I was thinking a million miles a minute, and the next my nerves were all lazily waking up to the sound of my rooster crowing. I flexed my muscles here and there, curling up and yanking the covers with me. When they didn't come, I yanked harder. I just need a few more minutes. What the heck!

Then I popped one eye open. I was suddenly aware that I was not the only thing in the bed. The night before flooded back to my memory. I sat up in a big gasp, clutching the covers to my chest as much as possible with this big lug holding them down. He stirred, his dark eyelashes clinging to the top of his cheek as he started to rouse from sleep. I suddenly felt a little guilty for trying to yank the covers.

His face was so unassuming. And he looked absolutely ridiculous with the fluffy robe flanking his frame. It was hilarious.

I remembered his clothes were in the washer. I inched ever so slowly toward the side of the bed, cautiously dangling my legs off and sliding down. He would feel better in his own clothes, despite how much I was enjoying him having to wear mine.

I crept over to the washer and dryer and tried to pull open the door without making noise. I was unsuccessful. I had never realized how loud the door mechanism was until this moment. It might need some WD-40.

I shot a look over to Jack, who was definitely awake now. But he didn't look upset. I wasn't even sure that was what woke him up. He just sat up, looking at me thoughtfully. He didn't look as bleary-eyed as I would've expected. Maybe he was a morning person.

"Sorry," I said sheepishly, "just wanted you to have your clothes."

"It's ok," he said, his voice deep and husky from lack of use and sleep.

My spine tingled.

Laundry.

Focus.

I took the pile of wet clothes, opened the dryer door, and threw everything in. I jabbed the button to start it. In the time it took me to fix our breakfast, he'd hopefully have some clean clothes.

"How do you feel about scrambled eggs?" I said, a hand on my hip as I turned to him.

Jack sat in his fluffy robe — er, my fluffy robe — like a kid in a candy store.

"I love scrambled eggs."

He bolted out of bed in the most ungraceful way. He stood, trying to keep his robe down.

I grabbed the basket that hung on a hook by the door.

"You can come with if you want," I offered without looking back.

The front door creaked lightly as I opened it and stepped out into the fresh morning air. It definitely smelled like it had rained recently. And in the morning light, I saw just how much cleanup there was to do.

I'd need to seed the part of my lawn that got torn up. There was still some debris I needed to clear out. And the roof needed repaired ASAP. I might need to barter with a local handyman for it to be fixed properly. I didn't want a big company with people I didn't know ripping me off.

My bare feet met the dewy grass right as Jack came out. I smiled as he followed me to the chicken tractor to see about some eggs for breakfast. As I suspected, my rooster and hens were not happy being in a smaller space, but there were a few eggs.

I reached in and harvested what I could see and get to. We would need to move the thing later, but for now, we just needed breakfast. One thing at a time. Chores always felt less daunting when there was food in your belly. That's what my grandma always said, and she was usually right.

Jack wandered around while I dug for eggs. When I looked up, he was on the other side of the yard looking at the scrap pile that was his truck. A twinge of sadness twisted in my stomach. That had to be hard for him. But he didn't seem to be stressed or upset, just intensely inspecting. Maybe he was looking for anything that could be salvaged.

I put each egg softly in the basket, careful not to knock them against each other. I locked the chicken tractor back up. The chickens could roam later when we could supervise them while we worked in the yard.

"You alright?" I asked, the basket hanging from my arm as I caught up with Jack near the wreckage.

"Yeah," he said, elbow-deep in what used to be the truck window.

I was surprised he could even get his arm in there to begin with. I hoped it didn't get stuck. I didn't want to be standing in my yard in PJs with a man in my pink robe when the fire department showed up to help. That'd probably get published in the local paper. With pictures.

"My phone is on 2% and I have a charger in here, but I can't seem to find it," he explained.

Oh. I hadn't thought about him needing to charge his phone up.

"What kind of phone do you have?" I asked.

I could see if my charger would work.

He pulled it out of his pocket. It was fancy. Much fancier than anything most people around here owned. I hadn't gotten a good look at it before. But now, with it in my hands, I could see it was a touch screen without any cracks or blemishes. And the charging port was shaped nothing like mine.

"My phone charger wouldn't work I don't think, but I can take you into a city nearby to get a replacement when my truck is fixed," I assured him. "Or we can ask in town to see if anyone has a charger that would work."

"Thanks," he said. "I'm just going to send a quick email to let my boss know so he doesn't have a coronary when I don't respond."

"Ok," I said, leaving Jack in my pink bathrobe out in my yard by himself. I could only imagine what anyone driving by might think. I hoped they didn't have a wreck from rubbernecking. The thought made me giggle.

I set the egg basket down on my kitchen counter, Olivia waiting anxiously at my feet. She was so spoiled. She knew that she could beg and get almost anything, as long as it wasn't going to hurt her. It was time for her breakfast. I diverted to grab a can of wet food on the counter and put it on her food dish in the corner. Then I went to wash my hands and check the pantry for things to spice up breakfast with. I had plenty of canned goods in the cabinets. Some of them were from the elderly ladies in town. In fact...

I opened the door and reached for a strawberry preserve jar that I had been saving for a special occasion. Considering Jack's love for strawberries, and my lack of guests to spoil, it seemed like as special of an occasion as I was going to get. I had a few slices of bread left for us to eat it on.

My mouth was watering. I pulled the frying pan off of its designated spot on the wall and placed it on the stovetop, firing it up.

A dollop of butter went into the pan to heat up. I grabbed two plates and set them to the side. I warmed up the pieces of bread in the pan for less than a minute each and then put them on the plates.

I cracked the eggs into the pan, careful to keep the shells out. Then I threw in some fresh red peppers and a little bit of onion from the garden. As the egg cooked and rolled up at the edges of the pan, I desperately wished that I could make an omelet. This would've made such a beautiful omelet. But alas, I was incapable of flipping eggs. Which is why I always made scrambled.

Jack opened the front door and Olivia abandoned her food to go greet him. She must really be smitten, I thought, but then I realized I was hardly one to talk.

"It smells so good in here."

His tall frame filled the doorway. I felt so small in comparison.

"Breakfast will be ready in just a couple more minutes. You can go ahead and sit down if you'd like."

I opened my silverware drawer to collect utensils and stuck them on our respective plates as the eggs finished up, setting a butter knife on top of the preserves. I shut the door with my hip.

I looked over to see Jack watching me intensely. I suddenly felt very self-conscious. My hair was a mess, my nightshirt was hanging off of my shoulder, and I wasn't exactly worthy of a cooking show.

"How did you sleep?" I forced my voice to work, but in my nervousness, it came out quiet and raspy.

Jack smiled as I used a spatula to dish out eggs onto plates.

"I slept really well, thank you. How about you?"

"I slept well, too," I said, flipping off the stove and taking the plates to the table. I went back for the jam, salt, and pepper and set them on the small table.

"That's good," Jack said, followed up with a thank you as I set his plate in front of him.

"I'm glad Olivia didn't keep you up." I gave her a little glare, that she returned. "She sometimes likes to eat my hair or my toes in the middle of the night. I have no idea why."

His eyes crinkled as he laughed. "That little angel would never do a thing like that."

I rolled my eyes. Maybe she wouldn't to him!

I picked up the jar of preserves and tried to open it. The lid was sealed tight. It wouldn't budge.

I tried again from a standing position, but that didn't help.

"One second," I said, fleeing to the kitchen to get my drying towel.

Satin PJs were not the best tool for leverage against jars.

I came back to find the lid placed next to the jar on the table. My jaw hit the floor.

"What? Did you?" I sputtered, absolutely flabbergasted.

"You loosened it." He credited me.

I narrowed my eyes at the jar, as though it were my mortal enemy.

"Thank you," I grumbled, embarrassed.

"You're welcome," he smiled, stabbing a puffy clump of eggs with his fork.

I took the jam and spread it onto my toast. This was going to be incredible. It smelled heavenly.

"Did you know you talk in your sleep?"

Chapter
Thirty-Five

Jack

A lly looked as though she might faint.

"I do not!" she shrieked at a pitch I wasn't even aware she was capable of.

"You do," I said with amusement. "It's cute."

"Oh my gosh," she covered her face with her hands, but her red ears were still visible. "What did I say?"

The answer to that question was something I should take to my grave. I smirked, my knee bouncing beneath the table. She was so fun to tease. It shouldn't be legal, honestly, to have this much fun.

I could never tell her that she had murmured my name on and off during the night. I didn't realize how good it would sound to hear. But she didn't need to know that.

The first time I thought I was dreaming. Olivia walked across my stomach and woke me up to realize it was definitely not a dream. I would've paid good money to know what she was dreaming of, but since I knew she wouldn't tell me even if she did remember, I settled into my seat and waited to see what she would say next.

I spread some jam on my toast, waiting for her to drop her hands from her face. This spread smelled good. I breathed deeply. When was the last time I'd truly had a leisurely breakfast outside of the last couple of days? I couldn't remember one except maybe when I was a kid. What I wouldn't give to wake up every day next to Ally and eat the breakfast she made.

Wow. I was smitten. I pushed aside the thoughts of having to leave soon, choosing instead to be delusional and indulge the fantasies of seeing Ally cook in her satin PJs every morning.

"What did I say?" she groaned, placing a hand on the table in desperation. Her eyes met mine, pleading, begging me to tell her.

"What do you think you said?" I asked coyly, setting my toast down.

"I don't know, I probably was ranting about the chickens or something," she remarked offhandedly.

But I knew that couldn't be what she was worried about.

"That would've been funny," I admitted.

"Tell me what I said," she demanded, her dark eyes lightening just a little with the morning sun coming through the window now.

"Or what?" I sat back, hanging one of my arms over the chair in the silly pink robe. I must have looked like a deranged supervillain or something.

Her eyes turned to slits. I was pretty sure she was planning ways to murder me. She was plotting something devious. I saw it.

"Or I'll take a picture of you in that robe and send it to your work."

That... was actually a scary threat. I put up my hands in surrender as she pulled her phone out of her pocket.

"No need to be hasty," I said, walking it all back.

"Tell meeeeee," she whined.

"Blackmail is illegal, you know," I told her sternly.

"Who cares?" she said. "You really think Barney Fife is gonna come arrest me? He won't. He's too busy running a speed trap and chasing his own tail to care about things like that."

The dryer buzzed at that exact moment and I saw my opportunity to retreat. If I could grab my clothes and duck into the bathroom quick enough, all her leverage would be gone.

I stood up and bolted to the dryer, scooping out the pile of laundry and ducking into the bathroom.

Ally knocked on the door as I started putting legs through holes in a haphazard fashion. It felt weird getting back into dress clothes. I really had gotten accustomed to her fluffy robe.

"Tell me, Jack!" she yelped. For a second, I wondered if I should. I didn't want her to start crying or something.

I looked in the mirror, making sure I hadn't put anything on inside out. My reflection startled me. I didn't recognize the person looking back at me. That person was professional, had his act together, knew what he wanted (or at least pretended to) and looked like he was confident and collected. But my eyes didn't match. My smile didn't fit the aesthetic. It was real. There was genuine happiness gleaming in my reflection.

Could I really go back to the corporate world? I wasn't sure.

I opened the door to find Ally on the floor sitting crisscross applesauce. I nearly tripped over her. Her eyes were in fact watery as she looked up at me.

"Was it really embarrassing?" she looked like she was barely keeping it together. For such a tough exterior, she was quite the softy.

"No."

An absolute lie.

"Then tell me."

She stood, looking up directly at me now. For a moment, I thought she was going to put her hand on my chest, if only to push me playfully. My heart beat in anxious anticipation. But she didn't.

"It's not a big deal. It was cute," I reassured her. "I'm sorry. I wouldn't have brought it up if I knew it was going to stress you out."

Olivia came over, purring like a motorboat to comfort Ally.

"I just want to know," she said as we sunk back into our chairs to finish up our breakfast.

I felt far more comfortable sitting knowing that if I lapsed into a more comfortable position, nothing was going to fall out. I was not cut out for skirts, at all. I didn't know how men in kilts did it after all of that.

"You promise not to be upset if I tell you?" I asked her.

She looked away. "I don't know..."

"That's the only way I can tell you, sorry. It'll have to be a pinky promise, too."

That stuff was unbreakable. Even as adults.

"Hmmm," she looked at me as though she was assessing me. Then she stuck out her pinky, curiosity getting the better of her.

"Tell me," she said, confidently this time. I watched her take a bite of her toast with jam, a little bit sticking to her lip. How I longed to kiss it off...

"You said my name," I whispered, as though I was dropping a bomb or sharing top-secret information.

Maybe I was. I would've definitely been embarrassed if roles were reversed. It didn't have to be a big deal, though. We could laugh it off. We could pretend it never happened. Or we could dive in head first, fearlessly plunging into unknown waters.

Chapter
Thirty-Six

Ally

T he room felt like it was spinning. Was I going to throw up? Maybe.
It was a distinct possibility.

What did he mean I said his name in my sleep? Was I yelling it? Whispering it? Moaning it? OH gosh.

I held my now throbbing head in my hands.

"Hey," he said, coming to sit on his knees beside me. He took my wrists gently in his hands. "It's ok. It's not a big deal."

It was a big deal. It was a very big deal. My mouth was betraying me in my sleep. I had caught feelings for the city slicker that I spent nights trapped in a tornado shelter with. And he was leaving. And no man would ever measure up after this, and no one ever had before. It was ruining my life. How was I supposed to go back to what I'd known before Jack? And how was I supposed to face him now? I was so ashamed.

"I'm sorry," I murmured, nearly in tears. I hoped he hadn't felt uncomfortable. And I hoped he didn't think I was a horrible person. I barely knew him. My soul tried to leave my body from embarrassment. I could feel it floating away.

"There is nothing to be sorry about." He moved my hair back behind my ear, sending a thrill down my spine. I shivered, and his smile turned down into an intense, steady expression.

"I'm serious." His voice was a low and soothing balm. "I can forget about it right now."

"I could make you forget about it for real if I whack you with that frying pan," I joked, pointing to the stove.

"Not necessary, Rapunzel." He winked. "I don't think Barney Fife would look as kindly on assault and battery as he would on blackmail."

Had he said something after he winked? I hadn't heard it. He needed to stop doing that. It was maddening. I couldn't take any more.

"We should finish breakfast," he suggested. "We have a big day ahead of us, don't we?"

Right. Breakfast. Things to do. People to see. Yes. There was more to life than my embarrassment in the moment. I appreciated him bringing me back to reality.

Jack made small talk, clearly trying to get my mind to settle after teasing me so thoroughly. When we had cleaned our plates, I was pleasantly taken by surprise when he scooped them up and washed them in the sink.

"You don't need to do that," I said.

Guests weren't supposed to help clean up.

"I want to." His voice was warm and enveloping.

I liked having help. I went to make the bed and I grabbed some lilac overalls to change into for the next part of our day. When I emerged, he was hanging the murder weapon — I mean frying pan — back on its hook.

"Ready?" he asked excitedly. This man was far more stoked to clean up my yard and sort out things post-tornado than I was. Maybe because he didn't live here. For him, it was an adventure. For me, at least in part, it was responsibility and duty.

I nodded. Our first order of business was to let the chickens out. Olivia followed us, turning up her nose as we approached the chicken tractor and unhooked the latch. The hens and rooster came flooding out like they'd been trapped in the tornado shelter all over again. I couldn't blame them. It was far more cramped than what they were accustomed to. They scurried around, pecking at the yard.

"I'm going to see if I can get a hold of the mechanic," I told Jack, leaving him to watch over the critters.

I made my way to the singular corner of the yard with reception and dialed up the number. I wasn't sure if he was going to pick up the phone when I called. Sometimes he didn't hear it over the sound of the shop radio. But a "hello?" came through after the second ring.

"Hey," I said, "can you hear me?"

"Yeah," he said, sounding bored. I sometimes wondered if he just hated everyone and everything, or if he just sounded bored talking to me. I pushed down my social anxiety.

"I was just calling to get an update on the truck. I probably need to hitch a ride with someone one way or another tomorrow for work. And I need to figure out how I'm going to get Jack home."

"Yeah," he said simply.

Ugh. That wasn't an answer to my question. Why were some boys like this?

"So, is there an update?" I prodded again.

"Yeah, the part will be here late Tuesday."

"Oh," I said, needing a moment to digest. "OK, thank you."

"No problem."

He hung up. A man of few words.

Tuesday. That meant that Jack would be here tonight and Tuesday night. I'd have to take him home on Wednesday. But at least that meant I got another day with him. Though if I was taking off Wednesday to travel, I might ought to work today so that I didn't miss too many days of work. I couldn't really afford to, truthfully. And with harvest coming up any day now, time was of the essence to get all the machinery up and running.

Chapter Thirty-Seven

Ally

"What's the status?" Jack asked as I returned to his side, looking out at the sea of chickens.

I grimaced. "It may be Wednesday before I can take you home."

He sighed, his shoulders sagging.

"Boss won't be happy about that, but he'll just have to get over it. I have vacation time to burn. I've never actually taken any since I started with this company. He didn't want me to."

"You've never taken any of your vacation time?" I sputtered. "How long have you been there?"

"Three years," he responded, realization seeming to dawn on him how absolutely insane that was.

"No wonder you're not having a good time. They text and call and email at all hours and any day, and you haven't had a real vacation since you worked there!"

Not that I could say getting caught in a tornado and stranded was a real vacation, but it was something different for a change.

"My dad didn't like to take vacations, and I guess I was just kind of following in his footsteps. If he takes a break, he feels behind."

"Good thing you aren't your dad," I reminded him. "You can be your own person, making your own decisions about your time and what you do with it."

"Suppose that's true," he said, chewing on his lip.

Gerald the rooster came up and pecked at the ground in front of us both. The chickens seemed delighted to be running free. Olivia was glaring at them with an expression that said she believed them to be inferior beings. But if they got too close, she skittered away as fast as she could.

We watched them, amused, basking in the quiet for just a moment.

"How do you feel about tractors?" I asked him when I couldn't wait any longer.

If I was going to work today, I was going to have to get a move on. I could always leave him here, but I figured I'd give him the option.

"Never seen one up close," he admitted. "Why?"

"Do you want to see one up close?" I broached.

He tilted his head, looking at me sideways, "Yeah, that could be fun."

"OK," I said, "give me a second."

I retreated back to the part of the property that had the best service and called my boss on his landline phone.

"Hey Earny," I said as he picked up.

His voice was weathered, but friendly.

"Hey Ally, is everything alright? Heard the tornado passed by your place the other night."

"It did," I confirmed, indulging the small talk until we got to the meat and potatoes. "Everything is mostly fine, just lost the chicken coop and the roof has some damage. My truck is at the mechanic's being fixed right now, but I'd still like to come into work today if you'd be up for picking me up?"

"Oh my," his voice warbled. "Sounds like you've had quite the excitement. Sure sweetheart, I'll be there in a few minutes."

"Thanks Earny," I said cheerily. "I had one more question for you."

"Sure sweetie, what is it?" he asked warmly.

"Can I bring a friend?"

I remembered I had another phone call to make. As soon as Earny hung up, I dialed into town to the Co-op. Sheryl answered the phone. Just the woman I needed to talk to.

"Mornin' Sheryl," I said with a little bit of trepidation. "I have a question for you."

"What is it?" Sheryl said, her voice oozing irritation.

I wondered if I should've called later in the day so that she would've been more chipper, but it was too late now. I had to press on.

"Well," I said, wondering how best to word this, "Jack, my house guest, his phone charger was destroyed when his truck was hit by the tornado.

And now his phone is dead. Would you check in town to see if anyone has an extra charger for a newer, fancy type of phone?"

"Sure hon," she said.

She sounded like she was bored out of her mind. I wondered if she would even do what I had asked, but I had to leave it in her hands now. She was the best bulletin board, outside of Mayabell, in town. Asking them to disseminate something was more potent than putting it in the local paper.

"Thanks, Sheryl, just let me know what you find!"

She hung up before I could raise my phone down to hang up. I hoped she'd be in a better mood later. But more than that, I hoped that someone would actually have a phone charger for him. I didn't want him to have to wait until Wednesday to charge his phone.

Chapter Thirty-Eight

Jack

The next thing I knew, Ally and I were barreling down the dirt road with a wrinkled old man in a beat-up truck. If this man had never been an auctioneer, he'd missed his calling. He could talk a mile a minute without so much as taking a breath. I was amazed. And it was nice to not have to carry the conversation.

"So where'd you say you're from?" Earny asked me for the third time.

I wondered if he was going to give me enough time to actually answer this time.

"I'm from Texas," I blurted.

"Ohhhhh," Earny said, delighted. "Whereabouts in Texas? I have family in Texas."

His voice was nearly swallowed up by the sound of shaking tools in the back of the truck bed.

"In the Houston area, the traffic there is crazy. It's way quieter out here, much less noise."

"Oh surreeee 'nuff," he said. "That's a whole different world in that big city there."

I could only nod. It was true. This place felt like another planet in comparison. No big shopping malls, no high-rise buildings, no ambulances out of the window every day. The craziest action out here so far was tractors blocking the road. And tornadoes, of course.

"Well, are you liking your stay here?" he asked, talking over Ally squished in between us.

She didn't seem to be phased by his chatterbox ways. She seemed used to it. How did she ever get any work done for this man? I would never be able to focus for long enough to get anything done!

"Is Ally treating you alright? She can be feisty, ya know!"

"Hey!" Ally glared at him playfully.

"Oh yes, she's been wonderful," I said politely, and it was true. "She's only threatened to kill me with the frying pan one time."

I held up a finger for emphasis.

Farmer Earny burst into laughter, which led to a coughing fit. I worried about him for a moment as he gasped for air. Meanwhile, Ally playfully smacked me with her arm.

"Oh that's my Ally girl," Earny said proudly.

This man was so sweet, he seemed like a second grandpa to her.

"She's just a softie under all that, ya know," he whispered, as if Ally was not sitting right there.

"You hush," Ally said, her cheeks flushed like a little schoolgirl in front of her crush. "You don't gotta tell him all my secrets, you know?"

Earny just chuckled.

We pulled into a long, perfectly well-kept drive, with trees lining either side. I recognized some of them to be cedar, but others I wasn't sure what they were.

Up ahead, I saw a house flanked on three sides by wheat waving in the wind.

"Harvest is coming up quick," Earny said excitedly. "Ya ever seen a harvest season?"

"No sir," I said. "I'd love to, though."

"You should stick around a spell. Be here for this one," Earny recommended as he pulled the truck into an area with a bunch of farm equipment and other trucks.

"He's gotta get back to the real world sometime, Earny," Ally told him with exasperation.

"This is the real world," said Earny with a smile, throwing the truck into park. "Here we are."

We all piled out and Ally looked like she was in business mode now. Two men were standing around tinkering with parts outside of trucks. Then a third appeared from underneath a big combine and made his way over to us.

"Didn't know it was bring your boyfriend to work day, Ally Cat." The man spit into the grass beside him.

I tried not to make any sudden movements, but out of the corner of my eye, I saw her clench her jaw. I hadn't actually seen her genuinely mad like this.

Was Ally Cat a nickname she actually liked? Was she close to this guy? Or was he just another one of the guys in this town who wanted to get in her pants and use that as bragging rights? Seemed to me that there might be an abundance of those around here.

"It's not," she growled. "He's not my boyfriend, and you better be nice to him or I'll—"

"Leave her alone Jim," Earny piped up, "and while you're at it, dig up some southern hospitality. I gotta go finish breakfast with the Missus. Nice to meet you, Jack."

He disappeared up the gravel pathway to the two-story, cream-colored house. A little dog followed close behind him, his tongue happily waving outside of his mouth as he walked.

When I turned back, I found the other two men were sizing me up. They were looking from my shoes, to my head, and back. I supposed I couldn't blame them. I did look out of place. But it was this or the fluffy robe. And I was fairly certain they would bully me more if I was wearing the fluffy robe. Maybe I could help Ally with her work, prove that I could be just as much of a manly man as these three goons.

"Come on," Ally said, grabbing hold of my forearm and dragging me toward a barn that looked like it had seen better days. "Sorry about those three."

"They've got problems," she added after we were out of earshot,

"Oh really?" I said, trying to make a joke. But she laughed so hard, I wondered if it was actually true.

"Probably, honestly," she said once she had recovered, climbing up the stairs to the loft.

There were little rectangular hay bales piled in the corner. It looked like something out of a picture-perfect family photo in the fall. All that was missing was some pumpkins.

"Here," she said, slinging something down at me. I held my arms up just in time to catch a small bag full of tools. "We're gonna need these."

I looked inside, not recognizing half of the things or their potential uses. But I was happy to carry a bag around. This was definitely a nice change of pace compared to being on the phone all the time getting yelled at and staring at numbers until my eyes crossed.

"What are we working on?" I asked. What if she asked me to hand her a tool, and I didn't know which tool and I looked stupid? I suddenly felt very inadequate and unmanly. Was I failing at life because I had different proficiencies than the Jim Bobs out there?

"I think let's do the tractor first. That way, you can really get up close and personal with it. They are pretty cool."

I nodded, gulping as she turned around. I followed her out to where it was sitting behind the barn. It was a lot taller than I had pictured, and the tires in particular were huge! It was a little intimidating, honestly. I was a tall guy and they were even taller than I was. How many people did it take to change a tractor tire, I wondered?

But Ally was already on to the next thing. She tried to explain what she was doing, using all of this technical jargon, and I wondered if she was speaking in a different language. But when I heard her say wrench, I snapped out of it.

"Sorry, did you need the wrench?" I asked.

"Yes please," she said, patiently waiting for me to place it in her hand.

I dug in the bag.

"Here you go," I said confidently as I placed it in her hand.

I got a little ego boost from that. I could be helpful. I wasn't useless. And I thought about how she had a mechanic looking after her car. Maybe she wasn't just an encyclopedia on machine repair either, maybe she just specialized in some things.

"Crap!" she exclaimed, her voice angry.

"What?" I faltered. One minute she was jabbering about the underside of the tractor, and the next she was backing away, holding her hand.

I got closer and saw blood. The whole earth started spinning.

"Do I need to go get Earny? Are you ok?" I gasped. I was not a blood person. Far from it.

"I'm fine," she hissed, applying pressure with her other hand.

"Let me see," I pestered her, though I actually really did not want to see. I wanted to make sure it really wasn't bad, though. My concern for her overshadowed my fear of potentially passing out.

Her palm oozed blood. She had sliced it pretty good.

"We need to get that cleaned up." I grabbed her other hand, hauling her toward Earny's house. I was sure he wouldn't mind me inviting myself in with her for some clean water and bandages.

I knocked briefly once we got up the three steps at the door. It was flanked by beautiful vines with flowers and yellow roses on each side. If I hadn't had adrenaline pulsing through my veins, I would've stopped to admire it more.

An elderly woman no taller than five feet flat answered the door.

"Hello dear," her voice was friendly and welcoming.

"Ally hurt herself," I blurted out.

"I'm fine, really," she said, trying to hide it.

But the old woman narrowed her eyes and took a glance.

"Oh, good heavens!" she exclaimed. "Come in and let's get this taken care of."

"What happened?" Earny called from a dining room table nestled back behind the living room.

Their house was beautifully decorated with wood furniture and what I suspected were oil paintings of landscapes, nature, and the occasional woodland creature.

"Ally's cut her hand," the old woman's voice quavered.

She shuffled as she led Ally to the kitchen sink to rinse it off. I awkwardly followed behind, unsure what to do with myself. I was practically wringing my hands like a helicopter parent over her getting a cut, but in my defense, it looked pretty deep.

Ally groaned through clenched teeth as the old woman held her hand under the running water.

"You really buggered it up," she declared.

"Sonny, would you get me some ice from the fridge?"

It took me a moment to realize that was me. I was Sonny.

"Yes ma'am," I said, hopping to it.

I procured a cup from the cabinet and filled it with the ice dispenser on the front of the fridge, then handed it over to her.

"Thank ya," she said.

She had wrapped Ally's hand in clean paper towels around the cut and was holding it tightly. Then she left Ally to hang onto it and pulled a bottle of rubbing alcohol from the cabinet.

Lifting the paper towel, she announced that it had stopped bleeding so badly. She held Ally's hand over the sink to pour the alcohol.

Ally cussed, even in front of this nice old lady, which I got the impression she didn't normally do considering how profusely she apologized after the alcohol pouring was over with. The old woman didn't even bat an eye. She took the ice, poured it into some paper towels, and made a little bundle with it, then pressed it onto the cut.

"Hold that there for a bit," she told Ally.

"Come sit down while I go find some proper bandages," she said to the both of us.

"Days off to a great start, huh?" Earny said to us both.

Ally nodded solemnly. I wondered if she would've treated the cut at all had I not insisted on dragging her inside. She needed to take care of herself!

"Some days are just like that," said Earny, then he turned to me and winked, "even in Oklahoma."

Chapter
Thirty-Nine

Ally

My hand stung like crazy, but the first rule of keeping up with the boys was not letting any of them see you in a moment of weakness. So when Jack freaked out over my cut, I was a little confused.

Any of the other men that I worked with would've just told me, "Suck it up, buttercup!" Except for Earny, of course. He had a heart of gold, and a sense of humor to match it.

He was more of a manager at this age; he was starting to not get around so well. Which meant I was mostly alone with the three goons in the front yard who would've been completely unsympathetic to my plight.

Meanwhile, Jack was losing his mind over it. Dare I say, overreacting.

I would be fine, it was just a cut. I felt a little dizzy, but who didn't when there was an accident like this? I hadn't realized how sharp that rusted edge was going to be and bam! It got me.

I was planning on washing it, calmly, later. But Jack had other plans. I hoped that none of the guys had seen him parade me to the door in a flurry like that. I was fine, really.

Ethel seemed to side with Jack, though. I could tell all of the wrinkled lines on her face were exaggerated from stress as she inspected it. That rubbing alcohol made me feel like I was going to pass out worse than the actual cut had. But she knew what she was doing. Farmers never went to the emergency room unless they were dying, so farmer's wives were essentially an emergency room unto themselves. I was in good hands.

When she went to get bandages, I snuck a peek and immediately regretted it. The ice helped me and gave me something else to focus on.

Jack and Earny made small talk while I got fixed up. I was grateful that they seemed to get along so well. I hadn't considered that before their introduction, but I could see how they would. Even though they were at vastly different positions in life, Earny was always up for talking to people.

I think they both offered each other some valuable perspective. Earny on remembering what it was like to be young, and Jack on what it was like to be an old, stable man who didn't go into finance or corporate America. It was never too late to see things from a different perspective.

"Was this young man here distracting you too much, Ally?" Earny teased as Ethel came back into the room, tsking with her basket of bandaids hung on her hip. Her gray hair was losing some of the hairspray that kept it in place from her frantic pace.

I would've shot him a glare, but Ethel was already on it.

"He's a perfect gentleman," she crooned. "He'd never do such a thing."

Earny gave a hearty laugh and downed some coffee that I knew was as pitch black as it could be.

Jack's face was multiple shades of red, and I couldn't help but feel a little embarrassed myself. I had, admittedly, been a little bit distracted trying to show all of my knowledge off to Jack. It was hard for me to interact sometimes.

How else was a gal supposed to woo a man? Blasting him with a million facts about whatever you were proficient in was as good as it got, wasn't it? Isn't that how men wooed women? So why wouldn't it work in reverse?

I couldn't see his face, so I didn't know if it was working exactly, but judging by his voice, it might not have been. Maybe I needed to try harder. Or maybe I needed to stop trying to woo him at all. After all, he was leaving.

"You two crazy kids are free to go now," Ethel said, releasing my hand.

She'd bandaged the whole thing while I was having an internal war with myself. She was nimble and efficient. I supposed she'd learned to be that way because of Earny. He never sat still as it was, let alone if he was injured. Unless, of course, he was watching TV. Then that man was as still as a statue. Sometimes he'd even fall asleep and sit there snoring. But if you said a word about it, he'd argue with you in his sleep.

There was truly never a dull moment around here. And that was just the way I liked it.

We went back out. Jack looked a little sheepish.

"I'm sorry if I distracted you. I don't want you to get hurt again. Maybe I should get out of your hair," he started rambling.

"You're fine," I said, brushing it all off. "You didn't distract me. Don't worry about it. I just wasn't being careful enough. That's on me."

"But you'll be careful now?" He searched for reassurance.

It was touching how genuine he was about wanting me to be safe. It was a little difficult to fully accept being coddled when I was used to the exact opposite, though.

"Uh-huh," I said, heading back over to the tractor. "Let's go. This thing won't fix itself."

I was quieter this time, but I tried to ask Jack questions periodically so I could listen rather than talk. It seemed easier to do that safely. The morning was fairly mild, thanks to us being in the shade. But it was still summer in Oklahoma; I felt sweat dripping down my back here and there regardless. I was sure he was even hotter in his fancy getup.

I heard him move, and when I turned, I found him sitting under the tractor with me.

"Hi," he said, like a little kid. So full of innocence and lack of malice.

"Hi!" I laughed.

He looked absurd. I wished I could fish into my pocket and find my phone to take a picture, but I had to have two hands to put this bolt back in place. I resolved to etch the scene into my memory forever instead.

"How'd you learn all this stuff?" he asked. "About the tractor, I mean. How do you know what's wrong with it?"

"I've just kind of picked it up over the years," I explained. "Trial and error, you know? Nearest place to take it to get fixed is a long way away, and super expensive. So we try to avoid that. But I actually don't know what is wrong with it most of the time. I have to guess and experiment."

"Oh," he seemed to be taken off guard by that.

"Yeah," I explained, "It's not an exact science. Especially when what you're mostly working with is just the weird sounds it makes. It is kind of funny to hear different people give wildly different renditions of the same sound, though."

"So you're just guessing?" Jack asked.

"Yeah, usually," I admitted.

I was happy to share trade secrets if it made him feel better about his own abilities. Not that I could ever see him working on farm equipment, but there was no need to feel insecure when nobody knew what they were doing most of the time.

"Interesting," he said, stealing a glance in the direction of the other men.

I wondered if he was applying this newfound knowledge to them as well.

Honestly, he should.

The lunch bell reverberated through the yard. It was a real cowbell hung from a tree in the yard. Mrs. Ethel would go out to ring it when she was finished cooking and had the table all set and everything, and we would all come in to eat. Usually, by this time of day, it was getting too hot anyway. It was good to come in and cool off for a while.

"Lunch," I told Jack, pointing to the porch, "I bet she's made you a plate too."

"Oh," he said, following my lead.

Ethel always made good food. We never went hungry, and her meals made up for the pay not always being the best. What other job would feed a person homemade, homegrown food every single day? Sometimes she'd send us home with leftovers or cookies. I was grateful to her.

I needed to come can with her one of these weekends like we'd been talking about for a while. I just hadn't made the time yet. I was too chicken to try it on my own because I didn't want to get something wrong about the process and then get sick eating the results.

We walked into the house behind the guys, who were all taking off their caps as Earny stood near the table ready to say grace. I bowed my head respectfully as he did, and Jack did the same. Earny and Ethel were good Christian folk, which couldn't necessarily be said about everyone who claimed the title. I had a lot of respect for them.

As soon as "Amen" was uttered, there was a mad dash to sit in chairs. Ethel pulled in an extra one for Jack and put it next to mine at the table.

Ethel poured us each a glass of milk and SOME OF US passed the salt and pepper shakers and butter down in a polite manner. Not the boys, but some of us. Earny gave them a disapproving glance that tempered their enthusiasm for mischief, at least temporarily.

It almost felt like I'd brought Jack home for family Thanksgiving. These were the people that felt the most like family, honestly. I saw them pretty much every day, all day. Ethel and Earny definitely took care of me like I was family. The three bozos were the crazy brothers or cousins. A sense of peace and calm washed over me at the realization. My family had accepted this man. It didn't matter what the town would say or think after he left, Ethel and Earny would know he was a good man.

I gave a contented sigh as I ate, one that drew Jack's attention. I smiled at him, and he visibly relaxed. He ate so much more prim and proper than the rest of us. Ethel didn't let us put our elbows on the table, but otherwise, it wasn't exactly perfect table manners around here. The men would let out pretty large burps, especially if Ethel had excused herself to the bathroom or outside to get a fresh herb. Meanwhile, Jack was over here with proper fork and knife handling, eating reasonable bites, and not talking with his mouth full. Crazy.

Bubba, who was sitting next to Jack, decided to strike up a conversation. I suddenly felt very nervous.

"You ever been huntin'?" he asked. Jack fully chewed and swallowed his bite of green bean casserole before responding.

"No," he said, "but I think it would be a good bucket list item. I have been fishing though. Do you like fishing?"

Yes. Good. Make Bubba talk instead so he doesn't grill you for the next hour.

And it worked. Bubba started incessantly talking about all his fishing trips, complete with taking out his phone to show pictures and pantomime "It was this big" when he didn't have one of his hauls. It was honestly pretty fun to watch. And Jack seemed genuinely into it.

"How bad are the repairs going to be for your house, dear?" Ethel asked me.

I swallowed hard. I honestly had been trying not to think about it. Especially because I knew, even with insurance, that the roof repair was probably going to set me back quite a ways.

"Just the corner of the roof and the chicken coop," I told her. "The chickens are in a chicken tractor which... they aren't thrilled about, but they are safe."

She chuckled. She knew how my chickens were. So feisty and opinionated.

"Let me know if I can come help. I don't want you getting overwhelmed."

"Thank you, Ethel," I said politely, knowing full well I would not ask her for help.

She was already doing so much work, keeping this place running. Ethel was tough as nails and had seen so much in life. She wasn't really scared of anything. I think if the tornado had come this way, it would've been more scared of her than she was of it!

I wanted to ask for seconds, but I wasn't sure I wanted to do it in front of Jack. I remembered what he had said in the Co-op though, about the other girls he had known and how oddly they had focused on their diets. I decided that he would not judge me for getting seconds of Ethel's casserole.

I excused myself and walked to the stove, scooping another helping out of the ancient dish that surely was even older than Ethel herself. Her kitchen had a bunch of matching, grape-related paraphernalia. The side of the casserole dish had grapes and vines painted into it, she had fake grapes and vines hanging from her cabinetry, and the paintings on her fridge from her grandchildren were held up by grape refrigerator magnets.

My plate nearly slipped from my hand when I walked back in to find Jack arm wrestling with Bubba. Only my fantastic reflexes and will to live kept Ethel's fine china and savory meal from hitting the floor and shattering into a million tiny pieces.

Earny looked at me and winked. Jack hadn't noticed me step back into the room yet. He sat looking very focused, the veins along his face bulging. There was no way he would win this, but there was no denying he was putting in a valiant effort. Bubba probably had 100 pounds on him. I just hoped that he wouldn't break his arm. Of the three, Bubba would be the nicest to him. Applause broke out all around as Jack's arm flattened Bubba's to the table.

Bubba grunted in respect to Jack, who was sweating from his temples but grinning proudly. I gave him a thumbs up, then took a bite of the still-steaming hot casserole. I was contemplating all of my life choices, but really, this wasn't a choice. This was a man who had been thrust at me by the literal winds of fate. Who was I to argue with the winds of fate? Just a mere mortal.

Jack seemed to earn some serious brownie points after that little display. All the boys seemed to take to him more after that, and there was no more mean-spirited banter when we returned to our work outside. At least, no more than usual.

Chapter Forty

Jack

I couldn't believe that this was what Ally did for work. Despite her having to guess at the problems any given vehicle was having, she was tenacious and driven. She wasn't idle by any stretch of the imagination. I admired her resolve and fortitude.

My job was annoying and long hours, but at least it was air-conditioned and didn't involve getting cut in the hand as a hazard. Unless you counted paper cuts. Which, while annoying, were nothing compared to this.

But none of it phased her. She loved this. She was positively radiant as she popped out from under the tractor; her face covered in black marks from where she wiped the sweat from her brow. She had given me some tools to organize from a clasping case that had broken open in the back seat of one of the vehicles. I went scavenging for the pieces, then sat organizing all of them as she worked on the tractor.

Ally occasionally would pop out and say, "How's it going?"

Then she'd sit for a second to see the progress I'd made. Her tan skin and dark hair were glistening from perspiration, but she looked like something out of a beautiful painting. I couldn't take my eyes off her.

"Did you need help?" she asked, and I realized that I had zoned out and hadn't paid attention to a single word that she said.

"No, sorry, I've got it."

She smiled. I gulped. She knew I'd spaced.

The temperature started dropping outside. The air was easier to breathe and the stuffy feeling began dissipating. I looked over to find the sun dipping toward the horizon. I supposed Earny would probably be taking us home soon. I honestly couldn't wait to go home and get in bed.

Well, to Ally's house. It... it felt like home. It was more home than anywhere I had lived in a long time.

"Finished!" Ally declared, and for a second I didn't understand.

"Want to take it for a test spin?" She grinned proudly.

"Sur-sure," I stuttered. I was a little nervous about how ornery she looked.

"Come on!" she said. She bounded up to the stairs that led up to the door.

I watched her climb up, trying very hard not to stare at her butt. It was a nice butt. The kind that would be lovely to stare at. But now was not the time! We had important tractor things to do.

The door was significantly smaller than I had originally taken it for, and so was the actual cab of the tractor. A bag of sunflower seats sat on the floor, as did a cup filled with... something... I was scared to ask what.

Ally saw me staring at it and simply said, "That's a dip cup."

As though that explained everything.

I decided that whatever a dip cup was; I didn't want to touch it. I didn't recognize any of the controls on this thing. We might as well have been in a spaceship for all I knew. Maybe this was why aliens made crop circles, because they thought farmers were close enough technology-wise to them to understand each other.

Ally sat down on a seat that was being held together by duct tape and prayers, and I realized there was a smaller seat with foam visible in patches.

"You can sit in the bucket seat," she explained, "or we can share this seat."

She said it so matter-of-factly and without any flirtatiousness, but I couldn't see us both fitting on that seat unless one of us was in the other's lap. And I wasn't sure that she had thought that through, so I hesitantly sat down on the bucket seat. It made my butt hurt.

Ally messed with some things on the ceiling and off to the side on a panel. Whatever she did made the tractor lurch forward unexpectedly. I flew into the glass front window pane, my hands bracing me on impact.

"Sorry," she said, wincing, "it's not exactly a smooth ride."

"It's ok," I said. I straightened myself back out.

We escaped the barn in the tractor, which was impressive.

I had never driven anything this big, and I couldn't imagine the pressure to navigate it out of an enclosed space without hitting anything. But to Ally, it was all second nature. She navigated confidently, and the jostling didn't seem to surprise or bother her at all. We drove down the property toward a little pond along a flat path. It looped around the pond and back up. I flew into the side window as the tractor tilted, catching myself yet again.

"Seriously," Ally said, "you can sit with me. It's not a big deal. Here."

She moved over as much as she could, which wasn't much since the chair was fairly small, and motioned for me to sit next to her.

Would Bubba and the boys have my hide for cuddling up on their little girl? I didn't want any smoke with them. But she insisted, so I shimmied over and into the seat as best as I could.

I was essentially squatting, with a little support, and smooshed up against her at every dip in the road. Ally seemed quite pleased with herself, and I wondered if this had been her plan all along. Was she really that devious? That calculating? Her body accidentally bumping into mine was maddening.

I wanted to stop the tractor, turn to her, and pull her in to hold her for a while just so it wasn't a bump here, a bump there. I wanted to soak in her softness and her beautiful, muscular frame. Just for a minute.

Another jolt crashed us into each other again, and she giggled like a crazy person.

"Having fun?" I said, smirking at her.

I'd never met anyone like Ally, and I was quite certain I never would again.

"Yep," she said, proudly tipping her chin up, "lots."

Chapter Forty-One

Ally

J ack looked like a fish out of water in the tractor. I couldn't help but giggle as he looked around the cab and out of the window. I supposed if you'd never been in a tractor, it would be an interesting new experience. I decided to use it to my advantage. Anything could be a wingman if you were creative enough!

In the end, he didn't seem to mind the jostling. Forbidden romance always lent itself to creative ways to flirt. And it had worked. My whole body was unnaturally heated as he sat next to me. It was like I was a teenager sitting next to my first crush. But I leaned into it, literally and figuratively, and so did he. The sun faded into an orange and yellow on the horizon, with pinks and purples streaked across it.

Jack stared, mesmerized. The reflection splayed across his light-colored eyes. I hoped that when he was back in his big city with his fancy job, he would remember this. Remember that life could be like this. That peace was just a tractor ride away. Maybe he would come back to visit, I told myself. Maybe he would miss it. Miss the smell of dust and wheat, of chickens and homemade food, and all of the little places we had explored.

But more than anything, I hoped that he would miss me. It felt so scary to admit that to myself, but it was true. A solemness fell over me and I took in the weight of it all. I had truly fallen head over boots for this man. And while he flirted back, I didn't know if he felt the exact same way.

"Ally," he said, "are you ok?"

He must have noticed my change in demeanor.

"Yeah," I rasped.

"It's just getting late," I added, trying to walk back the way my voice had betrayed me. "I need to get you back home. All princesses need their beauty sleep."

"Oh no," he groaned. "Are you going to make me wear the pink robe again?"

His face was twisted with fake horror as he teased me.

I dished it right back, "Well, I can't very well have you sleeping in my bed in dirty clothes."

Sleeping in my bed. It all sounded so much more scandalous than it actually was, and I honestly felt like that made it more embarrassing. What I felt for him wasn't fly-by-night. It wasn't a hook-up situation. I genuinely wanted him.

He blanched. "I suppose I can survive one more night as a pretty, pretty princess."

"Perfect," I laughed. "Olivia will be happy to have company as the other princess in the house."

"Oh," he asked, "are you not one?"

I laughed, looking down at my dirty clothes. "Don't think so."

The lines on Jack's face deepened. "Why not?"

"Look at me," I reasoned. "I'm not princess material."

"You think that you're not princess material because you work hard and get dirty?" His voice was high with incredulity.

"Well, I can't think of any other princesses that look like me. Maybe Cinderella or something. I guess she gets dirty and does hard work, but she still wears dresses all the dang time."

I waved my hand around dismissively.

"Hmmm." He looked like he was deep in thought. "Maybe you're a new kind of princess."

I shot him a look with a raised eyebrow.

"Yeah," he said excitedly, "that's it. You're a prairie princess."

I wanted to tell him he was silly and being ridiculous. But honestly, I liked being called a princess. I just didn't want to admit it. To myself or out loud. And I liked the idea of a prairie princess. Of being able to be feminine and admirable, without having to change core pieces of myself. Without having to change who I was fundamentally to fit what was stereotypical. Was that possible? Was it too much to ask? Was it allowed?

"I like that," I said softly, pulling the tractor back into the barn at the end of the path. I turned the key and pulled it out, hyping myself up to get up and get out.

Jack smiled, standing and lending me a hand as he vacated my personal space, "I do too, princess."

Maybe tractor rides could be romantic, after all.

Chapter Forty-Two

Ally

E arny was waiting for us in the front porch light. The truck sat running with the A/C on full blast. In the summer, even the nights could be sweltering. Even though the relative temperature had come down, I appreciated the gesture. So did Jack.

"Wait!" Ethel bolted through the door, stopping us mid-step into the truck.

I turned just in time for her to shove something into my arms.

"I figured that man of yours might appreciate a change of clothes. My cooking has put a few too many pounds on Earny for him to wear these."

Her voice was not quiet, but she acted like she was whispering, nonetheless.

"Heard that," Earny said with a smile on his face. She tsked at him, telling him to drive us safely home.

"Thanks, Ethel," I said, squeezing her arm before we loaded up.

We'd not even made it a quarter mile down the road before Earny started yapping at a very tired, but always polite Jack.

"What'd you think of your first day on the farm, Sonny?" Earny asked.

"I learned a lot," Jack responded. "I have a lot of respect for the work. It's a different kind of hard than what I'm used to, but it's a nice change of pace."

"Glad to hear it, glad to hear it." Earny nodded, taking his chewing tobacco cup and spitting into it. I saw Jack's eyes widen in shock. I had to stifle a laugh that would've doubled me over if I let it. Jack quickly fixed his face before Earny saw.

Guess that cat was out of the bag. Jack looked a little green with the newfound knowledge of chewing tobacco cups, but thankfully we were only a few minutes from home.

"Thanks for coming to get us and taking us home, Earny," I said. "I think Wednesday will be the day I take Jack home. If my truck is fixed up by then, of course. I'll owe you a day this week."

"Don't worry bout it," Earny said, his voice seasoned with age. "We'll be sad to see you go, Sonny."

He looked over to Jack.

"If you ever decided you like it around here, we'd love to have you back. Even if just for a visit."

"Thank you, sir," Jack tipped his head to Earny.

Earny's headlights illuminated Olivia sitting on the porch as we pulled in. I could see her mouth opening and closing as she meowed. She was probably hungry. I spotted something else, too. Something white was taped on my front door. What could that be?

I thanked Earny again for the ride after we had piled out. Jack helped me down with my arm full of clothes. He was ever the gentleman.

We waved goodbye, then I made a beeline for the door. I unlocked it one-handed, flicked the porch light on through a cracked door, and yanked the envelope with tape on it off the door. I plopped it on top of the clothes pile as Olivia danced on my feet.

The note inside read:

"Here's that charger you asked for. Hopefully it's the right one. One of the kids helped us look through the extra ones people brought by today. It wasn't being used, so your guest can keep it if he needs to. Sorry about his truck, and I apologize for being short this morning. Hadn't had my coffee yet."

I laughed. At least she recognized she had been short with me. I pulled out the crimped phone charge. It had been tightly wound and kept together with a twisty tie.

"Does this look right?" I asked, handing it to Jack.

"I think so," he said as he took it.

He crossed through the entry to go find his dead phone on the bedside table, too prematurely for Olivia's liking. He didn't pay her entry fee, so she followed him in to stomp on his feet. Jack plugged the phone and charger in. We both stared at it, waiting to see if it would come to life.

After a few seconds, I decided I better get a move on bedtime. It would either work or it wouldn't and no amount of staring would change that.

Tomorrow was another full day of work. I hoped that maybe tomorrow would be the day harvest started and I could show Jack the inner workings of that. I set the clothes Ethel sent for him down and went to scrounge up some dinner for us both before bed.

"How do you feel about pasta?" I asked him, eyeing the contents of my cabinets.

"I love pasta," he said cheerfully.

Good.

Pasta was my holy grail around here. My "girl dinner" as the kids said. It would be easy to start the water boiling while I went and took my shower. Then I could finish babysitting some noodles and fry up some spam while Jack showered. I wondered if he had ever had fried spam, but I decided not to ask. I'd just let it be a surprise if not.

I took out my pot, ran some water in it, and flicked on the burner. The stove did its customary tick, tick sound as the gas flames ignited.

"Alright," I said, "I'm gonna go take a shower. I'll be quick."

I joined Jack over at the bed to look through my dresser drawers. How could I manage this discreetly? I barely opened them at all, sticking my hand through the small crack in the drawer. I couldn't risk him seeing inside and making fun of my cheetah print satin night sets.

"Ok," he said, looking distractedly at his phone.

"Did it work?" I asked, sneaking a peek at his phone. I was being snoopy.

"Yeah."

The screen boasted over 100 missed calls, texts, and emails.

I was starting to think that these people were a little too attached to Jack. I couldn't imagine going on vacation for a few days or even getting stranded and Earny blowing up my phone like that. He'd certainly come and get me if I was ever stranded, but these people didn't seem like the type to do that. It didn't seem like a family so much as a labor mill. You didn't matter except for being a cog in a machine. I hated that for Jack.

"Good luck," I said, excusing myself to the bathroom to take my shower.

I heard some distinctly male voices from the other side of the door, but I didn't think there was any way that they could be from an actual phone call. Maybe a voicemail that he was able to retrieve, though. I could sometimes go through voicemails in the house.

I turned on the water to drown out the sound so I couldn't eavesdrop. The steam filled the room. I inhaled deeply as hot water massaged away all of the tension from the day.

Chapter
Forty-Three

Jack

D ad had called me? I rarely got calls from him. And I had missed five calls from him in the time my phone had been dead.

A wave of dread crashed through my body as I thought of all the possibilities of why he would call that much. I didn't get to see my grandparents much, and I would be absolutely beside myself if they passed away while I was off galavanting in the countryside.

I saw a few voicemail notifications, so I started going through them. The transcriptions didn't seem to be working, maybe because of the poor cell service, so I had to listen. They were so quiet I had to plaster my ear to the phone to hear. Even then, I couldn't decipher what was being said.

I put it on speakerphone and hoped it wouldn't disturb Ally. The first two were of my boss, exasperatedly asking what day I thought I would be back. He sounded like a man going through the five stages of grief.

The third one was the office secretary asking if she could temporarily give my work to another person until I returned. She sounded apologetic, almost embarrassed about it. I made a mental note to shoot her an email in the morning to calm her down before I reached out to anyone else.

Then I got to my dad's voicemail.

I opened it with shaking hands, unsure of what to expect. He didn't call often, and it was never just to chat.

"Jack," he said in a stern voice, "I heard you've gone on a rather abrupt vacation under the excuse of recovering after an alleged tornado. I also heard you're not sure when you'll be back and that you took this time off without giving your work any notice. I am so disappointed in you. I raised you better than this, son. You need to honor your commitments. There will be time to relax when you retire. You should've gotten over yourself in the first place and gotten on the plane. We have a lot to talk about when you get back."

An angry click sounded when he hung up. My shoulders slumped.

All my life, it had felt like I would never measure up to what he wanted me to be. I wasn't allowed to be my own person, with my own hopes, dreams, and fears. I wasn't allowed, apparently, to decide what was too much for me and what I could handle. I was just supposed to go along to get along with whatever whims he or my corporate boss had. They might as well have been twins.

Yes, we would have to have a talk. But I wasn't sure it would go the way he wanted it to. I didn't want to live like this. I was a hard worker, and I was willing to learn new things and get my hands dirty. The fact that they were always casting my efforts in a negative light drove me crazy. I thought about it, and I wasn't sure my dad could even measure up to his own expectations. He might not take many vacations, but how often did he take Fridays off to go golfing with his buddies?

Just because he took his leisure time on a weekly basis rather than a yearly basis didn't make it any less hypocritical on his part. And my own boss was constantly leaving early. Some of the guys lived at the office, sure, but they had no interest in doing anything else. No hobbies. No life outside of work. They would never have a family, a wife, or children. I couldn't live at this pace forever. And I was finally coming to terms with that in a direct, undeniable way.

I switched over to my email app, which was well into the hundreds in terms of unopened emails. That... would be painful to deal with later.

Ally's cat, Olivia, must have sensed my growing agitation because she came over and started hugging my legs while purring. I bent down to pet her, setting my phone on the nightstand to charge more. I decided I would be turning it off overnight.

Getting a full night's sleep without being interrupted by a ping these past few nights had been amazing. Just because other people didn't have good work-life balance didn't mean I had to do the same.

Now that I had had a taste of freedom, I wasn't sure I could ever let it go.

Ally stepped out of the bathroom, jolting me from my thoughts. Her beautiful dark hair was piled into a towel, with a few ringlets escaping out from under it. She scurried over to the stove, tending to the boiling water that I hadn't even realized she'd left out here.

"Your turn," she said, casting a glance over her shoulder at me.

"Thanks," I said.

Perhaps a shower would help clear my head.

"I set the clothes Ethel sent home with us out for you. They're clean."

"Oh." That was so kind of Ethel and Ally.

I needed to write Ethel a personal thank you note for sparing me from another night of the fluffy pink robe. I wondered if Ally was disappointed not to see me in it again.

I stepped into the bathroom and found that Ally had left the clothes all folded on the side of the sink, with a fresh towel and mat for the floor. She was so thoughtful.

I could never repay her for everything she'd done for me on this trip. My world had been completely changed with every little attention to detail she showed in caring for me as a complete stranger, as well as the care that everyone around her showed for me. I thought that had made the biggest difference. That was what broke my ability to tolerate being disposable any longer.

Chapter
Forty-Four

Ally

J ack had seemed a little downtrodden when he stepped in the shower,
but I hoped introducing him to the fine dining cuisine of fried spam
would perk him right up. He would either love it or hate it. And honestly, I
wasn't sure which. The man was a bit of a wild card. I wasn't complaining,
though.

I took down my trusty frying pan and set it on the burner with a pat of butter. Then I cracked open a can of spam and started slicing. The pan sizzled as I carefully placed four pieces into it and watched as they curled ever so slightly on the ends. My mouth watered. This would hit the spot after the long day we'd had. I was thankful we'd had some vegetables in Ethel's lunch because I had no energy to prepare any tonight.

Olivia meowed irritatedly, and I realized I hadn't given her food yet.

"Sorry honey," I said, bending down to put some dry food in her bowl out of the plastic bin.

I had to be quick. If I didn't flip the spam, it would burn. I closed the bin and washed my hands, catching the spam just in time. Olivia munched her food. The way her nose scrunched when she ate crunchy things was so adorable and satisfying.

I plated the first round of spam and started a new one, wondering what tomorrow would hold. My heart ached that soon, Jack would be gone. His ghost would haunt my house, I just knew it. I'd never get over the phantom sounds of the shower running without me, or the steps outside the bathroom door, or the bulk of his frame in my bed.

I resolved to try to forget that he was leaving until Wednesday morning when we actually had to do something about it. There was no need to mourn something that wasn't over yet. Too many things in life were ruined that way, and I didn't want this to be one of them.

I heard the shower turn off as I was draining the water from the pasta. I hoped that he wasn't too much of a snob when it came to whether pasta was al dente or not because I did not throw food at my walls to figure it out. I wasn't fussy about the doneness of my pasta. Food was food, and if some of my experiments were unpalatable, they were opossum food.

Which reminded me, I hadn't seen Olivia's opossum friend she sometimes frolicked with in a while. I hoped he was doing ok, as long as he was leaving my chickens alone. It was a delicate balance sometimes, wishing the wildlife well as long as they stayed away from my chickens.

At least the deer hadn't gotten into my garden this year. Yet, anyway. Maybe the coyote pee had actually worked this time.

Jack stepped out of the bathroom.

"Almost done," I called.

"Sounds good," his voice was rumbly. It reminded me of the first night in the tornado shelter. I wondered if it was his overly tired voice. Whatever it was, I liked it.

I grabbed an unopened container of spaghetti sauce out of my pantry, deciding that was what I wanted on my noodles tonight. Sometimes I buttered them, but tonight I wanted something a little different. I realized I hadn't had my customary nightly routine since the night of the tornado. It was dangerous to change that routine, clearly...

I finished plating the food and shut off the burner. I turned to find Jack sitting at the kitchen table, his hair still damp. The flannel shirt that Ethel had given us fit him so well, not just in shape... it did something to me. I wasn't sure what. He looked like a different man. Maybe he acted like one, too.

"That looks so good," I blurted out.

My cheeks flushed. Why was my brain always betraying me?

"The new clothes, I mean."

Yeah, I'm sure that's what he thought I meant. That did not lessen the embarrassment one iota.

Somebody should've started digging a hole, because I was dead.

I sat a plate down in front of him, my face hot.

"Sorry, that stove is so warm sometimes."

I looked up; his grin told me he wasn't buying any of it. UGH. I wanted to throw something at him.

"Shut up," I said instead.

His shoulders shook from laughing so hard. "I didn't say anything, Ally."

"Yes you did." My words were punctuated. "You said it with your eyes!"

"Oh I see," he said with a laugh. "I didn't know you spoke the language of eyes."

I crossed my arms. "You just hush."

"What are my eyes saying now?" he asked.

He leaned in with his elbows on the table. Jack certainly had not broken out this lack of table manners at Ethel's table.

I looked up at his eyes, humoring him, and my stomach dropped. His expression was serious now. And his eyes were intense, searching and wanting something that I couldn't comprehend. Was it me? Was I the object of desire?

I gulped, reaching for my silverware.

"I don't know," I laughed dryly. "I think they've switched to Spanish."

His eyebrows shot up and twitched.

"Wow," he said, "I didn't know my eyes spoke Spanish. I gotta write that in my diary when I get home."

"You have a diary?" I said with surprise. I guessed I could see him having a diary, but I couldn't imagine what he actually wrote in it. And now I felt like I needed to know the answer more than I needed life itself.

He looked down at the food. "What's this?"

His tone wasn't trepidatious or rude. He seemed genuinely curious.

His table manners were out to play once again, with his elbows off the table and his fork and knife ready to go.

"It's fried Spam," I said.

I tried to sound nonchalant, not wanting to let on that I was waiting with bated breath to see if he would like it or not. I opened the jar of spaghetti sauce to keep myself busy instead of blowing my cover by making faces.

Jack took a bite of the spam. I couldn't detect what he thought one way or the other. And I was so focused on him that I poured a little too much spaghetti sauce down onto my noodles. It was now spaghetti sauce with spam and noodles rather than noodles and spam with spaghetti sauce. But that was ok, a little tomato never hurt anybody.

"I like it," he said at last. "What's it made of?"

"It's pork," I told him. "I'm glad you like it."

He nodded, taking another bite.

"May I?" he said, pointing to the pasta sauce. I passed it over to him, and he poured it much more carefully than I had.

Olivia had finished her kibbles and was now walking through the legs of the table and chairs, and rubbing up against us, begging for scraps. She would be sorely disappointed not to get any tonight.

Jack looked down at her, smiling. He was a sucker. Putty in her perfect little paws.

"Ready to do it all again tomorrow?" I asked him.

"Yeah, actually," he said. "Do you think there is more that I could help with? It wouldn't necessarily have to be outside. I'd just like to earn my keep for the meals Ethel is giving me and just be a help in general. Maybe I could help them with some paperwork or small building projects or something? They seem like such a nice old couple."

"I think they'd probably have something for you to do. Ethel has been getting overwhelmed lately with that sort of thing. And I'm sure her honey-do list is big enough for both you and Earny. We can take the wheat trucks out for test drives too, if the boys have them up and running tomorrow. We're so close to harvest, it's crazy!"

I appreciated that he wanted to give back the effort that Ethel and Earny were putting into him. I liked that he didn't just want to freeload on their good graces.

Soon my stomach was stuffed with pasta, and so was Jack's. I had to laugh when he asked for seconds of the spam. I gladly gave him some. I wondered if he would tell the people in his office about this delicacy he had tried here. Oh, to be a fly on the wall for a conversation like that.

I cleared the dishes before Jack could get up, so he grabbed the spaghetti sauce and stashed it in the fridge. I smiled. He was a sweetheart. As he walked away toward the bed, I became acutely aware of the fact that the jeans Ethel had given him happened to fit him like a glove.

"Stop staring!" I told myself.

But I couldn't help myself. I lingered a few more seconds on his cute butt before turning back to the dishes. I needed to bake that woman some thank you cookies or something.

He pulled the covers back, sliding into bed. He picked up my book, combing through the pages. My mind froze for a second.

"Hey," I said, nearly dropping the dish I was washing, "what do you think you're doing?"

His smile was ornery. It made my heart beat just a little faster. Was I going to have to wrestle it out of his hands? I mentally prepared myself to as he read the back.

"What's this about?" he asked, not at all innocently as he skimmed the synopsis.

"Girl stuff, now give it back!" I jumped on him and swiped it from his hands.

I froze as I realized I had one hand pressed to his chest, my book in the other. I was hovering above his face. His upper lip twitched. He was waiting to see what was going to happen next.

"It's a good book, huh?"

A great book, really, and if I didn't love it so much, I would've whacked him with it.

"Maybe," I said, slowly backing away.

"Cool," he said. "I need a new book to read. I'll have to get a copy when I get back home."

The blood drained from my face. I felt it oozing away.

"Don't you dare," I growled at him.

"I'm a grown man, Ally," he said, gently pushing me to the other side of the bed. "I can do what I want."

My jaw hung open. My brain scrambled. He could not read this book. I mean, he could, if I never saw him again...

"Fine, but then we would have to avoid seeing each other again for the rest of our lives."

He turned, propping his head up with his hand.

"Oh yeah? Must be a pretty interesting book," he taunted. "But I don't know. I think I'd like to see you again, so maybe I shouldn't risk it."

My heart skipped a beat. Not just at what he had said, or how he was reclining, but also at how his eyes dropped down to my lips.

I couldn't take this. I covered my face with my hands.

"You're leaving, remember?" I reminded him. Reminded myself. There was no way to make this work long-term. We lived in different worlds.

"Doesn't mean I can't come back and visit, right?" He flipped back over onto his back, staring up at the ceiling. "If you want me to, that is."

I did. I did want him to. So much. I felt myself sinking into this possibility. This was dangerous. If I wasn't careful, I was going to fall too far and not be able to get myself out.

"Yeah," my voice was barely above a whisper.

He gave a soft, side smile. Then he moved gently toward me and whispered, "I thought so. After all, I owe you a chicken coop."

Then his lips brushed my forehead. They were feather soft and warm. I melted.

There was a man, in my bed, kissing me. Never mind the fact that he slept a foot away from me and it was a forehead kiss. I was dizzy from the sensation.

I blinked in shock, too stunned to speak.

He looked back at me with his calm, confident demeanor.

"Goodnight, Ally."

"Goodnight," I breathed out.

Olivia stomped on both of us as she found her spot between us and curled into a ball, purring us both into dreamland.

Chapter
Forty-Five

Jack

That was quite possibly the best night of sleep I'd ever had. Made all the better by waking up to find Ally nuzzled into my arm. I didn't dare move. Olivia popped an eye open and seemed to understand the assignment, because she didn't move either. Ally's hair was a tangled, wavy mess. But her face was so peaceful. She almost looked like she was smiling in her sleep.

I couldn't believe that she had let me kiss her on the forehead last night. It was a risk, but one that was worth it.

I laid there, content. I wondered if I was delusional to consider a way to make this work. Would I get bored, living on the outskirts of a small town? Would I grow tired of not having a good internet connection or cell service?

What if this was just a temporary thing, and I'd hate it if it was my every day?

But my heart told me no, that wasn't true. I was drawn to this, to Ally, like a moth to a flame.

Ally shifted slightly, which was helpful because my arm was fully asleep. I was starting to wonder if I was going to have to have it amputated.

She groaned, her eyes opening to slits, and slid off my arm, muttering a half-asleep apology.

"You're ok," I assured her.

She rubbed her eyes, looking at the clock on the wall.

"Guess it's time to get up," she said, stumbling off to the bathroom in search of a hairbrush.

I seized the opportunity to put some leftovers on the table for breakfast. Her eyes got misty when she walked out and saw the spread on the table.

"Jack, I..." Her morning voice was a little hoarse. "Thank you."

"You're welcome," I said, beckoning her. "Come sit and eat."

She was oddly quiet this morning. Anxiety started eating away at me. Was she mad at me? Tired? Contemplative? I couldn't tell. Maybe she just needed some space.

She had spent days on end with a complete stranger without a break. Though maybe I shouldn't consider myself a complete stranger anymore. We'd spent more time together than any casual relationship I'd ever seen in my life.

I decided not to say anything. I didn't want to overwhelm her or make anything worse. If she wanted to talk, I'd be here.

We had a few bites left of breakfast when there was a knock at the door. I nearly jumped out of my chair, and Ally spooked too. I went to the door, unlocked it, and greeted our guest with a polite but tentative, "Hello?"

Earny beamed at me, "Hey kids, you ready?"

Ally groaned, "Yeah, sorry, I overslept."

"Don't worry about it Ally girl. I'm not in a rush. Today'll be a short day anyhow."

That would be nice.

Ally changed into work clothes as I talked with Earny, or rather he talked to me. She emerged, her hair tamed into a braid and her eyes a little less burdened. I smiled, and she smiled back, but it didn't quite touch her eyes.

The ride to work went much the same. Ally sat quietly, almost sullenly, as Earny explained the different breeds of wheat and what time you could plant them and harvest them. He also complained about a neighbor that flung rye across his fence. It seemed to be quite the feud. I had no idea there were such agricultural wars in the world. While it seemed annoying and perhaps stressful, it seemed much less high stakes than crossing someone in the corporate world.

The guys were waiting in the yard at Earny's place, tinkering on things. But now they outnumbered the projects since we were down to two of the harvest trucks with the bins on the back of them. I remembered Ally telling me about how they go down to dump the wheat kernels. I wished that I could stick around to see that.

"Ally, would you mind working on the downed fence today? I noticed it yesterday, and I'd like to get it taken care of before the cattle find it," Earny asked.

She grimaced.

"I know it ain't your favorite, but you're the most competent one to do it."

I stifled a laugh. I didn't have a hard time believing that.

"I got it," she said, taking off toward the barn and coming out with a bunch of things I didn't recognize.

"She's a moody one today, eh?" Earny said as we stood near the house.

I swallowed hard. "I don't know. She's been like that all morning."

He laughed. "Women are funny sometimes. You'll know soon enough what's stuck in her craw."

Her craw? What was that? Did I want to know? Maybe not...

"I hope so," I said, confiding some of my anxiety into my voice. Earny was a safe space, I knew.

"Come on in," he offered. "I'll get you some coffee. Might ought to give her some space."

I followed him down the cobbled path into the house.

"Oh, good morning, Jack!" Ethel said from the dining area.

She disappeared into the kitchen, returning with an extra coffee mug.

"Good morning," I said when she was in sight again, "thank you."

"Sure thing. Those clothes look like they were made for you. You like 'em?"

"I do," I said. "Thank you so much. These are much more comfortable than running around in business clothes."

She nodded. "I'm glad, Sonny."

She sat down and sipped on her coffee. She scrunched her nose, picking up an instrument that looked like a stick with a honeybee hive on the end. Ethel poured a little bit of the sticky substance into her coffee. She stirred, took another sip, and cleared her throat.

"That's better."

"Ally is in a bit of a tizzy today," Earny told her bluntly. I braced myself, unsure where this was going to lead.

"Oh, yeah?" she asked. "Whatever for?"

"Don't know," Earny said, taking a large swig of his jet black coffee in a mug with a chicken painted on it, "neither does he."

He hiked his thumb toward me.

"Uh oh." Ethel's eyebrows went up. "Didn't make her mad, did ya?"

She turned to me expectantly.

"No," I said, then qualified it, "not that I know of."

She hummed, taking another sip.

"Well," she said, "we'll probably know soon enough."

"You got something for him to do in here?" Earny asked. "Ally's out there fixin' fence, and I don't want her to clobber him out of frustration. Her fixin' fence is never pretty, but with her already moody, I think it'd be a disaster. Unless Jack wants to go help the boys..."

"Oh I think I've got some things for him," she said, saving me from a fate that may have been worse than fixing fence with Ally. I think without her around, those men would eat me alive, even with the little bit of rapport I had gained with them. Except maybe Bubba.

"Sounds good," Earny said, downing the dregs before he headed out the door.

"I'm pretty good at paperwork," I volunteered to Ethel.

"That's good, Sonny. I definitely have some of that to go over. They've made all of this tax stuff so complicated. I filed for an extension. I always do it myself, but I don't know what some of this new jargon means. I do have all my receipts, though."

She hopped up, heading down the hallway and returning with a basket packed with papers.

Ethel cleared the table, then started making stacks. Compared to the papers I saw at work on a daily basis, this was going to be a cakewalk. Might be a slower process since Ethel seemed like she could be a certified yapper. That was fine by me, though.

Once we got our piles more or less organized, it was time to dig in. Ethel told me about what receipts she had saved, all the papers that came in the mail, her itemized list, and all of the other miscellaneous papers she had kept.

"Do you have everything?" I asked.

This was manageable. But I felt like maybe it wasn't complete.

"I think so, but there is one paper I can't find."

She was right. She was missing a paper. And with as organized as she was, I couldn't imagine that she had misplaced it.

"Do you have an online account for anything?"

I double-checked the papers.

She frowned. "Let me look."

I wasn't sure that Mrs. Ethel could get around very easily on the internet, but I supposed I was about to find out.

She pulled out several notebooks, licking her finger and thumbing through with a pair of readers on the bridge of her nose.

"Here we are," she said, sticking a bony finger into the paper. "Follow me."

I dutifully obeyed.

We passed through the hallway with wooden cabinets that smelled distinctly like pine. I had to believe that they were homemade. In fact, I wondered if Earny had built the house, or at least built a lot of the things inside of the house.

He seemed handy enough to do something like that. I wondered if he would help me learn how to build a chicken coop for Ally, but then I remembered I was on borrowed time. Maybe if I was able to come back... but by then, Ally would probably already have it built. And I doubted my boss was going to be in the mood to approve time off after something like this. I wasn't sure he would've ever cottoned to it in the first place.

Ethel rounded a corner and opened the last door to the right in the hallway. In it sat an ancient computer, complete with a monitor and a tower. Was it still on dial-up? Were there any computers still on dial-up?

Was that thing going to start up at all? I grimaced. This might be harder than I thought.

At least dial-up might be more stable than the Wi-Fi and data out here, I told myself.

She took her notebook in hand and sat down in the computer chair. It sat on one of those clear plastic-y mats so it could roll, with the spikes on the bottom that no soul ever wanted to step on. Those were worse than Legos.

I watched as she pushed a large button, making the machine hum to life. As soon as the screen booted up, it prompted her for a login. She typed a few letters, looked down at her notebook, and repeated. This was a bit of a painful process to watch, but she didn't seem to be in any rush, so I wasn't either.

By the time she typed in the URL for the website, I was ready to jump in and take over. But then she had to put in another login and I thought I might be in my grave before we got what we needed. I wanted to make it go faster for her, but I didn't want to take away her autonomy, so I stopped myself.

"What's that say?" she said, squinting with her glasses on, then repeating the process with them off.

I leaned in. In microscopic font on the top of the screen, there was a place to download and print tax paperwork. How was an elderly person supposed to be able to read that? I could barely read that! I was sure they'd probably sent an email, but how frequently did Ethel and Earny check their email?

"That's where you can get the paper," I explained. "Do you have a printer?"

"Oh," she said, "yes, I do."

She went to bend down.

"Here, let me get it for you," I insisted.

"It's under there." She pointed.

It was nestled under the desk. I didn't want her to hit her head, so I bent down and pulled it out for her. There were about a million cords coming out of it. I found a wall outlet to plug it into, and then traced the other cords to the respective ports on the computer. Then I hoped for the best.

The screen popped up with a recognition message that it had connected to the printer. I took the mouse and clicked on the small text, then clicked download.

"Almost there," I said to Ethel, who was frowning in confusion at all this.

"They sure don't make it easy to do your taxes, do they?"

"No," I laughed, "they sure don't."

I plucked the paper off of the printer and we went back to the kitchen table to work in earnest.

Chapter Forty-Six

Jack

L unch came and went without Ally uttering a single word to anyone. Her smiles were fake, her eyes were tired, and her face was streaked with red dirt. Earny seemed to be more affected by it than Ethel was, but he didn't say anything. I could just tell in the way his face jumped further and further every time he looked over at her. I helped Ethel clean up the plates and put away the food. She'd made cheesy enchiladas for lunch, and while enchiladas couldn't possibly top her casserole, they were in fact a close second.

"You've got her head over heels, I think," Ethel said as she scrubbed away at a dish with her green dish gloves that reached her elbows.

"What?" I asked in surprise. Had she been stewing over this mess this whole time, silently working through it?

"Ally," she said, "I think that's why she's mad. She's smitten and she doesn't want to be."

"Oh," I said, a little confused. "Are you sure?"

She shot me a look that simply said, "Men," and continued with her explanation.

"I've known Ally since she was a little girl. She's never been smitten over a boy. Nobody was ever able to get her attention enough to make her stop and think... And she's so independent, ya know? I think you've really turned her world upside down."

"I think it was the tornado that did that. She's probably just tired of me being a house guest. How does the saying go? That they smell like fish after three days? Maybe I smell. Maybe that's why she's mad. She's ready for me to leave," I offered alternative explanations.

Ethel laughed. "No, Sonny. I don't think so. I think she's anything but ready for that."

I chewed my lip. Could that be true?

Chapter Forty-Seven

Ally

T he sun beat down on me, sweltering and uncomfortable. Could it be any hotter? Wait, never mind. Don't answer that. This was Oklahoma in June. Of course it could be. In fact, it would be very soon. I didn't want to think about that. Or this stupid fence.

I looked up, wiping sweat beads away from my eyes. I caught a glimpse of someone heading toward me. Earny? Uh oh. Was he coming to check up on my progress? Fixing fence was a huge undertaking. I hoped he wouldn't be disappointed with what I had gotten done. I set my tools down, waving at him as he closed in on me.

"That boy of yers is helpful," Earny said with admiration. "He figured out the missing piece of paperwork Ethel needed to finish our taxes."

"Oh?" I said, trying to keep my voice level. But I failed miserably, and I knew it.

"Not sure he's mine, but I'm glad he's being helpful."

Earny sighed, picking at a piece of long prairie grass and twiddling it in his hands.

He gave me the look. The look that said, "I know something is up. Why aren't you telling me what it is?" The grandfatherly look of "I've lived long enough to see everything. What makes you think I can't see through you?"

I hated it. Just let me stew. Just let me mourn.

More had happened this week than had happened in most of my life combined. Except for maybe losing my grandparents. And I was about to be handling it all mostly alone again.

The insurance lady had left a message on my phone earlier about getting the roof assessed and handled. They were going to give me a little money for the chicken coop, but not near what it was worth. And of course, a call letting me know I was in a disaster area and asking if I needed any assistance.

The problem was, no amount of phone calls or temporary help was going to fix the fact that I could handle it all on my own, but didn't want to anymore.

But I couldn't chain Jack to my cellar. I couldn't keep him here. It was better to let go now than spend another day attached. We couldn't keep growing at the hip with each other, just to say goodbye sometime tomorrow. This would make it a clean break, for both of us.

"I think he's the real deal, Ally," Earny said, throwing some of the grass to the side that he'd split down the middle. "I've never seen you like this."

I pouted. Arms drooping, face sullen. Like a toddler.

"I've never been like this before. I don't know what to do... There is nothing I can do. He's leavin' Earny!" My drawl came out.

"Maybe," Earny said, "for now. But I have a feeling we'll see that young man again someday."

"No! He's gonna forget about me, forget about us, the second he gets back to that job. They're gonna suck him in and not let him go ever again. He'll probably get with some hot blonde secretary and marry her and they'll have lots of babies. And I'll be here all by myself with the chickens and cat."

Hot, stupid tears ran down my cheeks. The nice thing about men like Earny is that they had aged like wine, mature enough to no longer be afraid of a woman's tears. He scooped me up in his arms, holding onto me like I was his own flesh and blood granddaughter.

"That boy is not going to forget about you Ally," he reassured me. "I promise you. Yes, he has obligations in his normal life, but he gets to choose if those are the obligations he wants for the rest of his life. Those decisions are not set in stone. Everyone is always one decision away from a different life, and he is no different. Neither are you, Ally."

I couldn't tell how much time had passed that he stood there, hanging onto me like my life depended on it. All I knew was that I appreciated it, because I felt like I was falling apart at the seams.

I looked up at him, blinking through salty tears. "You think so?"

"I know so, Ally girl," he said, "I know so."

Chapter
Forty-Eight

Jack

M y phone started ringing in my pocket.

"I'm so sorry, Ethel. Would you excuse me?"

She smiled sweetly, "Of course, Sonny. You can go out to the patio if you'd like some privacy."

"Thank you," I mouthed as I clicked the answer button on my phone and held it to my ear.

It was my dad. I owed him a call back, but I wasn't mentally ready for this. I didn't want him sending the cavalry to come get me, so it was best to appease him.

Ethel unlocked the patio door and slid it open. I stepped out into a room with an abundance of plants and a mosquito net door to the outside. There was quite a lush paradise out here.

"Hello?" I said. "Dad?"

"Oh, I'm here, just waiting for you to give an explanation for your behavior," he said sharply.

"I see," I said evenly.

I was not willing to play into his outrage. If he just said what he wanted to say, berated me however he wanted to, he'd eventually run out of steam and I'd hopefully be able to calm him down. I'd assure him that I wasn't leaving my good job with my good pay that he wanted for me so badly. Though it wasn't turning out for me the way it had turned out for him, and I was sure at this point that that was a good thing.

He raised his voice as he launched into a tirade, similar to what he had left on my voicemail. Even though he wasn't physically here, I could picture his face turning red and the veins in his head bulging as they always did when he yelled at me or Mom like this. The man needed blood pressure meds and some therapy; I was convinced.

I tried to at least somewhat listen in to what he was saying so I could allay some of his concerns when he was finished yelling. But I had to admit, my eyes were glazing over and I was mindlessly scanning the plants in the room.

"Are you even listening to me?" he shouted so loud my ear rang.

"Yes," I said, pulling the phone away from my ear. "You're mad that I got stuck in a tornado shelter with a farm girl for a couple days. But if a few unexpected days when I've never, ever gotten a break is going to cost me this job, then so would getting really sick from the flu and ending up in the hospital. I cannot control forces of nature or illnesses. It's a wonder that I haven't gotten super sick from the stress at this job, honestly."

He interjected about how he has worked even with the flu, at which point I promptly tuned him out again. I forgot the only acceptable absence from work was death in his eyes. What an awful way to live! Maybe if he hadn't worked on his and Mom's 25th anniversary, they'd be in a better place. Or all of our birthdays. And Christmas. I felt even worse for Mom now than I ever had.

"I'd rather do other things besides work before I die, Dad. I'd like to have at least one or two days a week that are actual rest days like everyone else gets at a normal job."

And again he launched into a tirade about how those people are poor. This was useless talking to him.

"What would make you happy?" I asked him point blank. Because honestly, I really wanted to know.

"If you'd just listen to me," he sputtered.

"I have been, and that hasn't worked, and I've been doing what you've asked, and that hasn't worked either. So it must be something else. Are you happy with your own life? With your own choices?"

"Why I!" he yelled. "How dare you talk to me this way? Kids these days are so disrespectful. I-I-"

He disconnected the line before I could respond further or hear more of his monologue.

Just as well. I needed to get back in and help Ethel.

I was sure I'd hit a nerve. I might have finally found the cause of all his miserable controlling of my life and future. He wasn't happy himself, so he was trying to take the reins on my life as a way to be fulfilled.

I hoped he'd think about that question long and hard. I didn't know if he'd be waiting for me when I got home, but I hoped not. I'd like a few days off from talking after that. His voice was still ringing in my ear when I stepped back inside.

Ally seemed to be in a better mood when we got ready to head home. I didn't know what accounted for it, but I was grateful. Earny seemed to have played some hand in it. He winked at me when I came out to load up in the truck. Ethel wrapped her leathered hands around mine.

"Thank you for the help, I'm so grateful to have that done. I couldn't have finished without you."

"No trouble at all," I told her. "It is hardly a fair trade for the food you made. It's delicious." I rubbed my belly for good measure.

"You flatter me." She covered her mouth with her hand to hide her smile.

The road home was yet again filled with Earny talking a million miles a minute. This time Ally was roped into all of the conversations. He told embarrassing childhood stories about her, which I was all too eager to hear.

"She was so gullible as a child. I gave her a cow tales candy, and when she took a bite of it, she asked what it was. So I told her cow tails. I've never seen a kid spit out somethin' s'fast."

Earny laughed as Ally's face flushed.

"It took three months of convincin' that it wasn't a real cow's tail and just the name. I wouldna told her that if I thought she was gonna take it that seriously."

"Awwww," I said, looking Ally right in the eye. For the first time today, she didn't look away.

"That's adorable. I'm sure she's recovered."

Ally glared at Earny, but it was playful.

If Ally ever got married, Earny needed to be the one at her wedding telling embarrassing stories. And I hoped I'd be there, one way or another. The thought sent a pang to my heart. I really did love this woman.

"Oh come on Ally, you don't want him to hear about you treating the duck like a doll? That thing hated everyone but her. He let her pet him endlessly, pick him up — or at least try to — and even put him in little hats and sweaters!"

Ally facepalmed in the middle seat. She really was a rough around the edges princess.

"How does Ethel take you anywhere?" she bemoaned, dragging her dirty hand through her equally dirty hair.

"Oh," Earny laughed. "She threatens to leave me at home all the time but I'll tell ya what, I think she likes my company. She'd be bored without me, ya know? She gets quiet and sad if I'm not pestering her. She likes it, she just won't admit it."

Earny and Ethel were quickly becoming goals. Not in the same way that work had been, not all-consuming or an exact replica of what they had. But I wanted to make it like they had. I wanted to be 40 or 50 years down the line, still loving and pestering the crap out of each other, you know?

"Well kids," Earny said, putting the truck in park all too soon, "here we are."

I felt my eyes sting. This might be the last time I saw Earny. At least, for a while.

"You take care of yourself, young man." He looked me in the eye in the dim glow of his overhead truck light. "You always have a seat at me and the Missus' table."

I choked on my own voice. "Thank you, sir."

Ally looked like it was only just now hitting her. She reverted to a bit of somberness that I fervently hoped wouldn't last the rest of the evening.

"You drive safe tomorrow, Ally. Let us know when y'all get there, when you head back, and when you get home. And don't stop at any sketchy gas stations, OK? Let Jack pump the gas on the way there. And make sure to double-check the air in your tires, and the oil, and the windshield wipers, and..."

"I will, Earny," Ally said, slowly closing the door. She looked equally like she was about to laugh and cry at all his advice and warnings. "I promise."

He smiled, waving us both goodbye as he pulled away and down the road.

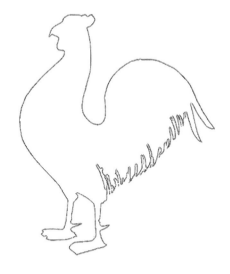

Chapter Forty-Nine

Ally

"I 'll be inside in a minute. You can go ahead and get a head start on a shower if you want," I told Jack, in a nicer tone than I had used with him all day.

I needed to make my rounds on the chickens. And cry. Mostly cry.

He nodded silently, stepping through the door with Olivia hot on his heels. He moved too fast to let her step on his feet, so I knew she was going to rectify the situation.

The chickens started carrying on when they heard their feed bag. Salty tracks ran down my face as I threw it in handfuls to them.

I wasn't ready for this to end. I was terrified of being alone again. And I was even more terrified of what I felt like I needed to do.

Tell Jack.

I didn't want to guilt him into staying. I never wanted anyone to be in my life because of guilt. I wanted him to be here, if he wanted to be, solely because he wanted to. I'd survived before alone, and I would do it again if I had to. I just didn't want to.

I wondered what people would say if Jack left and I became sullen. Would I have to deal with nasty rumors about how I couldn't keep a man that I hadn't even been looking for? I hoped not. I hoped that Mayabell would shut them down. She loved to gossip, but I think if she realized how badly I was hurting, she would make sure and do her best to protect me.

Turning to put the feed away, I saw something fly by in my peripheral vision.

I furrowed my brow. What was that?

Then I saw it.

"Jack!" I screamed.

My brain struggled to move. To think of what to do.

A coyote was coming up on the chicken tractor. He was hunched down low, teeth bared.

I wasn't sure if he could get into them, but I was still out here alone. I didn't want him anywhere near them, even if he couldn't find a way in.

I needed my shotgun.

But it was too late.

I heard a commotion in the house that startled the coyote.

The next thing I knew, Jack was barreling out the door.

I heard him before I saw him. Which was good, because I needed to have some time from one shock to the next to recover.

He ran up to me, throwing his arm around me with nothing but a towel wrapped around his waist.

"Ally, what is it?" His wide eyes searched mine.

The coyote took a tentative step back that caught his attention.

This man, in all his shirtless glory, charged at the coyote.

He yelled in a deep, frightening voice that made even me feel like I was in trouble. I wasn't sure I had ever seen a coyote more confused, but it ran nonetheless. It bounded over the fence. At a certain point, it became so scared that it stopped looking back to even try to understand what was chasing it and yelling.

Jack looked back after he was sure that the coyote was far, far away.

"Are you ok?" He jogged up to me.

I wanted to know how he had tied that towel on. I needed a tutorial, stat. That sucker was not budging. Impressive.

Not as impressive as his bare torso, though.

Adrenaline and grief were surely messing with my brain, I told myself.

When I forgot to answer, he wrapped his arms around me and pulled me straight into the aforementioned bare chest. His body still had water droplets clinging to it from the shower. He was warm. Any reservations I had about not sinking right into him were gone as I melted. Since he was already wet, maybe he wouldn't notice the tears sliding down my nose and onto him. I hoped, anyway. This was embarrassing, and that made me want to cry all the more.

In that moment, I was thankful that I didn't have close neighbors. I had enough privacy that I could harbor a half-naked man, or a man in a pink robe, in my yard with no one to witness it.

"Let's get you inside," he said, taking charge gently.

I tried to keep my face down as I walked in step with him. I was not able to dry my tears before he saw them as we stepped into the glowing porch light. He opened the creaky screen door for me, extending his hand in a gesture for me to go first.

"Ally, are you hurt?" he asked again.

I shook my head no. Because I knew he meant the coyote.

Jack took my hand in his, leading me away from the incidental water spots on the floor from where he'd made his mad dash. I was far too tired of fighting to pull away from it or deny that I wanted his hand holding mine. He brought me to the end of the bed and patted the spot right next to where he sat down.

"Let's talk," he said. "What's going on?"

I didn't feel like words could begin to describe the answer to that question. I had gotten a taste of not being alone. And not just not being alone, but not being alone with someone that was actually worth not being alone for. And now I couldn't imagine life without him, but that was the reality I was staring down. I didn't want him to leave. Even for a little while. I didn't want him to just visit occasionally. I was scared. Of a lot.

"I'm scared," I admitted.

That seemed like the easiest thing to say. The smallest. The least incriminating. Maybe he'd think I was talking about the coyote. Plausible deniability and all that.

"Well apparently I am scarier than a coyote, so I don't think you have to worry about that one anymore. He probably went home and told one of his friends about a deranged hairless bear that nearly ate him. Maybe they won't come around anymore, either."

I leaned into him as he pulled me closer, laughing softly. That sight, in hindsight anyway, was definitely going to be pretty funny.

"You are pretty scary," I said, nestling into his arm without looking at him.

It was so interesting listening to him talk while being able to feel the rumble in his chest and the beat of his heart. It was faster than it should have been, but he had just charged a coyote, so I decided not to be too worried about that.

"Am I?" he said, stroking my hair.

"Mhmmm." I nodded, still not looking at him.

"Why do I get the feeling we're not talking about the coyote?" he asked, trying to get a glimpse of my face. I tilted even more so he couldn't see the way my face was breaking trying to force me into tears again.

"Because we're not."

Chapter Fifty

Jack

I took her in my arms, wrapping her in a hug.

"I'm sorry, I didn't mean to scare you," I said, feeling terrible that I had scared her at all.

She took in a fragile breath.

I was confused.

"What scared you?" I asked, hoping she would take pity on my clueless self.

"Everything." she gestured vaguely. She looked up, taking a single, tiny peek at my face.

"That's very specific," I teased her. She choked as she laughed and cried at the same time.

"You scare me," she whispered, burrowing into my arm again. I was glad I had at least gotten most of my shower in before she was close enough to smell how sweaty I had been all day.

"What do you mean?" I asked. "Am I scaring you now? Should I stop?"

It was completely instinctual for me to wrap her up and hold her like this. My talk with Ethel had softened my heart even more toward Ally. I didn't want to hold back anymore from the fact that, despite only knowing her for a few days, I really loved her. I never thought I'd say this, but I was thankful for the tornado. Even with my truck gone. Even with the inconvenience. Even getting stuck in the shelter with claustrophobia and an army of chickens and Olivia.

This woman had my heart. She owned it.

"No," she blubbered through her sobs. My heart squeezed.

"I am scared you're gonna leave and then you won't come back, and you'll forget about me."

"I am not going to forget about you!" I exclaimed.

That was so ludicrous. Did she hear herself? Honestly!

She was overly tired, I thought. We probably ought to go to bed early tonight considering the trip in the morning. If I was honest, it was making me a touch emotional, too.

"And I will come back to see you, I just don't know when yet," I assured her. "But I know I simply cannot live without the Spam you cook. I'll crave that every day that I'm gone."

That elicited a laugh and a weak smile from her.

"My grandma always said a way to a man's heart was through his stomach. I didn't realize how true that is," she blurted out.

I smiled. "Well, believe it."

"I still don't want you to go."

"I don't want to go," I said, throwing all of my cards out on the table.

I wasn't tricking her. I wasn't stringing her along. I wanted her to know that. I was tired of keeping it in trying to protect myself. It had clearly done no good at all.

"Really?" she said, the raw hope clinging to her voice.

I brushed her hair back, looking directly into her dark eyes. They were so rich with emotion and depth. I could get lost without trying and maybe never come back up for air.

"Yes Ally, really."

She buried her face in me yet again. I heard a muffled, "Ok."

I stroked her hair with one hand and her arm with the other. She took some deep, clarifying breaths as the sobs that wracked her body slowed, then ultimately stopped.

I soon realized that she was nodding off to sleep, which was probably for the best. We had so much driving to do tomorrow. We were both going to be exhausted, but she was the one who had to make the trip there and back. Maybe I could arrange for someone to meet us sooner than my apartment so she wouldn't have to go so far.

As soon as she sounded like she was fully asleep, I moved so that she could lie all the way down. Then I pulled back the covers on her side of the bed and picked her up, placing her in her spot. But as soon as I pulled away, her eyes popped open.

"Stay with me," she said, her eyes glazed as though she might still be asleep. I frowned, looking at the wet spots on the floor that I really needed to clean up. I crawled into bed next to her, and she rolled over into me. She was so cute. My heart was in danger of exploding.

I waited until she was sleeping deeply and I quietly rolled away. I ninja-maneuvered onto the floor like in the videos I had seen people do with their newborns sleeping. I had to say, I was pretty good at it. I didn't even make a sound despite the floorboard's propensity to creak. I still hadn't figured out exactly which ones were the worst offenders.

I worked quickly to mop up the mess I'd made from bolting out of the shower, but I had barely finished when Ally called for me yet again. I stashed the wet towel into the laundry bin and got to my feet as she propped herself up looking for me and whimpered, "Don't leave me."

And that's how I found myself crawling back into bed in a towel, cuddling a softie of a tomboy all through the night. There were worse fates.

Chapter Fifty-One

Ally

I woke with a start. I didn't remember falling asleep. The sun was already shining diffused light coming through the curtain. What time was it? I shot up, then flattened myself against the headboard when I caught sight of Jack.

He lay on the other side of the bed, completely shirtless, with Olivia curled up at his back. I rubbed my eyes, trying to recall what had happened. How had we gotten here?

I suppressed a groan as images of the coyote, Jack running out in a towel, and me crying flooded into my mind. I dug my palms into my temples. Ugh, I was so stupid.

Then I realized today was Wednesday. He was leaving. I had to take him home now.

Banishing the quiver in my lip, I sucked in a breath. I had barely glanced at my phone yesterday, but I had caught that the mechanic had texted me that he was on track to be done with my truck.

I extricated myself from the bed, carefully sliding inch by inch down to the foot and gently standing up. I spared a look at Jack, his beautiful, peaceful face still smushed into my favorite pillow.

I stepped out to shoot a text, but then I saw my truck in the yard. Guess Adam had been right on time. My hope for one more day with Jack evaporated.

Walking up to it, I pulled open the door and snatched a note off of the dash.

"Good to go. I'll catch you at the Co-op for payment soon, no rush. Safe travels with Jack." The message was scrawled in slanted handwriting, smudged with motor oil.

It felt weird for him to use Jack's name, and it was even weirder that I sensed some kind of acceptance of him. Not that it mattered now, but something about it touched me and warmed my heart. I folded the note, tucking it away. I'd have to stash it in my pile of mementos for a scrapbook I had every intention of starting but never did.

I rounded to check on the chickens before heading back into the house. They seemed entirely unfazed and undisturbed from last night. Crazy critters didn't realize how badly that thing wanted them for dinner.

My bare feet padded along the grass, the morning dew clinging to them. The wooden stairs felt steadying as I climbed up them and opened the door.

Jack stood, still in his towel, trying to maneuver way too thick of slices of Spam on my frying pan. I laughed for a moment at the sight. Then I saw a pop of grease fly in his direction and sprung into action, pushing him by his pecs away from the stove and turning the heat down.

"Sorry," he grimaced, "I just wanted to surprise you."

"Color me surprised," I said, laughing, "but I can't have you scarring your beautiful body for the girls back home."

Oops. I hadn't meant to say that. I hadn't meant to think that, either.

His expression dropped.

"There are no girls back home."

"I highly doubt that."

I tried to grab the spatula from his hand, but he tugged it away. And his height made it so he could hold it out of reach from me infinitely.

"There are no girls back home that I am interested in," he clarified.

He could just be saying that.

But he wasn't. I sighed. This sucked.

"Well," I said, trying to move past my pouting remark, "you should probably put a shirt on or something. Though it should pop less with the heat down where it is now."

"Thanks," he said, grinning. But did he listen to me? No. He just took a defensive maneuver as he went to flip the Spam. I sat down at the table in the seat he normally took so I could watch his antics. It wasn't every day that I got breakfast and a show.

"What do you usually cook at home?" I asked as he brought plates over with the Spam on them. It was cooked unevenly, but I didn't care. I was just grateful for the effort.

He sat down, pulling his chair in and casting his light eyes up at me in a way that made it hard to breathe.

"I eat out usually, but I do like ramen noodles and hard-boiled eggs."

Oh. A true bachelor. I couldn't judge. If I lived closer to conveniences, I might eat out and eat ramen noodles regularly too. As it stood, my guilty pleasure was the Creamery.

"That sounds good," I said, digging into my meat.

"It is," he said, proudly taking a bite of his. "This is not as good as yours."

"It's your first time cooking Spam, and besides, have you ever even used a gas stove before?"

"No," he admitted, "it does seem a little less..."

"Consistent?" I offered. "Yeah, they are notorious for being a little uneven. You did good."

"Thanks," he beamed.

Olivia meowed incessantly under the table at us, and I didn't think much of it until she nibbled on my leg.

"OW! Liv, what the heck?"

I leaned under the table to look at her. She gave me a look that said, "Why are you so stupid?" Then she meowed again, forcefully.

She stared at me in judgment, then she walked over to her food bowl.

"Oops," I said, "sorry girl, I'll get you some breakfast too."

I turned to Jack. "She does not like to be left out."

He laughed, "I see that."

Jack was apparently a carnivore, or he just hadn't wanted to snoop through my pantry and fridge too much. But I was ok with that, we could stop for snacks as we went. We could even stop and eat at a real restaurant if he was up for that and we had the time. I didn't get out of the surrounding small towns often. This would be a treat for me. We could make the best of the time we had left together.

End things on a high note.

I scarfed down the rest of breakfast, wiped out the dishes, and left them soaking in the sink for later. Jack disappeared into the bathroom and came out changed into his now tattered office clothes that he had come in only days ago. They didn't look nearly as flattering on him as Earny's old clothes had. My heart ached a little. He looked so different now. His eyes were wild and free compared to what they had been. He'd been a prisoner in his own life. I hoped that he could carry the memory of freedom back home with him, even if it meant going back to a terrible job.

It was crazy that he was walking out of here with only the clothes on his back, what he'd come into the shelter with. And maybe some worsened claustrophobia.

Chapter Fifty-Two

Jack

C onsidering I'd only ever ridden with Ally in the driver's seat of a
tractor, and she'd intentionally made it a bumpy ride to try to force
me to be closer to her, I wasn't actually sure what kind of driver she was.
Which was why I was sweating a little getting on the road.

Her truck was immaculate, but I suspected that wasn't always the case.
At the very least, I would've predicted some dirt on the bottom. The
mechanic must've cleaned it out.

She'd packed a few granola bars, some trail mix, and beef jerky into a bag.
She'd even packed a case of water that she kept under her kitchen sink. The
woman was nothing if not prepared. She'd thrown it all into the small space
between the seats and the back window of the truck. There was a beautiful
engraving on it. It had cracks running through it and I didn't know if that
had been the case before the tornado or if it had come about as a result.
Still, it was beautiful craftsmanship.

Olivia purred at my leg as I stood on the front porch with Ally while she locked the door.

"I'll be home late, baby," Ally said to her.

It was hard to say goodbye to the sweet little cat that I'd grown so close to over the course of a few days. I wasn't sure I'd miss the chickens as much, but I definitely preferred the rooster over my alarm clock still.

All I had to take was my phone and the charger I had been given. It was weird to be returning home with less than what I'd come with. I was lighter in more ways than just that, and that was a blessing.

"Here we go," Ally said, leading me to the truck.

She'd worn a pair of jeans that seemed fancier than her work jeans. They were more flattering on her. She'd also put on a button-up blouse and pulled part of her hair back. Ally was beautiful. I wanted to see her in every outfit she owned. I wanted to see her on rainy days and sunny ones, every hour of the morning and the evening, every season under the sun. My feet wanted to cement themselves to the ground I stood on and never leave her land.

But I couldn't do that.

It was time to go.

Both of our doors slammed in unison as we climbed inside. The truck started smoothly, and soon enough, we were off down the road.

The neighbors on the way into town had made some progress on repairing their outbuildings that had been harmed by the tornado. A pang of guilt hit again as I remembered my promise to help with the chicken coop. I shoved it down. I'd deal with that later, when I was alone. I didn't want to bring the mood down.

We rolled down the Main Street of town, and I was surprised to find that the mechanic was out of his shop, waving us on our way. A few people were standing outside the Co-op, and as they saw us, they must've called for the others, because people began pouring out of the doors. A few men scowled at me, but most everyone, including Mayabell, waved us goodbye.

"I didn't know they were going to do that," Ally said, her voice choked.

"That was nice of them," I said, waving back and smiling. "I feel like royalty."

"Everybody dies famous in a small town," she laughed.

I was curious about where Ally would take us. I wanted to know, if I had been able to successfully keep driving that night, what road I would've stumbled upon. Would I have found the right way on my own? I knew they were silly what-ifs, but they raced through my mind, regardless.

Ally reached for the radio dial but quickly turned it down when the static was deafening.

She flipped to a country channel and left it there, a coy smile on her face. She remembered that I'd told her I liked country music and had to listen to it in secret. My heart swelled as I sat back and listened, lazily watching her as she drove. I looked out at the fields through the window occasionally, so she didn't feel like I was just staring at her. It seemed as though the wheat had really shot up in the time I had been here. It seemed taller in comparison to the fences.

Ally told me about each area that we came upon. We saw a speed limit sign that said 55, and she blurted, "This is a speed trap."

No sooner had she said that, another sign that said 45 popped up, and then another that said 35. They were in pretty quick succession. If a person had blinked, they would've missed it. And sure enough, at the top of a gentle hill sat a local sheriff.

And here I just thought she was a grandpa driver when it came to being on the road.

"Have they ever caught you before?" I asked as she passed the sheriff.

She gave a little smirk. "No."

"Is that because you don't speed?"

"It's because I don't let them catch me."

I laughed so hard it hurt.

"Are you telling me that little Miss Ally is a speed demon?" I teased.

"Only when the opportunity presents itself." She looked over at me and winked.

I shook my head. "There is so much I still don't know about you, Ally."

The aura of joy and denial dissipated. I hadn't meant to puncture it. I regretted it instantly.

"There is always more to know about a person," she threw out a platitude, trying to cover up the awkwardness.

"I suppose that's true."

We sat, saying nothing as the radio poured out tunes with banjos and harmonicas.

I tried to fill the awkwardness with something. I looked around and couldn't help but notice that people out here had about a million cows.

Well, that was maybe hyperbolic. But it was a lot. I decided to find out how many there actually were. I counted each one as we passed. Then I refined my system to not only count the cows, but also the type and color of the cows. I knew that the boys had horns. I wasn't a complete buffoon. Eventually, Ally would start a conversation, so I just kept counting and keeping a tally.

Was it any wonder I ended up in finance?

When Ally did finally break the silence, I had to stop her.

"Wait," I said, "I need to tell you something!"

"What?" she asked incredulously. "What is it?"

"We have passed 52 black cows, 20 red cows, and 13 spotted cows."

She rolled her eyes so hard I could've sworn they'd gone to a different continent. "Oh really?"

"Yes, really," I said enthusiastically.

"Did you actually count all the cows we've passed so far?" Ally asked. She sounded hesitantly impressed.

"Yeah," I said, giving her a side eye, "I wouldn't make up something this important."

Ally laughed, with a snort mixed in there.

"Were you the kind of kid that tracked how many license plates from each state you saw on road trips?" she asked.

"No, we always flew. I've only done road trips as an adult."

"Seriously?" she looked at me fully, making me a little nervous. I needed her to watch the road.

"Yep."

Her face scrunched in confusion. "Where did you even go for vacation? Out of the country?"

"Only once or twice. My dad did well, but he didn't make that much. We usually went to Florida or California to resorts or theme parks."

"Wow," she said, her eyebrows knitting together, "so you've seen the ocean?"

"Yeah, hasn't everyone?" I said, not thinking.

"I haven't."

At first, I thought she was joking. But then her expression remained unchanged. She looked at me briefly, giving a half smile.

"You're missing out," I said. "It's amazing. The water isn't green or muddy or red, and you can surf, and..."

"Maybe someday," Ally said wistfully.

"I'll take you."

The words were out of my mouth before I could consider it. I was already picturing her on the beach in a little frilly grandma-like cobalt blue and white two-piece, her hair in two braids down her back, and her farmer's tan out on full display. I had to make this a reality.

"Really?" she said, and there was true hope in her voice. Her pessimism about me actually coming back was either waning, or she was giving into what she must think was delusion for the time being.

"I promise," I said, extending my pinky to her, which she briefly hooked with her own before planting her hand right back on the wheel.

Her expression turned into an easy smile. I would make good on this. I had to.

Chapter Fifty-Three

Ally

"We're almost out of gas," I said, thinking about Earny's warning to us. I didn't want to get stuck at a janky gas station, and I doubted that Jack wanted to either. "Can you help me look for an exit?"

"Sure," Jack said, sitting up attentively.

He had been in and out of dosing off as we were driving. I couldn't blame him. Several hour-long road trips were hard and often boring. We both had a limit, it turned out, with talking. But we were good to sit in silence together and that was as valuable as being good conversationalists in my eyes.

We were set to hit the state line in an hour or less, so this was a good time to get out and stretch our legs. I was getting weird cramps in my muscles and just generally restless.

"Looks like we've got one coming up on our right in a mile," he told me as he consulted the GPS.

Perfect.

The traffic to our left was zooming. They had to be going 80mph. But the traffic on the right wasn't much better. I had to go a little faster in my little farm truck than I would have liked to because of how aggressive and fast Oklahoma drivers were outside of the small towns. They acted like this was the autobahn. But at the same time, you had to admire the teamwork. They believed that if we all went 80mph, the cops wouldn't be able to get everyone. Just don't hang out at the back of the line and you'd be fine.

I shook my head, smirking. I wondered if Texas traffic was this crazy. I knew Oklahoma City could get pretty wild; we'd had a close call there just earlier today. But I didn't know if Texas metros would be better or worse. I hoped better, otherwise I might make Jack drive so long as he promised not to kill my truck.

I eased us off the exit, relieved to see the gas station. It looked well-inhabited and kept up, with lots of working pumps. The hard part was going to be going back home by myself. I'd need to make sure I stopped before dark and found a place like this to do it at. Hopefully, if I filled up at roughly the halfway point, I would be able to make it all the way home without having to stop again.

I parked at a pump. Jack jumped out, then came around to open my door. He was so sweet.

"Why don't you go use the bathroom? I'll take care of this. And here," he said, handing me a twenty-dollar bill, "would you get us both some ICEEs?"

"Thank you," I said, feeling awkward. But he was already gone, messing with the buttons on the pump.

I ran inside, not wanting to be here too long. I wanted him to get home at a decent time today and get some rest for the crapstorm he'd be walking back into tomorrow.

I did my business, then went over to the ICEE machine. I wished I had asked him what flavor he wanted. There were so many options! I decided to make one cherry and peach, and the other blue raspberry and coconut. I'd take whichever one he didn't want. The cups made my hands cold, so I set them down, then grabbed a few napkins to pick them back up. There were a few people in front of me either paying for their gas at the pumps or paying for assorted snacks from the aisles. I slipped the twenty onto the counter when it was my turn.

The bored attendant popped their gum. "You want a receipt?"

"Sure," I said.

Jack seemed like the type to keep receipts. I pocketed the change and the receipt and went back out to join him. My heart dropped when I didn't see him in the car or at the pump. I spun around, looking in each direction for him. Had he slipped in to use the bathroom behind me and I just missed it?

But then I saw him on the grass next to the gas station sign, stretching his legs. I checked my truck doors to make sure they were locked before I joined him. It felt nice to take unbridled strides after being cooped up.

"This one is cherry and peach and this one is blue raspberry and coconut." I offered up both the ICEEs.

"Oh, thank you! I love blue raspberry." He took that one, and I forked over the change and receipt once my hand was free.

I took a sip of mine, then my entire face twitched.

He laughed, "Brain freeze?"

"Yeah," I gasped.

"Sorry," he said, "I hate those."

His tongue was now stained with blue. I snuck a peek as he talked.

"You look like you ate a Smurf," I teased.

"The price we pay for deliciousness." He winked.

After a few more minutes of stretching, we hopped back in the truck and took off south again.

"Once we get close to Houston, I can take over," he said. "It gets kind of crazy. Though thankfully we'll be beating rush hour traffic. It would take us hours to get anywhere if we hit that."

"I bet I can handle it. I mean, I can handle the tractor," I insisted, but his expression said that he was not persuaded.

"How bad can it be?" I asked.

Chapter Fifty-Four

Jack

S he jinxed it. She asked how bad Texas traffic could be and now we were almost getting blown off the road by people passing us.

I knew I should've insisted on trading her places, but I didn't want to be pushy. She had out-of-state tags, so I'd foolishly hoped people would give us a break.

Now it was too late to trade off. We were doing trial by fire down a five-lane highway. We were about another hour out from my apartment. I couldn't believe how fast the trip had flown by. It wasn't fair. I wasn't ready to say goodbye.

My mind had been working through the logistics of how I was going to take her to California and how I was going to get back to visit.

A lifted truck flew by us, flipping us off as they passed.

I rolled my eyes. "People here have anger issues, just ignore them. You're doing great."

She looked like she wanted to shake but was holding it together nicely. If I hadn't spent a few years driving in this, I would be absolutely terrified. You just get used to it after a while.

"Once we get off the highway, it'll calm down a lot."

"There are more signs and messages jammed into one overhead highway rail than I've ever seen in my whole life. I can't believe people read all of them before they whiz by."

"Well, the thing is, they don't."

"Seems like your job isn't the only thing that's a little unreasonable around here," she scoffed.

Her knuckles were white on the wheel. I felt so bad.

She'd flipped off the music the second we got into the city proper. We'd found a lot more radio stations when we crossed the border into Texas. Ally and I had been taking turns introducing each other to the types of music we liked outside of country. As it turned out, we both had diverse musical tastes. Which was good, because I liked to change things up sometimes and I didn't want to have to hide my music again.

Miles passed in the blink of an eye at the speed we were going. Ally was right. The pace around here, in every aspect of life, was insane. Some people liked that, though. Some people were adrenaline junkies for bright lights and fast cars, risks and excitement. It just wasn't my kind of excitement, I'd learned. I wondered what brought my family here. I'd always figured it was probably dad's job. I knew from experience that the more in the metro you lived, the better the pay. It helped to keep up with the cost of living.

Every sign we passed that I recognized was one step closer to home. My chest ached. My palms were sweaty and my stomach continued to drop further than I'd ever felt before.

"Your exit is coming up in about five miles," I said.

We'd have about twenty minutes once we took that before we would reach my place. Had I cleaned it before I left? I'd lived through so much since then, I really didn't remember. I wasn't a slob, but I wasn't a neat freak either. And my place certainly wasn't decorated like Ally's was. I wasn't even allowed to hang pictures in my apartment. I wasn't a frat boy, I owned a bed frame, but I still was nervous. Would she come up with me to say goodbye, or would she drop me off and leave? New anxieties shot past the front of my mind.

"Are you ok?" she asked, looking toward me with down-turned lips.

"Yeah," I said, "just... "

She patiently awaited my next words, but I struggled to find them. I couldn't truthfully say I was tired.

"Anxious, I guess," I said, and maybe that was the closest thing to the truth.

"Oh, come on, my driving is not that bad," she said with fake offense.

"I don't know," I teased, leaning into it, "I think everyone that's passed us would say it is."

"Well, that's because they are wannabe NASCAR drivers. This is a highway, not a racetrack."

"Texas drivers don't know the difference," I reminded her.

She flipped on the turn signal. "This is it, right?"

"Yep," I sighed, "this is it."

The suburban streets and side roads were remarkably less busy in comparison to the highway.

Ally's shoulders came down from where they were glued to her ears from the stress.

The next thing I knew, she was throwing her truck in park in the space that was reserved for my truck. My now nonexistent truck.

"Oh," she blurted out, "I need to text Earny that we made it."

She pulled out her phone and furiously typed.

"It's crazy that things immediately send around here."

"Being close to cell phone towers and civilization helps with that," I joked.

"Hey um," she bit her lip as I pulled out my charger and phone from the port in her truck, "we never did..."

She gestured back and forth between our phones.

I tilted my head, questioning silently. I didn't understand.

"I don't have your number," she looked down, embarrassed. Color rose across her neck and climbed up her face.

"Oh." OH. I was so stupid.

"Of course, here, I'll put it in." I took her phone and typed in all of my information. That would've been crazy to have lost touch with her over that. There was no way I'd ever be able to find my way back to her house, even on accident.

"Thanks," she said, coyly tucking a piece of hair behind her ear.

"Thank you, Ally."

I desperately wanted her to look up so I could look into her eyes. A fervor clung to me as the realness of the situation set in. She was about to leave, and I didn't know when I would see her next. The last few days were gone and I couldn't get them back.

"I'd offer to carry your stuff up with you, but I guess there isn't anything to carry." She looked down. "I'm sorry."

I hopped out, walking around to her side to open the door.

"It's ok," I assured her, "things can be replaced, including the truck. But the time with you was priceless."

She looked bashfully up at me.

I walked up the flight of stairs with her following right behind me. My keys rattled as I fished them out of my pocket. I liked the pockets of Earny's old jeans better, they were more spacious. I missed them.

I fiddled with the lock.

"I have to get on the road again, so I'm not driving too much after dark."

I cracked the door open and turned to Ally.

"Ok," I said. I felt my heart shattering into a million tiny pieces onto the concrete below us.

"I'm going to miss you, Jack," she choked up.

She couldn't choke up. I would choke up. Then we would both be crying.

"I'm going to miss you, too, Ally," I said, wrapping my arms around her.

She grabbed me way harder than I was expecting her to. I made a funny noise, which prompted her to grab on even tighter. I hugged her back, taking in the smell of her, the texture of her hair, the softness of her skin.

I pulled away, tipping her head up to mine.

"Can I kiss you, Ally?" I asked, my stomach taking a nosedive.

She nodded, her eyes wide. I tipped my jaw down to meet hers in a gentle, warm embrace that lit a fire in my soul. Time stopped. Nothing mattered in this moment but us.

Chapter Fifty-Five

Ally

It was hard to cry and drive, but I didn't exactly have a choice. Leaving Jack back in Texas was the hardest thing I had ever done. I hadn't wanted to drive hours and hours home by myself. All that was waiting for me was an empty house. No offense to Olivia, of course. She was great company, but this was different. I had finally been able to sleep well, knowing I wasn't all alone out in the country by myself. I had help and companionship.

Now that was gone.

I tried to get my GPS to take me down some backroads out of Texas, but that did not turn out as well as I had hoped. I did seem to miss the worst of rush hour traffic, just like Jack had said, but Texas drivers were truly something else at any hour of the day.

My chest felt tight when I crossed back over into Oklahoma. Every mile away from him was another slice to my heart.

I turned up the radio, trying to drown out the sound of my own thoughts. They were moving faster than I could bear.

The only thing that shook me out of my fatigue and emotion-induced dissociation was the little red gas icon turning on in my truck.

I was thankful that it came on while it was still light out, because I'd completely forgotten about getting gas. I scoped out the nearest exit and found the cleanest gas station I could find. After I situated the gas pump, I got back in my truck and locked the door. My teeth hurt as I ripped open a packet of trail mix with them. I pulled my phone off the charger and dumped some trail mix in my mouth. I needed to let Earny know where I was and how long it would be until I got home.

I furiously typed away, smashing the send button before downing some more trail mix. I could've choked eating it that way, but at the moment, I really didn't care.

The GPS said two more hours. I was on the home stretch now.

I supposed it was time to get back to what I knew as real life. I needed to get the insurance adjuster out to look at the roof, and I needed to focus on harvest coming up, and then Friday... Oh no.

I popped out of the truck when the clicking sound came from the gas pump, then snatched my receipt and jumped back in, immediately locking the door again.

My white knuckle grip on the wheel persisted as I pulled out and got back on the highway.

The dance was Friday. I was going to have to deal with the moody cowboy again, and this time, Jack wasn't around. Was he going to be retaliatory? I knew how men were, especially men who weren't well... civilized. I could imagine him being pretty upset. I wasn't looking forward to it. Maybe I would just stay home on Friday night. The whole town would notice, but I could always say that I'd come down with something. It was believable after all of the stress.

I didn't want to dance with anyone there, anyway. All I wanted was Jack.

Chapter Fifty-Six

Jack

My footsteps echoed through the empty apartment, white walls surrounding me. It was so sterile and empty. Now that I had spent days living in a home with a woman's touch, the apartment felt like a prison. It was bigger than her house, but somehow less like a home.

I hated it.

My arms ached to hold Ally for just a few seconds longer. But I knew she'd had to go. I couldn't live with myself if she ended up getting hurt in Texas rush hour traffic, or stranded. At least she had my number, not that her cell phone would work at her house. It wasn't exactly like having direct access, but it was better than trying to mail letters or something.

I opened my fridge, staring blankly into it. My stomach squeezed. I didn't really want to eat. I didn't know what I wanted, except for her. No food could fix the gaping hole in my life. I grabbed the orange juice and poured a glass, sitting hollow-eyed on the island high top chair.

Work in the morning was going to be brutal. I doubted I would be able to get any work done. I'd probably be swarmed with coworkers asking about the whole situation with me being gone.

I wasn't looking forward to it.

Chapter
Fifty-Seven

Ally

O livia trotted right up to the truck, meowing excitedly. But when she peered in to find Jack wasn't there, she started wailing.

"You and me both, girl. You and me both."

I scooped her up, along with the remaining snacks, and shoved the truck door closed with my hip. My legs felt like jello. I could barely stand. I couldn't feel my butt for at least the last fifty miles.

I didn't want to go on another road trip anytime soon. That was brutal. At least, the second half when I was alone. The first half being entertained by Jack was great.

I put Olivia down so I could unlock the door; the chickens clucking in the background. I needed to feed them.

Olivia stomped on my feet, a little gentler than usual. Then she padded in, her fluffy tail held high.

"Be right back," I told her, dropping the snacks on the counter.

I peered around the house to check for coyotes. Nothing.

The chickens clucked and carried on as I threw the food into the chicken tractor. I really needed to get started on a coop. I might need to dip into savings or take out a small farming loan to get everything around here back in shape after the storm.

A light emitted from my pocket. I fished out my phone, blinking at the bright light. It reminded me that I needed to text Earny that I was home before he sent a search party.

"Miss you already."

My breath caught. It was Jack.

There was a picture attachment that must've loaded while I was still on the road. It was the sunset from the balcony of his apartment. Dramatic hues of orange, red, and yellow slashed across the sky in jagged marks.

"I miss you too." I typed, then deleted it all.

"I'm home." I typed again, then deleted that too.

"That's beautiful!" My fingers made satisfying clicking sounds as I pushed each key on my phone. "I miss you, too. I made it home. Olivia is UPSET that I came home without you."

I walked over to the fence, hoisting my phone in the sky and begging it to send. The little checkmark popped up, thankfully, and I headed back into the house.

I washed the dishes from this morning, then dug around in my PJ drawer for something to wear. My own laundry had really piled up over the last few days, but I hadn't wanted to wash it with a man in the house. I went over to start a load and found the clothes that Ethel had given Jack on the top of the pile. I pulled them out, sniffing them like a deranged weirdo.

They smelled like Jack.

Tears threatened to form at the corners of my eyes. I decided that tonight I was going to be pathetic. I wasn't going to wash these. I took the shirt and found some tattered shorts in my junky clothes drawer, throwing them on as pajamas.

Olivia laid right on top of me when I reclined in the bed. I didn't pick up my book to read. I just stared at the ceiling fan blades spinning until I passed out.

And all my dreams were filled with black, swirling masses heading straight for my house.

Chapter Fifty-Eight

Jack

I was thankful I'd had a quiet Uber ride to work. Now that I was alone, I realized just how close of a call that tornado had been. The adrenaline and company had kept me from processing the experience. I found that I was not doing as well with it as I thought I was. It didn't really occur to me until raindrops were falling on my window when I got to my desk. I flinched as flashes of the rain on the windshield of my truck that night came back to me.

"Are you ok?" Rachel asked.

"Yeah, sorry," I told her, "just a little tired."

She nodded, taking me at face value.

I sat down, booting up my computer. I could already imagine the endless emails I had waiting for me. All the lines and charts and numbers I had ahead of me today. Then I noticed the thick stack of papers sitting on my desk.

I groaned. All the policies and procedures I was supposed to have read.

My boss came stomping in, beckoning me to his office. I followed him around cubicles filled with people who looked as thrilled to be there as I did. How had I never noticed that many of them were also just mindless zombies clocking in and out, too? The gray carpet and beige decor really didn't do much for the spirit either.

"Sit," he commanded, pointing to the chair across from his desk.

I did as he asked, keeping my expression blank and pliable. I didn't have the energy to be berated.

He looked angry at first glance, but something must have changed his mind because he softened a little.

"Jack?" he addressed me.

"Yes, sir," I said, like a dutiful soldier responding to a commanding officer.

"Son, you look awful. Are you ok?"

I sat back, mentally calculating. Did I really look that bad? I had made sure I didn't forget to comb my hair this morning. I'd set out a good set of dress clothes the night before, so I wouldn't have to worry about it this morning. I'd forced myself to choke down a passable breakfast. I even took a shower, which I had to say was not as luxurious of an experience without Ally's fluffy pink bathrobe.

"I'm fine," I lied.

He narrowed his eyes at me, tilting his head to the side.

"Take a break if you need to today. You do have a lot of work ahead of you, but you can always work on Saturday and Sunday to catch up."

Ah yes. The compassion only extended so far. Like he wasn't already going to have me working Saturday and Sunday in some capacity already.

"Thanks, I'll keep that in mind," I said, rising as I looked at him to be dismissed.

He waved his hand, slipping back into his normal robotic persona.

I was not looking forward to lunch. If the two people who had seen me today so far had decided that I didn't look good, there would be a never-ending stream of "Are you ok?" at the buffet table.

Sitting at my desk was a difficult task. The mind-numbing work in front of me wasn't so much the problem as the rain pelting the glass behind me was. Every little sound brought back another scene from that night. Either of the dark, stormy road ahead, the sounds and lantern light from inside the shelter, or Ally's restless face as she slept.

Maybe I hadn't slept well last night. I did recall waking up a few times, tossing and turning. I had gotten so used to Ally being right there. To being able to wake up and see her beautiful face any time, and going back to sleep peacefully. I'd even grown accustomed to Olivia using me as a mini trampoline during the night.

It was just going to take some adjusting; I told myself. I had been through a major natural disaster.

Which reminded me... I needed to email my insurance lady and see what the next steps were. Somebody either needed to go check my truck remains at Ally's house or use the pictures I had taken to file a claim. My fingers flew over the keys as I composed the email. At least I looked like I was being productive. I pressed send and checked my phone. I wanted to text Ally so badly, but I didn't want to bother her or be too clingy. I told myself I needed to wait, even though I really, really didn't want to.

Chapter Fifty-Nine

Ally

"**A**re you ok, sweetheart?" Ethel patted my shoulder.

"Huh?" I sucked in air. "What?"

I'd been lost in thought, though I couldn't remember what I had been thinking of. Behind my eyes throbbed from lack of sleep.

"Are you ok?" she asked again, and this time, all the guys were looking at me now, too.

"I'm fine." I touched the top of her hand. "Just tired. Long drive, ya know?"

Earny frowned in disbelief.

"You've not touched your food," Ethel prodded, "and I made your favorite."

Three perfectly crafted deviled eggs sat on my plate. Ethel had made sure to save me some before the boys devoured them all. I'd been in my own little world in the yard, engrossed in my own thoughts until I realized I didn't hear anyone out in the yard. When I noticed, I'd hightailed it into the house for a late lunch. But I hadn't eaten anything at all. I'd spent the whole time pushing things around with my fork.

"I'm sorry," I said, picking up an egg and forcing myself to smile. "These are wonderful. Thank you so much!"

But the food tasted like sand in my mouth. Even though I knew it really didn't. I didn't know why. I wished I could taste the deliciousness that was Ethel's deviled eggs. Maybe I could put these in the fridge and take them home for dinner tonight or breakfast tomorrow.

I returned to mending fence down the way. The boys' talking made my head throb. My irritation mounted as I struggled to concentrate. I brought the mallet right down on my own thumb.

Red colored my vision as I danced around hooting and hollering and saying things my mama would've washed my mouth out with soap for. And when I had blinked away the tears, there stood Earny.

"I talked to Ethel," he said matter-of-factly, "she said you can sleep in the guest room for a few days if you need, after everything."

"Oh," I said, unsure of what to say. I appreciated the offer, but did they think I needed to be watched?

He took my hand in his, inspecting my thumb. His wrinkles creased.

"What's going on, Ally? Is this about Jack?"

"No," At least I didn't think so. I did miss him terribly. Maybe it was.

"Is it about the tornado?" he asked.

"Maybe it's both," I said. "It feels like they're inseparable at this point."

I could handle the stress when he had been here. I'd felt impenetrable. But without him, especially looking at the damage to the house and his truck, my resolve melted.

What if I had been trapped down there alone and died? What if nobody had come to get me in time? What if he hadn't made it to my house in time and died? It was all too much.

Earny caught me up in a hug. I realized that I was sobbing. Before this week, I never cried like this. Not in a long, long time.

Chapter Sixty

Jack

"What was it like?" one of my more precocious coworkers asked.

I chewed and swallowed some very bland potatoes. I missed the butter Ally cooked with. I needed to ask her if she got it locally and if so, if they shipped.

"What was what like?" I repeated back to her.

"The tornado," she clarified. She was promptly elbowed by another lady sitting next to her.

"Loud," I thought for a moment, "and really dark. And fast."

A picture might be worth a thousand words, but I couldn't come up with those thousand words in this state of mind.

"Wow," she breathed in awe.

I supposed maybe at one point I would've also been in awe of a tornado had I not actually been through one. Now I was perfectly comfortable respecting them from a distance. A long, long distance.

That reminded me. I needed to check my email for a response from the insurance lady. If they were going to have to physically go out and see the remains of my truck, I needed to give Ally a heads-up.

I fished out my phone, pulling down to get my email to refresh. Nothing yet.

I stowed it in my pocket again.

"Did you get any pictures of it?" My coworker continued her curious interrogation.

"Diane!" the lady sitting next to her exclaimed in exasperation.

"What?" she mumbled, "I was just wondering..."

"Um, no," I said, processing her words, "I didn't have time. I wasn't really sure what I was looking at until it was a little too late to be taking pictures."

My lunch sat in front of me, barely eaten. I didn't know what I needed, maybe some sleep. I couldn't find the motivation to think about work, or eating, or anything productive. I didn't even have the usual carrot dangling of getting done so I could go home.

I could've gone for a walk to clear my head, sometimes I did that, but I didn't care to in the rain.

One by one, my coworkers got up and went back to their desks. The movement jolted my brain to snap back to reality. My nervous system suddenly forced me to take a breath. Had I quit breathing?

I realized I had been staring at the wall for what must have been a while. One of my coworkers dumped a paper plate in the trash with the remains of a pizza crust on it. They turned and gave me a pitying glance before slumping away.

This was not the normal I had planned to come back to. I would've almost welcomed the normal I was prepared to come back to at this point.

Was I going to be the class science experiment now? Randomly probed for information about the wild and mysterious beast that was a tornado?

I supposed I couldn't blame them for being curious. I wouldn't have asked questions like the one coworker, but she wasn't known for her social graces, so that didn't necessarily bother me. I concluded that yeah, I would've been curious. I would've listened in on any information I could've gotten. But even so, I wasn't enjoying being the center of attention at all.

I was already exhausted and feeling defeated as I stood from the table. Then I remembered I'd still have to deal with my dad before too long.

Dad was waiting on my doorstep when I got home. His suit was perfectly pressed, which I was sure Mom had done for him, and his shoes were polished and shined. They didn't show any wear from having walked in the puddles on the ground. Perhaps he had studiously avoided them. His black umbrella was folded at his side as he waited for me at the top of the stairs.

"I'd like to have a chat," he said, no emotion evident on his face.

I considered going back in my car and sneaking into the office to sleep for the night.

I unlocked the door, planning on just taking the lecture. I tried to mentally prepare for anything and everything he could throw at me. All the verbal abuse, all of the punishment. I could just shoulder it until he was satisfied and then maybe crawl straight into bed.

He set his umbrella inside the door, leaning it against the frame, and set his briefcase down beside the table.

Dad took a seat on the high top chair at the bar, looking at me expectantly to follow. Instead, I stood on the other side of the bar, getting some distance. I pulled icy water bottles out of the fridge, offering him one as a gesture of goodwill.

He sighed.

"Your mother and I had a conversation."

Which meant he talked while she listened...

"She told me that I need to hear you out... and she... was very persuasive."

I froze in place, pondering what it was that he had said. Was I hearing things, or had he really just said that he had listened to Mom? That Mom had insisted on telling him something? And he... had actually listened?

He had my attention.

"Ok..." I said hesitantly, nervously.

"Your mother thinks..."

He looked thoughtful, then practically backspaced his sentence and started over.

"She's persuaded me that there may be more to life than work. That maybe I have prioritized work too much, and am expecting you to do the same. I am not saying that work is not important," he interjected. "It is. It is very important. But I have maybe put it on a pedestal."

I sat my water bottle down on the counter, feeling a little lightheaded. Was the room spinning? Had someone replaced my father with a clone? Was this real life right now?

"Thank you, Dad," I said, a little stunned. "I really appreciated that, um..."

"I have more to say."

I clamped my mouth shut. Maybe the worst was actually still coming. Maybe I had let my hopes get up a little too soon.

"I was too harsh with you about what happened. It can be stressful to have a child in a dangerous situation in which you are helpless. Even if it's an adult child. I am sorry. I am very glad you are okay, and I am sorry that

I reacted the way that I did. Downplaying it can be the only way to cope, not that I'm saying I did that, you understand... You'll understand when you have kids of your own."

Honestly, this was a pretty good apology for my dad. This was definitely a dream. It had to be.

"I really appreciate that," I said, processing everything he had said. This was the most introspective I'd ever seen my father in my whole life. I wasn't aware he was capable of such a thing. What had Mom said to him? I needed to give her a call.

"I want you to live your life, and I thought that the best thing would be for you to live it like I live mine. But apparently, that hasn't made anyone happy, myself included."

I needed to sit. My legs threatened to give out on me. They were boneless, and I was suddenly sinking. I went to take a seat next to him.

Could I be as vulnerable as he was being? Could I bare my soul like he had, in his own way? Should I?

If there was one thing I'd learned being stuck in that tornado shelter, thinking about all the things I would regret if I died in there without ever seeing the sun again, it was that life was far too short and unpredictable for things to go unsaid.

"I'm thankful for all your sacrifices, Dad," I said. "Thank you. I am glad that you'll maybe be giving yourself a little break. I'm sure Mom is thrilled about that."

"Yeah." He chuckled, loosening his tie. "I'm taking her on a vacation. She is excited. I feel like I've been living in a haze, with scales on my eyes. Just a zombie. I'm looking forward to it myself."

"That's great!" I clapped him on the back.

I chewed on the inside of my cheek, contemplating the risk of telling him what I wanted to. But in the end, he was my dad. And I wanted him to tell me what he thought. I wanted him to be happy for me and supportive of the things in my life.

"Hey Dad," I said, trying to give myself an internal pep talk, "I met somebody."

"The girl you spent the night with in the tornado shelter?" he said, his voice even.

He didn't sound surprised, but he also didn't sound jaded or skeptical.

"Yeah."

He said nothing, and regret started to creep into my muscles and shut me down. But something told me to press forward.

"I really like her," I admitted. "I spent a lot of time with her while I was there. She's so..."

What words could I even use to describe her to someone who'd never met her? Hard-working, gorgeous, tenacious?

"I know," he said simply. "I could hear it in your voice on the phone."

A hint of a smile tugged at the corner of his lip.

"Seriously?" I asked.

"Oh yeah," he answered. "Men in love always have a certain way about them. It shines through, even if you don't want it to."

"Have you told her?" he continued.

In this moment, I had more of my dad than I had in a long, long time. Maybe ever.

"Sort of."

He stroked his chin in contemplation.

"One thing I've learned, at least this week, is that you have to lay all of your cards out on the table with your woman."

"I'd hate to have that conversation over text. Her phone barely works at her house. Hardly any cell service."

"So don't." He swiveled his chair to face me.

"What do you mean?"

"You should tell her in person," he encouraged.

"I think I'll have to wait a while, all things considered."

"Son," he addressed me as he pulled the tie all the way off his neck, "if there is one thing I've learned working in the companies I have, it's that they don't care about you. They care about getting as much out of you as they can and then replacing you with a cheaper, younger model. Your mother opened my eyes to that this week. From what it sounds like with this lady of yours, she's irreplaceable. You have to invest in people like that in your life."

I was glad that he felt the same about the corporate world, but I could hardly believe the words coming out of his mouth. He'd defended it for so long. Was this the same dad I had grown up with? The same man that had called me, furious, on the phone at Ethel's house?

"There's a dance on Friday night. She's going with someone she doesn't like who's kinda been bothering her," I said.

Was that too soon to go see her again?

"Go. Swoop in. Save the day."

"You think so?" I asked.

I supposed I could get a rental car and maybe grab a nice pair of blue jeans and a shirt to fit the occasion at the store. That way, I didn't stick out like a sore thumb.

"Yeah, I do,"

He stood up and walked to the door. My head felt like it was on a merry-go-round.

"And Jack?"

He picked up his umbrella and briefcase, though it didn't look like he'd need the umbrella anymore. It had stopped raining.

"Yeah, Dad?" I said, reeling.

"Bring her home soon. Mom wants to meet her."

I smiled as he shut the door.

"Yes, sir."

Chapter
Sixty-One

Ally

I sighed, resigning myself. I had to go to this stupid dance with the stupid farm hand.

My shirt was itchy, so I'd put a tank top underneath it as a buffer, but it was making me overheat. My jeans didn't sit right on my hips, I kept having to adjust them. I couldn't get my eye makeup to cooperate. I ended up wiping it all off and giving up. Nothing was going my way!

Olivia meowed at my feet, sensing my irritation.

"Sorry sweetie, it's not you," I said, giving her the head scratches she was searching for.

I checked the clock. Jonathan would be here in five minutes. I'd never driven with him before, and I wasn't looking forward to it. The guys around here weren't the best drivers, usually. I could see him being the type to lazily swerve because he got too absorbed in talking about himself.

Maybe I was being uncharitable. I sighed, closing the drawer in the sink cabinet with all of my hair and makeup stuff. I decided to just put my hair in a ponytail. Not enough time for anything else. The humidity would ruin anything else I did to it, anyway.

I wanted to be excited. I secretly loved to dance, even if I wasn't confident in my abilities. But I couldn't bring myself to feel excited when I was going to be dancing with Jonathan. I just felt repulsed, and he hadn't even touched me yet! Knowing my luck, he'd step on my toes.

A knock on the door made me jump about a foot in the air.

"Be right there," I called.

The door creaked open. Guess he wasn't going to wait for me. I rushed out, trying to get over feeling annoyed by this. He stood in my doorway, menacingly tall with dark features.

"Hey Al."

I hated the nicknames the men around here picked for me. I was sure they had others that I didn't know about that I'd hate even more. Earny's nicknames were the only exceptions.

"Hi," I said quickly. "Sorry I'm not quite ready. I just need to get my shoes on."

I reached down, which felt somehow oddly vulnerable around him when it hadn't been with Jack. And not in a good way. It was crazy how I could feel completely comfortable and safe with a complete stranger of a man in my house, but not one that I saw on a regular basis. I pulled the boots over my ankles, quickly grabbing my keys and tucking them into my pocket.

"All ready now." I smiled. It was fake, but he didn't seem to notice.

I followed him to his truck. He neglected to open the door for me like Jack always did. I tried to stifle my urge to compare. Olivia gave a disappointed meow as I waved at her. She bounded back up to the house to patiently wait for my return.

Jonathan droned on about the land he intended to purchase, the ranch he wanted to eventually own, and detailed his obsession over nice cars and types of alcohol as we drove.

I nodded politely, hoping that I was doing a good enough job of acting engaged in the conversation. I'd had wine once or twice, so I briefly talked about those experiences and what I liked and didn't like before he monopolized the conversation again. That way I could tell Mayabell that I had given a date with him the old college try. It wasn't that his hopes and aspirations didn't match some of mine, though maybe his were on a grander scale. It just didn't feel the same to me. I wanted a life I could be proud of, not a life that I could flaunt.

"This thing can go up to 120mph without rattling." His chest puffed proudly.

I'd known that he had liked to tinker on things to soup them up, but I hadn't noticed any big differences on this truck. At least not outwardly.

"Oh really?" I said, somewhat impressed.

"Yeah, I'll show you!" he beamed.

"Oh, that's not—"

But it was too late. He was already gunning it down a dirt road that definitely shouldn't have been driven on that fast. We couldn't have gotten up to more than 85 or 90mph, but I felt myself lifting off the seat. I couldn't believe that the people on the Texas highway just drove this fast naturally, even given that their road was smoother.

I clung to anything I could get a firm grip on.

Jonathan looked over at me, proud of himself and his truck.

"Impressive," I said, internally shaking in my boots. I could've done without the demonstration.

I tried my best to hide how shaken I was, because I feared that would only egg him on to do this sort of thing more. This was just one night. I could survive this and never agree to another date with him again.

"I could show you something even more impressive later," he smirked.

UM, NO. Nope. No thanks. Ew.

I... was going to text Earny and see if he could take me home. I could sneak away from the dance for a bathroom break and catch up with him when I was ready to leave. That sounded like a lot more than what I had signed up for.

Despite country men being perceived as gentlemen, that was often a trope confined to country songs. Reality was more of a mixed bag.

The streetlights of Blink glowed on the horizon, welcoming us. Jonathan parked down the street from the dance. The street for several blocks up to the Co-op was blocked off with barricades and caution cones.

I stepped out of the truck, again having to open the door myself. Jack had really spoiled me.

Jonathan came up beside me, walking a little closer than what I felt comfortable with. He just didn't seem to be able to read me for anything, or he just didn't care.

I was relieved when I heard familiar voices in the dark up ahead. I could pick out the voices of Ethel, Mayabell, Sheryl, and a few others laughing and carrying on. My shoulders dropped just a little.

"Oh, hi Ally!" Mayabell greeted me with a wink. "Hi, Jonathan. Good to see you two!"

I hoped that she wouldn't egg this man on. That was the last thing I needed.

"Hope you've been practicing your two-stepping skills, Ally," Sheryl said. "You're gonna need them. Lots of stiff competition tonight."

They'd all had some alcohol already, I could tell.

The town had a reputation for hosting a fine dance, such that the surrounding towns sent their young people out this way. It was a hopping place to be. Every small town was famous for something, nefarious or otherwise. This dance was what Blink was known for.

The smell of hot dogs and hamburgers permeated the air, along with cigarette smoke, perfumes and colognes, and the heat of the asphalt after a 100-degree day. The grilling going on created a haze in the air. Usually, it all felt magical. But tonight, I couldn't feel anything but dread and nerves. The DJ announced a raffle for an antique tractor; his booming voice pouring out of a speaker nearby. It was a little too loud for my ears. I took a few steps back from it before he kicked off another song.

Jonathan's arm snaked around my waist. Bile rose in my throat as he paraded me into the middle of the dance area. I ached for the natural way Jack touched me. I loved how it was a wordless conversation and not a lackluster, grabby demand.

Jonathan took my limp hand and interlaced it with his. Every fiber of me wanted to crawl out of my skin. I tried to listen to the music I had heard so many times and usually loved. I moved fluidly, but he seemed incapable of doing the same. I was thankful that my boots made it such that when he stepped on my foot, it didn't hurt. I had long been accused of wanting to "lead" too much when it came to dancing, but it was hard to dance when you didn't have a strong leader.

I didn't think I was to blame for that. Jonathan's movements were jarring, and as the next few songs played, his fingertips sunk deeper into my waist. My stomach lurched as I tried to ignore the sensory input.

A hand appeared and tapped him on the shoulder. Hope lifted me up and set me back on my feet. Was I going to get a break, even for just a brief song?

Jonathan's face twisted with barely concealed anger as he turned to see who was cutting in.

It was none other than Bubba. I cast a glance around for Earny as Jonathan stared Bubba down. I clocked him sipping a beer behind the barricade, watching. So maybe Earny had sent Bubba to give me a break. I was grateful for that. Bubba might not be graceful, but he could be nice when he wanted to be. And I was sure he was more than happy to put his hat in the ring to come selflessly save me.

After an inordinate amount of body language I couldn't quite read, Jonathan took a hesitant step back.

"I'm going to go get us some drinks," he told me as though that had been the plan all along.

Then he disappeared into the crowd, fading into darkness. I relaxed as Bubba took my hand in his massive one and started two-stepping with me.

"You doing alright, Sis?" he said, his swampy eyes focused on me. "He's not botherin' ya is he? We can get him off your back."

"I'm ok," I assured him as we went from one end of the dance floor to the other, navigating around other couples. It was easy to do with Bubba being so massive, people just made way for him.

I'd been too hard on him before. There were folks with hearts of gold around here. Familiarity really did breed contempt. Bubba had been relatively nice to Jack, and I appreciated him coming to help me tonight.

"Thank you."

"Sure thing," he said, casting a quick glance behind to find where Jonathan currently was.

I couldn't see him, and from the frown on Bubba's face, neither could he. Oh well.

"I wouldn't say he's bothering me," I decided to speak up before Jonathan came back, "but if you could pass along to Earny that I need him to take me home, that would be great. I don't care what kind of excuse he comes up with. I just need him to not take no for an answer."

"Will do." He scanned the crowd again while the song came to an end.

"Thanks, Bubba," I said.

"No problem Sis."

Jonathan appeared out of thin air. It was hard to hear footsteps when the music was so loud you could feel it more than you could feel your heartbeat. Bubba and I both jumped.

"Watermelon wine for the lady," Jonathan said, extending me a red cup of chilled wine.

"Oh," I said, "thank you."

In no way, shape, or form was I planning on drinking.

Bubba and I shared a knowing glance out of the corner of our eyes.

"Would you hold this for me?" I handed it to Bubba. "I need to use the lady's room."

He grunted, taking the cup. I tipped my head to Jonathan and headed to a secluded area near the porta-potties to get a breather.

Maybe I could say I had gotten sick and needed to go home. I doubted highly that Jonathan wanted to take home a puking woman in his precious truck. I didn't know how offended he would get when he realized I wasn't going to drink that cup, and I didn't want to find out. But I knew Bubba could probably "accidentally" misplace it for me. I owed that man a drink at the bar someday soon.

I was contemplating just how far I was willing to go to get out of this date when Jonathan came from around the corner.

"There you are, Ally!"

Right as I was considering faking my own death.

"Sorry," I immediately launched into yapping, "I—"

"They are about to play Peaches," he said, grabbing my hand, "let's go!"

Peaches was the redneck equivalent of the cupid shuffle or chicken dance at weddings, but for our town's little festival. What started out as a line in a local country song quickly morphed into an actual, proudly performed dance that we all did every year. I supposed I didn't really want to miss it.

I followed him out on the floor, just thankful it was a line dance and not a couple's dance. I saw Bubba a few rows back and felt a little bit better just knowing he was still close by.

I did all of the convoluted, hilarious moves that came with the dance as the speakers turned the town square into a honky tonk scene. I was squatting, about to pop back up and dig my heel in to turn, when I saw someone out of formation.

"Sorry, sorry, sorry," the figure apologized as they bumped into person after person. Then, in my state of rubbernecking, someone bumped into me, and I realized I'd stopped doing the dance myself.

I broke out of line, making my way to the voice that was so out of place...

"Ally," Jonathan's voice was muffled behind me. It was quickly drowned out by the music as I pushed forward.

Could it be?...

"Jack?" I stared in disbelief.

Dang, he looked good in jeans and a pearl snap shirt.

Chapter Sixty-Two

Jack

Two-stepping couldn't be that hard, could it? I set my phone on the bathroom counter so I could watch a tutorial while I brushed my teeth.

Practicing without another person was hard, but I was determined. I stepped in unison with the video, my toothbrush jutting out of the side of my mouth as I concentrated. I was so excited to see Ally, I could hardly stand it.

This was silly. But love was silly.

The talk with my dad had gone so well, I could hardly believe it. I hadn't even been nervous when I picked up the phone to dial the office and tell them I would only be in for an hour or two on Friday morning. The receptionist was nosy, but once she surmised that I would be returning to the tiny town, she said no more.

"Ooo," she said, "have fun!"

I could almost picture her smiling and kicking her feet at her desk.

"I will," I said, not even caring that it was going to cause gossip in the office.

I wondered what Ally was going to wear. I wanted to match her, but I hadn't exactly seen her whole wardrobe. I tried my best to pick something fairly neutral so that she would be the shining star. I thought about texting her, but I knew she might not get it. And I didn't want to give her any time to talk me out of it.

I dreamed of her face when she saw me there as I combed my hair. This was going to be great.

Olivia barreled into me when I stepped out of my rental car at Ally's house.

"Hi," I said, sinking down to pet her on the porch. She purred and carried on, rubbing against my leg as though she intended to knock me over. "I've missed you, too."

I didn't see Ally's truck in the yard. Maybe that meant she was already gone. I wondered if she would decide to stay home from the dance, but evidently not. I gave Olivia one more pat on the head before hopping back into my rental car. I had to be careful driving it on this road. The rental company wouldn't be happy with me if I buggered it up on the dirt roads.

Silence stretched on as I drove into town, nerves ratcheting up with every passing county road. I couldn't wait to see Ally.

Finding a place to park was more challenging than I had originally anticipated. I hadn't expected to find the town packed with people. I was pretty sure there were more bodies throughout the town tonight than there were people who lived here. I remembered her saying it was a big shindig, but I had drastically miscalculated what that meant.

I finally found a place to squeeze in between the lifted trucks that lined the small town blocks. Almost immediately, I started passing drunken people with red cups. Liquid sloshing out of the tops as they swayed without a care in the world. It wasn't even that late in the evening, I laughed to myself. These people partied hard.

Being in the city gave me every opportunity to do that, but I wasn't much for the scene. I would've preferred a quiet night in to a drunken, blacked-out bar hop. I had been the designated driver a few times in college, and there was nothing worse than babysitting an overgrown, belligerent toddler with bad breath.

I followed the music, darting in and out of the crowd as the amount of people thickened. Most of the attendees stayed inside the barricades that lined the road, swaying or dancing. That made it easier for me to walk along them and see the crowd inside without being surrounded. I started scanning faces for Ally, anxiously hoping that I would see her before she saw me. I wanted to see her reaction to me being here. I hoped she'd be excited.

My ears hurt from how loud the music was as I drew closer to the heart of the dance. I wasn't sure how there were actually people lingering near the speakers.

There seemed to be an area for a live band and instruments at the ready, but the music that was currently flooding through the streets was from a DJ. There were a lot of people busting moves on the dance floor, some that I recognized, and some that I didn't. But when the song changed and everyone started two-stepping, I was relieved to realize that I recognized it as such. I saw one of the farmhands from Earny's place dancing with a blonde lady. Keeping up with him proved to be a challenge. I followed him a yard into the crowd before I lost him.

What was his name? I suddenly felt bad because I couldn't remember. Had I ever learned it? I tried to push forward, careful not to bump into any rednecks. I didn't want to get into a fistfight with a drunken dude before I even laid eyes on Ally. I didn't want to spend the night sticky with beer on me, either.

The song changed again. To some kind of line dance, by the looks of it.

I dipped back out into the barricade area, trying to get a better vantage point. I saw someone that I thought was about Ally's height. It was hard to see, even with the streetlights on. Everything was a blur of shadowy motion. The loud noise made it hard to focus, too.

"Ally?" I called in the direction of the figure I'd seen. I pressed forward.

A few people looked at me in confusion as I wove through the area.

"Ally!" I called again. This time, I saw the head turn. My heart skipped a beat.

Before I knew it, she was within reach. Her mouth formed a perfect O shape. The man who stood next to her, that I recognized from the Co-op, was irritated she wasn't giving him attention in that moment. I hoped that she wouldn't be mad at me for crashing their date.

"Jack?" she said in stunned disbelief. "What are you doing here?"

"Correcting my mistake," I said simply.

The man scowled at me, but I paid him no mind. This was my girl.

"What mistake?" she asked, trying to compose herself.

"Leaving in the first place," I said with a grin, offering my hand to dance.

A shocked smile graced her face as she leaned forward and took my hand. The man standing next to her threw his arms in the air, stomping away. One of Earny's farmhands covered his face with his hand, stifling a giggle at the display.

"Sorry for crashing your date," I said, though I was not at all sorry. Ok, maybe I did feel a little bad.

"Don't be," Ally retorted, holding up a hand. "It wasn't going well."

I started working the dance floor with her. She was a natural! I was so thankful I had practiced before I came. After a while, I didn't even have to think about what I was doing. I just had to make sure we didn't crash into other people.

"How are you even here?" she said, loud enough for me to hear over the music.

"Well, I got a rental car, and I told work that I had to leave early..." I explained.

"I mean, why?" Her beautiful face was pinched.

"Because I missed you."

She chewed at her lip, looking as though she might cry. "I missed you, too."

"Anything exciting happen while I was away?" I asked, trying to stall the formation of tears.

"Not unless you count two teenagers breaking up. It's been the talk of the Co-op."

"That does sound exciting," I said, laughing. "What was it over?"

"Nobody knows," she said. "That's what the talk has been about. Speculating why. You know how it is around here. They were high school sweethearts and about to graduate. I figure maybe one decided to go to college, and they thought long distance was going to be too much. That happens a lot around here. People go to college, leave the other one behind saying they'll be back. But then they don't ever come back except for Easter and Christmas, if they come back at all. But, neither of them have told anyone what happened, and I respect that. Relationships should be private I think, except what people agree to share."

"I agree," I said. "I hope they are both able to move on."

My throat felt strained from trying to talk above the music. We both grew quiet for a while as we danced through the haze of night air, smoke, and a mixture of perfumes and colognes.

As we spun around, I saw her date glare at me with his arms folded, leaning up against a brick wall.

"Looks like your date doesn't like me." I pointed it out to her with a tip of my chin.

She didn't even look.

"I don't care. He was honestly a little creepy. I'm glad you came and rescued me."

Was she batting her eyes at me?

"Maybe I should've rented a white horse instead of a rental car," I said, stepping just a little closer to her.

Her eyelids fluttered. My pulse quickened. I made a mental note that she liked that sort of thing.

After about forty minutes of non-stop dancing, Ally maneuvered us over to one of the barricades to search for a drink.

"It's hot," I noted as I cracked open a water bottle Ally grabbed from a cooler.

I hadn't noticed the lingering heat of the day at first because I was too focused on getting to Ally through the crowd, but it was a little muggy. And dancing really worked up a sweat.

"It really is," Ally said, leaning against a tree.

She looked up at me, grinning from ear to ear. "But I know a way to fix that."

"Oh, do you now?" I geared up for her to splash her water at me.

"Yeah," she said with a devilish expression, "let's go!"

She took my hand in hers, a little callused from her job, and led me through the crowd.

"Where did you park?"

"Over there," I said, pointing way down the street toward the rental car. Its cherry red finish and lack of dirt coating it made it stick out like a sore thumb.

Her ponytail bopped up and down as she sped forward like we were fleeing the scene of a crime.

We reached the rental car, fireflies dancing in the trees ahead of us. I unlocked it, opening her door. She stepped down into it, pulling out her phone.

"Who are you texting?" I asked as I started it up. "Where are we going?"

"Earny," she said, "I had planned on him taking me home. I'm just letting him know it's not necessary anymore."

"The date was that bad?" I teased.

"Yeah," she made face a like something stunk.

"Wow."

"Take a left when you get down to the end of the road," she directed.

I squinted at her in the dark car. "Ok, but where are we going?"

"You'll find out soon enough."

Chapter Sixty-Three

Ally

This was a dream. I was dreaming. I had to be.

There was no way that Jack was here, back in Blink, on the night of the dance. And he was a good dancer!

I didn't want it to end, but once we were out of the crowd to get a drink, I didn't want to get back in it.

I wanted to go spend time with him. I'd had my fill of the noise.

"Take this right up ahead," I guided him.

He was perturbed by this wild goose chase, but dutifully obeyed all of my instructions.

"Are you taking me somewhere to axe murder me?" he teased. "I should've listened to my parents about talking to strangers."

I smacked his arm playfully.

"No, I could've done that last week if I wanted to."

He laughed, "That's true."

"Park right here," I told him as we got closer.

"There is nothing here?" he questioned me.

"Just trust me." I put my phone down in the middle console.

I got out as soon as he put it in park, then ran around to drag him out of the car.

"Let's go!" I said, bouncing up and down.

Jack's eyebrows were raised. He looked more than a little confused. I held his hand, leading him behind me.

The footpath was a little hard to find in the dark, but I managed to see it by brief glimpses of moonlight through the leaves above us. I held back the limb of a tree so that Jack could get through. He had to bend down so as not to hit a few tree limbs. I wasn't tall enough to have to worry about those.

Some leaves rustled right in front of us. Jack froze, peering over my shoulder. A blur of gray and white flashed before us on the trail. My hand flew to my ear as he shrieked like a little girl.

Then I laughed so hard I almost peed myself.

"What," he said breathlessly, "was that?"

It briefly occurred to me that I could make up anything to answer that. I could create a new urban legend that he could take back to work with him. Something he could tell his wide-eyed office mates. Maybe I should tell him it was Oklahoma's version of a fairy? But I decided to take pity on him.

"It was an opossum," I said between giggles.

"That," he said, eyes wide, "was the craziest looking creature I've ever seen."

I tilted my head, conceding.

"They are pretty crazy looking."

I pressed forward, Jack a little more skittish now. The trees parted in front of us, opening up into a clearing with a dock that went out over a small pond. There was a creek that fed it and ran out of it. It wasn't always full, but because of the recent storm, it had quite a bit of water in it right now.

I grinned as Jack stood there with his head turned. The only light was the moon streaming down, reflecting smoothly off the surface of the water. I pulled my shirt over my head, my back to Jack as I threw it over a branch near the edge of the water.

"Ally, what are you—"

I shucked off my boots and shimmed off my jeans, tossing them under and on the limb, respectively. I left my underwear on and tank top on. It worked out to be a pretty good hillbilly swimsuit. I didn't want to scandalize the poor man the first time he went skinny dipping, even if it wasn't truly skinny dipping.

I dipped my toe in, finding my footing so I wouldn't slip. Then I walked out until the water was over my clavicle, turning to Jack. He stood frozen like a statue, not even blinking.

I laughed. "Are you coming or not?"

He sputtered for a few seconds, then started fumbling with his shirt. I'd have to show him how to take off a pearl snap the right way, but I'd prefer to save those lessons for a honeymoon.

Once he'd shucked most of his clothes, he came to the edge of the water where I'd entered and dipped his toe in. I splashed water in his direction playfully, then swam a little further back.

He doubled back, going to the dock. My smile fell when he started running down it.

Jack cannonballed in, drenching me in his wake. He bobbed up out of the water with a grin, taking in my drenched hair and pout. I kicked toward him, splashing him back for good measure as he shook his hair out like a puppy.

"Told you skinny dipping is fun," I said.

He dipped under the water. It was so dark and murky that I couldn't see him, and I started to worry. What was he doing? I should've warned him not to open his eyes in a pond like this.

"Ack!" I cried as he tugged at my ankle and pulled me under. I held my breath, not wanting to have a taste of the murky water. My hands reached out, grabbing hold of him as we floated back up.

"Jack!" I chastised him.

His eyes were wild and joyous as he wrapped his arms around my bare waist, pulling me in.

"That's my name, don't wear it out."

I was about to say something sassy when his lips met mine. They were warm and steady, curiously searching mine. All of a sudden, he was pulling me under a different kind of wave.

Epilogue

Ally

"**O**uch!" Jack said, shaking his hand.

A tool belt hung around his waist. He pushed the hammer back into it and climbed down the step stool.

"I'm sorry," I said, offering him a glass of fresh lemonade.

I'd come outside just in time to witness his mishap.

"Thanks," he said, wiping the sweat from his brow.

"What do you think?" he stepped back, his boots heavy on the grass.

"It's perfect." I beamed.

The chicken coop was even better than the old one had been. A twinge of sadness came over me at the loss of the one my grandpa and I had built, but I had made plenty of memories with Jack building this new one. They weren't replacements; they were additions.

The chickens clucked, dancing around the new coop as they inspected it. Gerald, in particular, was raring to go inside. They all seemed to approve.

I was still shocked that Jack kept his promise about us building it together. We'd been able to reclaim some wood to keep costs down. It was bigger than the old one. It turned out Jack had a knack for drawing up plans and building things, even if he was a little clumsy with a hammer.

"Sheryl called," I told him, "she said she's ready for you to take over the position at the Co-op in October."

I was surprised she'd decided to go into an early retirement. She'd quietly been battling some health problems for months. I supposed that's why she had seemed so cranky the last several times I'd paid my bills. Maybe you could keep secrets in a small town, after all. But now that she was in remission, she wanted to prioritize traveling the world and spending time with her grandkids.

I could envision her leaning over the railing of a cruise ship, a martini with a fancy umbrella in hand. I was happy for her. I couldn't wait to hear about all of her adventures.

And I was forever grateful to her, because this gave Jack the ability to come here permanently. I couldn't believe he was really going through with it. I was so excited to have him here full-time. Going back and forth on the weekends was wonderful, but... I ached to have him here all the time. His job had let him come on the weekends with the understanding that he intended to either go down to remote or leave entirely. They agreed to it, so long as he agreed to train his replacement.

"What time are your parents going to be here?" I asked, nervously fidgeting with my dish towel.

I'd swept and dusted everything in the house, including the ceiling and walls. I wasn't sure what his parents were going to make of my tiny house, especially after everything I'd heard about his dad. He swore up and down that his dad's heart had changed.

I was hopeful, even through the nerves.

"Should be here about six. Let me come in and help you with supper."

He kissed me on the cheek, wrapping his arms around me. I leaned back, melting into him.

Jack was unrecognizable from the man he used to be. Confidence poured over his shoulders and down his back. He no longer hunched over like he was carrying the weight of the world.

I smeared a little bit of tomato sauce from the jar I'd opened on his nose, just to get him back for being so dang cute. His eyes lit up as he popped me in the butt with the dish towel.

Olivia purred at our feet as we made dinner, happily begging for scraps. I relented, giving her a small bite of chicken.

Then came a knock at the door.

"That must be them," I said, my expression dropping a little.

"They're gonna love you," Jack assured me, moving swiftly to open it.

His mom stood there, his dad behind her. In her hands, she held a bouquet of yellow flowers wrapped in ribbon.

His parents smiled.

"Hi," I said. "It's nice to meet you."

Should I shake their hands? I needed to wash mine first. I still had tomato sauce on them and...

"I got these for you," his mom said, handing me the bouquet.

"Thank you so much." I took the flowers and put them on the table. "They're beautiful!"

I hadn't had enough kitchen chairs, so Ethel had Earny drop off two extras. They were mismatched, but his parents didn't seem to notice.

"That chicken coop looks really good," I heard Jack's dad tell him.

"Thanks, Dad."

"Would you like to sit down?" I offered to his mom, making my way over to the food to stir it so it wouldn't pop. "Supper's almost ready."

Jack took his dad out for a tour of the property, leaving me alone with his mom. At first, I was nervous, but she had come fully prepared. She showed me every embarrassing baby picture they had of him and told every silly childhood story. I went back and forth, stirring the food and looking through pictures.

I hung on her every word. This must've been how Jack felt when Earny was telling him about my childhood antics. I supposed I could forgive Earny for spilling all my secrets...

"I wanted to show you this," his mom said, pulling something out of her purse. "It's a family heirloom."

A ring box lay in her hand. She handed it to me, patiently waiting for me to open it. I gave her a curious look before peeking inside. It was a beautiful ring with a ruby sitting in the middle, flanked by three diamonds on each side.

"What's this?" I asked, wide-eyed.

Olivia wandered up to Jack's mom, hugging her leg.

"It's been passed down for a few generations," she said, reaching down to pet Olivia. "I wanted to make sure you'd actually like it before I gave it to Jack. You know, for when he's ready...I didn't want you to have a ring you didn't like..."

Time stopped moving. My brain struggled to catch up with the implications of what she was showing me.

"I-I-" I stuttered.

This was big. That was so sweet that she wanted to make sure I liked it. My mind was racing a mile a minute. I was picturing it on my hand, dancing in the kitchen with Jack.

I closed the box.

"I love it," I said, tears in my eyes. I would've tried it on, but I wanted the first time I put it on to be when Jack put it on me.

She winked, taking it back and pocketing it. "I'll let him know."

I wondered when I'd get to lay eyes on it again, but I suspected it wouldn't be long. I smiled to myself.

We talked for another half hour. The men must've been as long-winded as we were, because we didn't see hide nor hair of them the entire time.

Jack looked surprised when he walked in and his mom and I were laughing hysterically. He shot me a look that asked what was going on, but I didn't let on anything. I had a whole new stock of ammo to tease him about now.

Dinner passed far too quickly.

I wasn't ready for his parents to leave yet when they loaded up. They'd gotten a hotel almost an hour away.

"We'll see them again tomorrow. You can give them a tour of Blink," he smiled, pulling me in and kissing the top of my hair.

I nuzzled into him, sighing with contentment.

My heart almost exploded when we drove into town the next day to give Jack's parents a tour. I slowed down, seeing Adam kneeling in front of the population sign with spray paint in his hand. He smiled and waved at us, winking at me as I read what it said now.

He'd marked out the 4 at the end and written a new number instead.

The sign now read: "Blink, Population 5685"

My life had changed in, well, the blink of an eye.

I had gone from being all alone, to having someone I couldn't imagine life without. I was surrounded by more love and support than I knew what to do with.

It was hard to imagine what my old life used to be like, before the tornado swept it all away.

I'd have to remind myself of that when the hammering from the roof repairs got to be too much. ;)

The End

About the author

Lainey Ross is just a small town girl who loves writing, good food, and her furry friends. You can find her on Facebook at

https://www.facebook.com/AuthorLaineyRoss/

Or on Instagram at

https://www.instagram.com/authorlaineyross/